Penguin Books
Hers

A. Alvarez was born in London in 1929 and educated at Oundle School and Corpus Christi College, Oxford. For a time he researched and taught in Oxford and America. Out of this came a critical study of modern poetry, *The Shaping Spirit* (1958). Since 1956 he has lived as a freelance writer in London, travelling a good deal and making occasional academic forays to the States. His Gauss Seminars on criticism at Princeton University in 1958 resulted in another book, *The School of Donne* (1961).

Alvarez has been poetry editor and critic of the *Observer*. He contributed to the *New Statesman* for ten years and was its drama critic from 1958 to 1960. In 1961 he received the Vachel Lindsay Prize for poetry from *Poetry* (Chicago) and in the following year he edited and introduced for Penguins their best-selling anthology, *The New Poetry*. Alvarez has also written, again for Penguins, *Under Pressure: the Writer in Society: Eastern Europe and the U.S.A.* A collection of essays (1955–67), *Beyond All This Fiddle*, was published by Allen Lane The Penguin Press in 1968, and a study of Samuel Beckett in 1973. *The Savage God*, a study of suicide, appeared in Penguins in 1974. A selection of his poems has been published in *Penguin Modern Poets* 18. He is at present Advisory Editor of the Penguin Modern European Poets series.

Hers

A. Alvarez

Penguin Books

Penguin Books Ltd,
Harmondsworth, Middlesex, England
Penguin Books
625 Madison Avenue, New York,
New York 10022, U.S.A.
Penguin Books Australia Ltd,
Ringwood, Victoria, Australia
Penguin Books Canada Ltd, 2801 John Street,
Markham, Ontario, Canada L3R 1B4
Penguin Books (N.Z.) Ltd,
182–190 Wairau Road, Auckland 10, New Zealand

First published by Weidenfeld and Nicolson 1974
Published in Penguin Books 1977

Made and printed in Great Britain by
C. Nicholls & Company Ltd
Set in Linotype Juliana

To Mac and Mary

They that have powre to hurt, and will doe none,
That doe not do the thing they most do showe,
Who moving others, are themselves as stone,
Unmooved, cold, and to temptation slow:
They rightly do inherrit heavens graces,
And husband natures ritches from expence,
They are the Lords and owners of their faces,
Others but stewards of their excellence:
The sommers flowre is to the sommer sweet,
Though to it selfe it onely live and die,
But if that flowre with base infection meete,
The basest weed out-braves his dignity:
 For sweetest things turne sowrest by their deedes
 Lillies that fester smell far worse then weeds.

WILLIAM SHAKESPEARE

I

She was ten years older than Sam, but looked younger. Not that he looked any older than he was, which was twenty-two. Whereas she was already in her thirties, with two children and a husband well over fifty. From where Sam stood, that was older than God.

Yet she looked like a child: blonde, fragile, with cool blue eyes and the smooth face of a fourteen-year-old girl. High cheekbones, delicate mouth, untouchable. 'Don't believe what you see,' she told him, 'I've got a witch's face. See, no wrinkles. I'm one of those awful women who still look like girls when they're sixty. One day it'll all collapse, cave in like a rusty old cistern when the power leaves me. Then where will I be?' Sam wanted to say something indignant and flattering, but didn't know how to without appearing foolish. And she had a gift for making him feel foolish.

At first he had only hung around her because everyone else did. All the bright young lecturers and would-be writers, their first books and ambitions fresh on them, flocked about her, chattering like starlings. It seemed the thing to do. Officially, they were merely being polite. She was, after all, the wife of the professor who ran the summer school, and the summer school paid well, brought in new and foreign faces, and somehow breathed a little liveliness into the gloomy university routine. It was informal. Nobody cared. So to teach at it was a plum they all clambered for. The least they could do was play up to the professor's young wife. He even seemed flattered by it. But secretly they were all besotted. The young foreign girls who came to that famous, ancient place to soak up the atmosphere and be bedded English-style were invariably second best. Not that they minded, really, provided they

9

got what they were after in the end. It was too brief an interlude to take offence, and not quite real. No hard feelings.

So Julie held court without competition. She had a sly, quick, sideways-on way about her which went with her deft body and cool stare. The young academics, who had all picked over the same drab books and spent most of their comfortable days taking in each other's washing elegantly and maliciously, didn't know how to cope with her. She never said the expected thing. Even her 'no' came like an aphorism, sighed regretfully just when the man she was with had decided he'd won. In the corners of old-fashioned pubs, in kitchens or darkened passages at other people's parties, on long romantic walks by the river, under the pollarded willows with cows looking on lugubriously, her answer was always the same. Sometimes she sounded mocking, more often plangent; occasionally the unsuccessful candidate was awarded a gentle, regretful kiss. But none of them passed. It simply amused her to keep a pack of tame admirers wagging their tails in anticipation. And probably it also amused her husband. Did they discuss the candidates together in the privacy of their Victorian terraced house?

It was difficult to imagine quite what they did alone. They seemed hopelessly ill-assorted: she slim and quick as a ferret, he stout and balding, with a booming voice and ponderous manners, his snout permanently lifted like a porpoise's in disdain of whatever was before him. He had met her soon after the war in the chaos of a south German university where he was doing a visiting stint. She was seventeen years old, a blonde waif hopelessly displaced in the jostling mass of young blackmarketeers and budding footnoters. She looked, and was, half starved, but turned out to be hungry also for an education and a life of her own. She was like no one Charles had ever met in his stolid, industrious life. No one at all. He didn't know what to make of her. Nor she of him. But his dullness appealed to her, his weight, his heavy belly and heavy mind. *Ponderismuskeit*. But also security. She had had a bad time in the war, though she kept the details to herself, saying only that her father had been arrested, then the Russians had come and she had slipped away ahead of them into the Western zone. No dates, no details, no family. Charles was safe; he was safety itself.

For him, already through his inexperienced thirties, her slender waif-like eroticism was a new world. His sluggish spirit moved slowly towards a sensuality he had never dreamed of, as massive and crushing as a Centurion tank. He became obsessed with the details of her body, forgetting everything he had spent his lifetime drilling himself in: the facts and trivia of literary history, the obsequious hierarchies of power above him and below. He felt like the woken Kraken, slowly, desperately coming up for air. Julie, in her turn, was overwhelmed, not by him but by her power in rousing him. It seemed disproportionate to her fragility, and also to her feelings. But when he asked her to marry him she accepted without hesitation. There would be no more hunger, no more drifting. What did a little distaste matter? By that time she was already pregnant.

So he took her back to England to have her baby legally. But the strain of the journey in packed, swaying trains and the exhaustion of moving into a new house were too much for her. She had a miscarriage. 'She's not strong,' said the doctor, 'and she's had a hard time. It's to be expected. Just let her rest, get her strength back. She'll be all right.' Charles stood at her bedside with the doctor, looking down at her small pale face with its shut eyes and down-turned, desolate mouth, thinking, My wife. What have I let myself in for, and at my age? They had a real marriage now, sealed in blood.

He was still serving time out in the provinces, where life was no less shabby than in Germany, though considerably more placid. They lived in a tall cold house in the suburbs, among sooty trees. The sun, when it appeared, was filtered through smoke. But mostly the skies were chill with rain. Occasionally, Julie would take a bus to the other side of town and wander through the industrial swamps. The long, grimy perspectives of the factory streets were oddly appealing. They had a certain finality. This is what life comes down to in the end: dirt and brick. They made her understand how far she had journeyed from childhood, from the deep, folded countryside of Bavaria, glassy in the heat. She had travelled downwards perhaps, but far. At least it was progress.

The barbarous nasal accents she barely understood were as exotic to her as those of a lost tribe. Her own English was lilting and upper class, but she was a good mimic and picked up the local slang.

'Bluddy deggin' agen.' She seemed to squeeze the words through her nose, registering mock horror at the rain heaving down.

Charles stared at her: 'Don't.' He was beyond amusement, beyond disapproval: husbandly. Married, married, married, he thought.

It was five years before she was pregnant again, but this time there were no mishaps.

As much as he could, he kept her hidden away, like a secret. He could make no connection between the life he led as a teacher, a scholar, a good committee man and administrator, and his private, night-time life with her. He would return harassed and buzzing from the day's routine, a heavy figure in his dark suit, tight collar, dull tie. His feet ached, he needed a drink. He liked to watch her putting the baby down, murmuring softly to it in a mixture of German and English, back in her own lost childhood. He would sit staring at her, unblinking, on a low nursing chair, dumbly reaching out a hand to touch her thigh or knee if she came near him, waiting like a man in a dream for the baby to be kissed and the light switched off. Then he would follow her out and loom, zombie-like, behind her while she softly closed the door. Almost of its own accord, his hand would reach out to the nape of her neck. He would steer her into the bedroom and make love to her with the whole weight of his middle-aged despair. For her part, she would have preferred to sit quietly with a drink, listening to music, exhausted by the baby and the day's emptiness. But she could no more have stopped him than she could have halted a landslide. She felt she was being overwhelmed by a natural catastrophe. Night after night. The force of it excited her but left her desolate. Three years later she was pregnant again.

Soon after the second child was born the call came, as Charles had always known it would, from the famous, ancient university. He had served out his time in exile, amassing two books of scholarly criticism and three competent editions of almost major writers; he had also applied the necessary dollop of grease to the axles of power. Now he was being rewarded. Through patience and industry he had made it to the top of his tree and their life changed. The ways of the ancient university were more indolent and social than those of the provinces. No one willingly talked shop; gentlemen don't. Food and wine and gossip: these were the passions. So the Stones began to entertain and be entertained. Julie, though Charles resented it, became an asset. She had been hungry so long during the war that food fascinated her. 'She cooks well,' was the verdict. 'She has a feeling for it.' More important, she talked well, intuitively, unpredictable, a perfect foil for Charles's preordained academic style. His older colleagues sought them out as a novelty, the younger ones clustered round her expectantly. For the first time in his stolid life he found he was cutting a figure. Nevertheless, he grumbled to her about her pack of doggy admirers.

She turned on him icily: 'Don't you see? I'm too old to be the only whore in the harem. When I was seventeen I didn't know any better. Anyway, it was exciting. Even when I was twenty-five it was OK. I used to think, Well, that's what I am. That's my role. But I'm a mother now, and soon I'm going to be thirty. I'm due for a life of my own, Charles.'

'But I want you. How can I help that?'

'That's got nothing to do with it. It's all I can do to cope with two small children. As you well know.'

He did indeed. The birth of their second child changed her, made her more definite. While she was carrying it the moon swelling of her pale body seemed to Charles like some prodigy of nature; it made him want her helplessly but, at the same time, it scared him, suddenly aware of his own grossness beside her. He hesitated and she knew she had won. For two months before the baby was born she held him off; then for two months after. And this established a habit of withholding. The children sucked her dry; didn't he see she was exhausted? He saw and acquiesced numbly, feeling again the weight of his own years. It was to be expected. Secretly, he had never believed his violent Indian summer could last.

They imported a German girl from Julie's village to help with the children and the housework, but this only added to their load. Now they had a teenager in the house, forever confiding to them

13

about her parents, her weight, her boyfriends. The intense privacy of their life together was broken. The atmosphere cooled. They made love now like they paid the milkman, once a week. They had settled belatedly into the habit of marriage. Julie began to blossom.

Her tame pack of talkative young men, always jostling each other for her attention, meant that she need never again be lonely as she had been in the chill, industrial north. There was always a volunteer to walk with her in the park with the children, to give her coffee in the morning or take her to the cinema at night when Charles was working. She let them hold her hand or occasionally brush her cool lips. But she took none of them to bed. Privately, they bored her with their obsessed literary chatter and envy of each other's tiny successes in a mini-world shaken by an article in one of the weeklies or two minutes on television. They dropped names assiduously and were eaten by a passion to be known. So this was the culture Europe had been broken in defending. She thought of the grey-faced Russian soldier, staggering with fatigue and looted booze, who had appeared like an exterminating angel one afternoon when she was thirteen; and the GIs who paid her in Hershey bars, which she ate, and packets of Camels, which she sold; and of her unbending Lutheran father who had disappeared in one of the camps. All so that these bright young men could play at their penny-poker literary life. She found them comic. At least Charles had his secretive and grim sensuality. That was enough, more than enough, for her. So she flirted vaguely and kept herself to herself.

Soon enough, she discovered that she had been co-opted unwittingly into the Muse business: the only begetter of several sheaves of love poems, mostly in lower case, and the heroine of a rather smart first novel by a thin young man who swiftly disappeared into television. Invariably, she found herself hard to recognize, even between the lines, but she did her best to appear flattered. In private she and Charles would giggle over the offerings. All that hopeless yet somehow complacent passion brought them closer together and inspired their intermittent sex. And because he knew their secrets Charles began to exert a kind of power over the assiduous young men. They listened to him almost with respect, bewildered because his wife remained faithful to him despite their attentions.

It seemed natural that it should be Charles who organized the international summer school. After all, he was in touch, wasn't he? He spoke German and had an interesting German wife. His older colleagues were as glad to escape this interruption of their long summer idleness as he was to accept it. In every way, he was now part of the structure, indispensable.

2

Someone was talking about the latest outrage in the latest American war. The voice was ripe and confident and did not relent. On and on, throbbing faintly with indignation and self-congratulation. Sam stood, as usual, at the edge of Julie's pack, since it seemed the place to be. On and on went the voice, on and on. He looked across at Julie. Her pale hair was knotted back, but a few wisps had come loose and hung along the delicate line of her jawbone, blonde on blonde. The voice went on dispensing its plummy vowels, drowning out the clink of glasses and the chatter of the other drinkers in the bar. Julie was looking down, nodding faintly, as if in agreement. But when she looked up her eyes were wide and full and elsewhere. It seemed to Sam that the whole of her life was pressing against their clear blue, and her life was utterly alien. I've never seen a real woman before, he thought. He shivered.

His sudden movement brought her back from wherever she had been. She smiled at him. 'A goose walking over my grave,' he said across the booming orator who paused, glanced at him contemptuously, and then boomed on : 'One would have thought that an induthtrial machine ath thophithticated ath the American' – rich vowels, cultivated lisp, the confident eye staring down its audience – 'wouldn't need an old-fashioned thtimuluth like war to keep it healthy. One would have thought it could diverthify into, thay, thpathe technology with a minimum of dithcomfort. Wouldn't one?' Indeed, one would, agreed the pack.

'I must go,' said Julie, 'it's the children's bedtime. I'll be at the seminar this evening.' She shook her head to the instantaneous offers to see her home and left.

Since Sam was nobody, nobody noticed when he slipped out after her. He saw her disappearing round the far corner of one of the colleges, walking fast, dwarfed by the grey gothic facade. He trotted after her. 'Hey,' he called as he came near, 'Mrs Stone.'

She turned, her face stiff with irritation. But when she saw who it was she smiled. 'Oh, it's you. I thought I was in for another lecture on imperialism.'

'God forbid, Mrs Stone. Enough is enough.'

'Julie,' she said. 'Everyone calls me Julie.'

'Julie then.' He fell into step beside her. 'Where were you during the sermon?'

'A long way from here.'

'Lucky girl.'

'I'm not a girl,' she said. 'Not any more. I'm a mother of two.'

'You don't look it.'

'But I feel it. And that's what matters.'

They walked on past an ornamental iron gateway, painted black, its flourishes picked out in gold; behind it a hundred yards of velvet lawn with deep borders of flowers. An elderly figure paced quietly in the dusty evening sunlight.

'It's a beautiful city,' said Sam, 'if only they'd stop talking.'

'They'll never do that,' Julie replied. 'Talk is what keeps them alive. It makes them feel they exist. Talking heads, hundreds of talking heads.' She sounded tired.

'How do you stand it, year after year?'

'It's only been two years. Anyway, I have my babies.' She pronounced the word 'bay-bees', lengthening it out as though in pleasure. For the first time in his young life Sam thought it would be nice to have children. Somehow sexy.

'They don't talk too much yet,' she said. 'At least, they don't pronounce. But I suppose their time will come. It's contagious.'

'What about the professor?'

'He's a quiet man.' Her voice was neutral.

They walked on in silence. When they reached the corner of Julie's street she stopped and faced him.

'I'll say good-bye now.' She held out her hand.

Sam took it. It was light and cool. He watched her mouth as she spoke, wondering how it would taste.

'I'll see you this evening at the seminar,' she said.

'You mean you're really going?'

'Of course. I'm the professor's wife. Anyway, I'm ignorant. I don't know about things.'

'Well,' said Sam, 'you could have fooled me.'

He watched her walk off down the road. Halfway to her house she turned and waved impatiently, as if shooing him away. He waved back and went. Two streets away the evening traffic was throbbing quietly home, its dull murmur a ground bass to his elation. What a lovely evening, he thought. What a lovely evening. But later, over dinner, the rattle of talkers depressed him more than usual.

During the seminar he tried not to look at her, not wanting to push his luck. But the ripe drone of the speaker went over him and round him and he knew she was watching. Once he looked up and caught her blue, amused stare. She smiled at him quickly, on and off, like an opening window flashing for a moment. And immediately he felt elated again, but looked away. When he joined in the discussion he ducked his bushy head forward nervously and his sentences came out without main verbs, shrewd enough but not quite coherent. Talking for her benefit, wanting to shine, knowing he had missed his chance. After two attempts he gave up and sat staring sullenly at the floor.

Like a large, nervous child, she decided. She was irritated by the elaborate charade of shyness he was playing out for her benefit. As if it mattered. He was livelier and more vulnerable than the smooth talking-machines around him, but he made her feel old – old and worldly and, at the same time, faintly absurd. None of this had anything to do with her. When the meeting ended she turned her attention to the assiduous pack, deliberately laying on the charm, and when she next looked round Sam had gone. Her irritation increased.

She and Charles walked home slowly through the sticky night. The stars seemed blurred above the trees, as though greasy with heat. As usual, Charles took her arm just above the elbow, part policeman, part proud owner. She shook herself free without speaking. Out of term the town always seemed to die a little without its swarm of undergraduates. The streets were quiet, the pubs long emptied. Gradually she became aware of someone walking silently, on rubber soles, fifty yards behind, keeping to the tangled shadows on the other side of the road. She glanced back once but could only make out a vague, surreptitious shape. She looked back again while Charles fumbled with his keys at the front door. Someone was hovering at the corner. She saw a triangular blur of face above a dark shirt before the figure moved quickly back into the shadows. Sam? She was certain it was, though for no good reason since she could make out nothing definite. She wanted to giggle. Between the Russians, the Americans and Charles she had missed her adolescence. Now she had a sudden insight into that overheated world of innocence, stupidity and conceit. She felt a little spasm of tenderness, as though it were a child out there, and smiled into the darkness knowing that whoever lurked there was too far away to see.

She went straight up to bed, saying she was dead tired, and when Charles came up pretended to be asleep. She watched him between her eyelashes as he slowly undressed. He moved without zest, pausing a moment naked by the bed to look down at her. His body was curiously hairless, his swelling stomach and soft shoulders grey and sad. She breathed regularly, seeming to sleep. Finally, he fumbled under the pillow for his pyjamas and went off to the bathroom. By the time he came back she had turned away to the far side of the bed. She heard him sigh and pick up a book. When he switched the light out at last he, too, turned resignedly to his own side of the bed. She waited until his breathing settled to a slow, faint snore, then rolled on her back and lay watching the shadows run on the ceiling, thinking about her dead father and her dead youth.

The next day, when she joined the summer school at the morning coffee break, Sam hovered uneasily near her, sheepish and speechless. He blushed when she spoke to him and mumbled something she couldn't catch. She felt sorry for him, thinking, How awful it is to be young, then realized that she was also sorry for herself because she couldn't remember ever being young in that way.

At the end of the morning he sidled up to her like a conspirator and muttered unsteadily: 'Why not skip lunch and come and have a beer and sandwich?' His face was stiff with nervousness, waiting to be rebuffed. She smiled encouragingly and said yes, but found herself glancing round the room to see if anyone had noticed. It's catching, she thought. Adolescence is a contagious disease.

The pub was one she didn't know; in a back street, small and full of elderly workmen who nodded at Sam when he came in. He parked Julie in a corner and went to the bar where the landlord perched on a stool, a tiny, purple-faced man, nursing a little round belly like a football. While his wife served the food and drinks, he and Sam muttered together intimately.

'Well,' said Sam when he finally rejoined Julie, 'there's flattery. He didn't want to serve you. Said you were too young and wouldn't believe me when I told him you had two children and were married to a professor.' He was hot with pleasure. Clearly, his stock in the pub had risen.

'They never do,' said Julie. 'It's one of the things I have to put up with.' She tried to sound indifferent but her face gave her away. After all these years she was crossing the lines into the ranks of the young.

The day was overcast and even stickier than the night before. Although the door to the street was open, the dim little bar gradually began to darken. When the landlord switched on the lights the gloom outside deepened. Suddenly there was a brief cough of thunder, then a moment of stillness. A faint, irregular drum-tap began, growing quickly to a steady roar. Through the open door they could see the rain bouncing off the pavement as if off a hot stove.

'Someone up there has turned the hose on,' said Sam.

'There isn't anyone up there.'

For ten minutes the rain bucketed dementedly down, then stopped as suddenly as it had begun. They ate their food in silence, subdued by the violence of the downpour. But when they came out of the pub the air was cooler and the sun made the wet streets glisten and steam.

'Let's go for a walk in the park,' said Julie. 'I still have a little time before the au pair girl goes off.'

They walked past the colleges with nothing to say. From time to time, Sam glanced sideways at her. Her pure profile and fair hair amazed him. He couldn't believe his luck. He sniffed deeply, inhaling the smell of the damp street and the occasional bursts of scent from the gardens.

In the park the rain had deepened the green of the leaves and the immaculate grass. The elms dripped steadily on them as they walked. Julie stopped suddenly. 'Look out,' she said and bent down.

The gravel in front of them seemed to be moving with an indeterminate, swarming life of its own.

'Aren't they beautiful?' she said.

Sam crouched beside her. The whole surface of the path was stirring uneasily. A river of tiny frogs moved across it, dark green, dark brown, shimmering black, moving blindly.

'I wonder if they've only just been hatched,' said Julie.

'Maybe the storm did it.'

'Maybe.'

She reached out and caught one. She crouched over it for a moment, brooding, then turned her cupped hands to Sam, leaning on him slightly as she did so. He looked at the tiny, dark creature on the palm of her hand.

'Feel it,' she said.

He ran his fingers over the frog's dank back, then, as though accidentally, over her wrist. He shivered, but not because of the frog.

'Creepy,' he said.

'Nonsense. It's beautiful. Look at the green.'

She put her hand back down on the ground, palm upward. The frog didn't move. She made a gentle clucking noise at the back of her throat, as if to encourage it. Still the frog didn't move. Instead, two more of the tiny, slimy creatures clambered heavily onto her palm, one of them trailing a leg behind it like a piece of forgotten luggage. They lay there, their chests swollen and heaving with effort, their eyes hooded slits. Sam put his hand over hers. He could feel the things stirring dankly.

'They seem to like you,' he said.

She replied: 'Of course. I'm a witch. Didn't you know?' She smiled at him slyly. 'That's why I look so young. I commune with the dead and they reward me by protecting me from wrinkles.'

'And naturally the frogs are your familiars?'

'Naturally.'

Sam laughed uneasily, his hand still over hers. Then he leaned across and tried to kiss her mouth. She stood up quickly.

'Don't be stupid.'

'What's stupid? It seemed right.'

'You're in too much of a hurry, Sam. *Trop empressé.*' She looked down at the dark mass still squirming across the path. 'If we go any further, we'll step on them. So we'd better go back.'

'OK.' His voice was surly. He could feel the weariness coming off her. He'd been made a fool of – and had made fool of himself.

Julie took his hand. 'You mustn't mind. It isn't worth it.' When he didn't answer she added, 'Give me time.'

Sam looked at her gratefully. Fool, she thought, Why did I say that? What am I doing? She turned abruptly and began to walk back towards the park gates. What am I doing? Sam padded along beside her.

'I'm sorry,' he said. 'Blame it on the thunder. Like the frogs.'

'All right. Like the frogs.'

A bond had been sealed between them. There was nothing more to say.

The next day Sam went off to the pub at lunchtime. He caught Julie's eye as he left the seminar room and made a small gesture with his head. But he said nothing. Ten minutes later she joined him in the bar. They drank their glasses of beer, ate their sandwiches and talked in a desultory way about nothing in particular. Testing each other out, moving blindfolded. There were no more walks together. A week passed like that, at once neutral and intimate. He was careful not to touch her.

In the evenings, when Julie wasn't there, he flirted laboriously with a chic Parisienne who attended his seminars: large dark eyes and a faintly glowing skin, as though her body had been carefully ripened in the sun like the grapes of an expensive vintage. She had the vague, insolent air that goes with promiscuity, though she called it liberation and marshalled a great deal of elegant French rhetoric to support her case. Sam argued with her, then slept with her, since that was what she wanted. It seemed to him the reverse of how things usually were: first sex, then arguments, like his parents. But the French girl, true to her theories, wanted nothing to do with him out of bed. 'I do not wish to lose my independence.' Her mouth was full but neat; her lips moved precisely, shaping each emphasis. She was full of emphases. 'We have an arrangement which gives us both pleasure. It is enough. It is necessary for us to be adult.' She was nineteen. Sam didn't argue. His brief afternoon interludes with Julie were easier now his nights were no longer lonely.

She knew of course, although he was discreet and as attentive as ever. She told herself that that's how it is in the summer school: everyone for himself; a highbrow meat-market. She told herself she was relieved. But underneath she was afraid. She had missed her chance. Something was slipping away that would never come back. The weather had turned brilliant after the storm. She stood in the park playground rhythmically pushing her daughter to and fro on the swing, saying to herself at each push, Too late, too late, too late.

When Charles next came at her with his blind urgency she didn't plead her usual weariness. But for once he left her unmoved and she was too depressed to pretend. He leaned over her, his face soft and smooth with lovemaking.

'What's up, darling? Is there anything wrong?'

'Nothing. I'm fine. Just blue, that's all. A bit blue.' The voice in her ear said, Too late. Julie Stone, this is your life. She was glad when Charles finally fell asleep.

That night she dreamed of her father. He was walking towards her down a long street between two high brick walls. She could hear the thud and clatter of a factory. The air tasted of smoke. He was dressed in black, his sombre face and iron-grey head twisted in some kind of pain. She wondered what they had been doing to him. When he came near he stopped, looked round carefully, and began to speak in a low, hurrying voice. But the din of the factory drowned out his words. 'I can't hear,' she said. 'Please, I can't hear.' He spoke again and the noise became louder. She shook her head. 'I can't hear.' Finally he stopped, looked at her contemptuously and began to walk back down the long, grubby perspective. She called after him, 'Don't go. Please don't go.' But he did not pause. She woke weeping and lay for a long while staring at the shadows on the ceiling. 'Don't go,' she said out loud. Then she remembered he was dead and began to cry again. Charles stirred in his sleep and put an arm across her. She moved away.

3

The summer school was coming to an end. As a final gesture, Charles had arranged a mass visit to Stratford and an evening at the theatre. Sam decided not to go, to the reluctant approval of the French girl who thought he was demonstrating his indifference.

'If we are not back too late,' she murmured, 'perhaps I will see you tonight.'

'You know where I live,' he said in the casual way she cultivated so strenuously.

'*Entendu.*' She seemed delighted.

At lunchtime Sam went off to the pub as usual. A beer, he thought, a game of shove ha'penny, then an afternoon's work. The prospect of a few hours on his own seemed terribly attractive .

Julie arrived as he was finishing his drink.

'I thought you were going to Stratford.' For once the sight of her irritated him; he felt intruded on and made no effort to disguise it.

She ignored his surly tone. 'I decided not to. I didn't want the au pair putting the children to bed. She's in one of her states. God knows what idiocy she'd commit.' When he didn't answer she went on, 'Why is it that au pairs have the curse at least once a week?' She was surprised how nervous she felt, and how placating.

'An occupational disease, I suppose,' said Sam and they both laughed dutifully. 'You want a drink?'

'Not particularly.'

'Me neither.'

They went out into the sun. Her frock was dark blue and dingy, her hair was scraped back in a bun, she wore sensible shoes. The brilliant light made her look hopeless and inept, like a child dressed in her mother's clothes. Sam's irritation increased. Why won't she let me be?

'I was going to work,' he said.

'Must you?'

'Not really, I suppose.'

'It's such a lovely day I thought it would be nice to go for a walk in the country.' She was pleading now. 'Just to get out of town for an hour or so.'

'All right,' he said grudgingly, 'for an hour or so.' He thought, She doesn't want me, she wants something of me. Why should I be used? They walked towards his car.

'You seem fed up,' said Julie.

'This course has gone on too long. I've had enough.'

'Will you go away when it's over?'

'I don't know. I should stay on. I've a lot of work to do in the library. But I'd like to get out. Enough is enough.'

'Anywhere in particular?'

'I don't care as long as it's out of England. But I'll probably stick around. I'm broke as usual.'

'Have you ever been to Germany?'

He shook his head.

'The south is beautiful. Bavaria and Schwabia. The landscape seems to move.' She lengthened the word out: moooove. 'Here everything is so settled. And there are beautiful little churches, *Schwabische Barock*.'

'You sound like a travel brochure.'

'It's my home.'

'I thought England was your home now.'

'I just live here. You feel differently about where you were born.'

'I suppose so.'

They climbed into Sam's old car and drove for a while in silence, northwards through the placid suburbs.

'You don't like me much today,' she said at last.

He glanced sideways at her and didn't reply. Eventually he said, 'Why do you wear your hair in that schoolmistressy bun?'

'If that's all that's worrying you.' Obediently, she lifted her hands to her head and fiddled with the pins. Her hair fell suddenly loose, a fine golden curtain round her face and down her shoulders. 'That better?' she said.

'Much better.' They both laughed.

'Where do you want to go?' Sam asked. 'Or don't you mind?'

'I know a nice walk. Turn left after Bamford. It's really nice.'

The main road curved smoothly through long alleys of trees, dipped steeply into Bamford, past grey stone houses and a grey stone church with a squat tower, then climbed again.

'Left here,' she said at the top of the hill. The hedges were thick with honeysuckle and brambles, and so high that the lane seemed to be burrowing down into the fields. Eventually, it began to climb and the hedges dwindled to stunted green lines between cornfields. At the top of the hill was a wood of old oaks and birch trees.

'Here,' said Julie.

Sam parked in a clearing at the entrance to a long, dim ride. They walked close together, without touching, under the arching trees, their feet making no sound on the turf. It was like being in a silent, green artery leading to the heart of the countryside.

'I love this place,' she said.

An owl, disturbed by the sound of her voice, lurched softly across the path in front of them and disappeared, offended and erratic, into the dark trees.

'You woke him up,' said Sam.

They walked on without talking. Occasionally, a rabbit burst out of the scrub oak and made a terrified dash for the undergrowth on the other side of the path. The ride curved slowly at its end and they came out onto an open grassy field sloping down from the crest of the wooded ridge. They sat down, the forest behind them, in front a cornfield shivering in the slight breeze like a horse's coat. Beyond, the fields stretched vaguely towards more hills, bluish and rounded, broken by the far spire of a church pointing above a fold of land. High above them, two hawks moved slowly round each other, waiting.

'It's so old, that wood,' she said. 'As though it had been there forever.' Sam stared up at the hawk turning, turning, and did not reply. She said, 'I'd like to have been around when all Europe was forested, like the Congo. All that darkness. No wonder they believed in evil.' Her voice was sleepy, talking to herself not to him. 'The Roman legions marched eastwards into Germany for three months without ever coming out of the forest. And all the time they were being picked off, disappearing.'

'Then what happened?'

'Oh, they just turned round and marched back again.'

'No wonder the place has never been properly civilized.' Sam lay on his back in the long grass watching the hawks.

'You've never been there. You don't know. It's just different from England. Its roots are elsewhere.'

'They produce bloody twisted flowers.'

'Not all of them,' she said. Sam didn't answer.

'Look at the hawks,' he said at last. 'I wonder what they're after.'

'Dinner, most likely.'

'It must be beautiful up there. Really free.'

One of the hawks stopped circling and began to soar slowly upwards on a thermal.

'The way they use the air,' said Sam. 'I've always thought they must see it, as if it were coloured.'

The hawk hovered, its wings faintly quivering. Then it dropped suddenly down, like the finger of God. There was a terrified explosion of small birds in a copse at the edge of a field, then the hawk laboured up again with something dangling from his pinions. He flew lazily above them towards the wood.

'The Romans never got him either,' said Julie.

'That's different.' Sam rolled over onto his stomach and watched the bird settle on a tree at the edge of the forest. For a moment the creature peered intently towards them as they lay, then began to jab with his beak at the broken animal he was holding. The other hawk still turned slowly high above.

'The world must look very simple from up there,' said Sam, rolling over onto his back again. 'Kill, eat, sleep and see things from a distance. If our eyes were as big as a peregrine's proportionately, they'd be the size of our fists.'

'Where did you pick up that bit of information?'

'I read a book about them. They fascinate me.'

'Oh,' she said ironically, 'do you fancy yourself as a predator?'

'No. Alas, no. But I wish my life was simplified.'

'Don't we all?'

They lapsed into silence again, listening to the faint summer sounds: the bees humming in the clover around them and the jumbled notes of the birds. The second hawk had drifted away and the larks rose and fell as they sang, as though balancing on jets of water. A butterfly flew vaguely over Sam's face and settled on Julie's stomach, its wings trembling, bright orange and brown against the drab blue of her dress. Sam sat up to look at it. She watched him, her eyes blue slits against the sun. When he leaned down and kissed her, her mouth opened under his and she put her arms round him. She tasted like she looked, of the light cool scent of her cologne.

All she said was, 'I was wondering how long you'd take.'

They went on kissing intently in the long grass: mouth, eyes, ears, throat. He undid the front of her dress, pushed up her bra and began stroking her breasts. Her skin was pale but faintly yellow, as if the colour of her hair had seeped downwards over her body. Her hands and tongue moved on him deftly. But when he slid his hand up between her thighs she pulled away sharply and sat up.

'I can't. Don't you see?' Her voice hissed like an aroused cat's.

'The hell I see. You want it. I want it. What's there to see?' His fingers locked round her wrist. He was trembling with anger and frustration. 'I know I'm young. But I'm too old for cock-teasing.'

'I can't. Not yet. There's too much ...' She made a sideways ducking movement, as though a great weight were pressing down on her shoulders. 'I'm sorry,' she said. Two tears oozed slowly out of the corners of her eyes.

'For Christ's sake,' said Sam, 'let's just call it off.' She was so upset that his anger seemed out of place. What did it matter? He began to feel sorry for her. 'You're a real mess, aren't you?'

'I'm sorry,' she repeated. 'I wish it was easier.'

'I think we'd better go.' He stood up and pulled her up after him. She stood passively as he brushed the pieces of grass off her dress. He looked at her critically. 'You'd better comb your hair.'

She did as she was told, like a chastened child, then followed him towards the wood. At their approach the sated hawk flew heavily off, loggy with after-dinner sleep. As they walked back down the shadowy ride, she took his hand tentatively, but he didn't respond. She stood helplessly while he opened the car door and steered her in. Her life seemed to have drained away and she moved like a sleepwalker. He got in, started the engine, then reached across, turned her blank face to his and kissed her gently.

'It's all right. Don't worry.' Her tears had run down into her mouth, leaving a faint taste of salt. 'What a mess,' said Sam.

The afternoon sun was thickening to gold as they drove back down the deep lane towards town. She closed her eyes, numb with fatigue and unable to tolerate the rich light.

When she got home the children were already screaming and splashing in the bath. They were sturdy, blunt-featured little creatures, like their father, though their blonde hair and pale colouring were hers. She helped the au pair wash and dry them. She buttoned their pyjamas and turned the pages of a picture book for them while they drank their evening milk. But she seemed to see them from far off, through the wrong end of a telescope. What had they to do with her?

After they were settled, she went into her bedroom, locking the door behind her, and lay down on the bed with her eyes closed. What had they to do with her? She sat up on the edge of the bed, numbly watching the evening gather in the trees outside the window. Then she stood up, took off her clothes and stared at herself in the mirror. Charles's picture watched her from one side of the dressing table, her father's watched her from the other. She ran her hands over her pale, unmarked body. Her youthfulness struck her as somehow indecent. She thought of the grey-faced, drunken Russian soldier and her first terror turning slowly to excitement as he laboured urgently inside her. What had that to do with her, either? What had anything? She put her hands on the edge of the dressing table and leaned forwards until her face was close to the mirror. She examined her smooth complexion carefully, like a cosmetician looking for flaws, her childishly delicate nose and chin, her pale mouth and long eyes, and the straight, fine hair, hanging forwards over her breasts. 'I don't even know myself,' she said out loud. 'Why won't they let me be?'

4

The lamp on Sam's desk cast a narrow pool of light, shutting out the rest of the room. The street was quiet, the house was quiet; he read. Occasionally, a moth drifted in through the open window and plastered itself longingly against the lampshade, stirring uneasily when he puffed cigarette smoke over it. Peace. Even the dullness of the book he was reading was reassuring: the definitive biography of a definitive master, every last detail day by day, from grandparents to gravesheets, saying so much so precisely that the man's troubled, indigent, laborious life somehow amounted to nothing at all. Five hundred pages of nothingness. One man's life and work transformed into another's lifework. What tedium.

Yet he felt at peace. The heavy-footed prose, the solemn accumulation of trivial fact after fact, the years of service in a dead discipline made up, if nothing else, a world apart. No mess, no tears, no grass in the hair. Should he, too, become a literary mortician inhaling the dust and silence of all those beautiful medieval libraries the city so prided itself on? To be at once dead and yet, in university terms, successful. Like Charles, old porpoise snout. It must be a satisfaction of a kind, or at least a release. Then he thought of a lifetime of bright conversation, evening after evening yapping at his colleagues over the port and walnuts. No peace there, despite the dark panelling, the old silver and odour of scholarship. Out: out of this town, this life, this idiotic flirtation. It's time to go.

The light knock on his door surprised him. He looked at his watch: nine-thirty. How could they have got back from Stratford so soon? he wondered, thinking of the French girl.

'It's not locked,' he called.

Julie came in, closed the door and stood with her back to it, in the shadows away from the pool of light over his table. When he got to his feet she walked quickly across to him and began kissing him as though parched. 'I'm sorry,' she murmured. 'Please, please. I'm sorry.' She unbuttoned his shirt, kissing his throat and chest, her hands moving on his spine and the backs of his thighs. 'I'm sorry,' she repeated, 'I'm sorry.' They clung together like two drowning people pulling each other under. Eventually, he picked her up and carried her across the landing to his bedroom, locking the door behind them. By the time he had his shoes and socks off she was already undressed. Her pale body was thin but supple in the darkness. Like a sword, he thought as they rolled together onto the bed.

'Look,' she whispered, 'will you go along with me on one thing? I don't want you inside. We can do other things. Please. You won't be disappointed, I promise you. But don't come into me. I couldn't face Charles again.'

'Does that matter?'

'Of course it matters. I have to live with him, don't I?'

'Do you?'

'You know I do. Don't be stupid.'

Thank God, thought Sam, then lay quietly for a while, watching her blonde head move intently on him. Well, he thought, well, well, well, well.

Later he asked, 'What do we do now?'

'I'll come to you when I can,' she said. 'I'll let you know. You must be patient. Don't push me.'

'Patience isn't my strong suit. But I'll try.'

'Do,' she said. 'There's no alternative.'

Her body seemed silvery in the dim light. He stroked her back gently. 'You create your own moonlight,' he said. 'Maybe you are a witch.'

'Of course I am,' she answered seriously. 'Why else do you think I'm here?'

'I had a simpler explanation. I thought you fancied me.'

'There's no difference.'

'There is for me.'

She left around eleven, suddenly panic-stricken that the bus might be back early. He lay watching her dress, thinking, I've always wanted her. Always. Long before I met her. She paused at the door, smiling. 'Soon,' she said and was gone. He fell asleep thinking about her.

Then came awake suddenly. Someone was standing silently by his bed. He rolled over and switched on the light: the French girl.

'You frightened me,' he said. 'What's the time?'

'One o'clock. You were sleeping very deeply.'

'Was I? What was the play?'

'*Othello.*'

'How was it?'

'*Passionant. Mais pas chic.*'

'What's not chic about it?'

'Jealousy. Jealousy is not chic. Not at all.'

'What is, then?'

'Infidelity.'

'Jesus Christ. Jesus Henry Christ. Where did you dream that up?'

'I did not dream it up. It's a truth.'

'Dumb,' said Sam.

'Do you want me to go?'

'It's up to you.'

His indifference was so obviously unfeigned that the French girl was overwhelmed. Had she misjudged him? She took off her clothes and slipped into bed beside him.

'You know,' she said, pausing in her knowledgeable kisses. 'It is as well the course is finishing. I could fall in love with you.'

'Yes,' he agreed without hesitation, 'it's as well.'

The girl's eyes darkened and widened. What had she been missing? For the first time, she stayed all night. Occasionally, Sam stirred in his sleep, half woken by her presence. He lay aware of her warmth, inhaling the mingled smell of her scent and sweat and sex. Then he would put his arms round her and drift contentedly back to sleep, thinking of Julie.

5

All the way back from Stratford Charles sat on his own at the front of the bus watching the driver's creased neck, his blunt hands on the wheel, thinking, Why did she stay behind? Why did she stay behind?

At his back the students and their young teachers were busy putting the finishing touches on their three weeks' business. Most were talking quietly just under the noise of the bus, one or two couples were kissing discreetly; a small group was singing in German:

Muss i' denn, muss i' denn zum Städtele hinaus . . .

The melody reminded him of his first days with Julie. Everything reminded him of Julie. He was besotted still. After all these years. Why did she stay behind?

He watched the long cathedrals of trees forming in the headlights. When the bus came out into open fields a yellow moon hung low in the sky, swollen and lopsided. Gibbous, he said to himself, from the Latin *gibbus,* a hump. A humpbacked moon. Why not a gibbous whale? It pleased him to know about things. He had knowledge, he had certainty, he was armoured. Or was he? Watching the enlarged moon peering down like a bloated face, slightly sinister, he felt only the vacancy of the night and the fields and the life he led. You need to be married, he thought, to understand real loneliness. Sleeping night after night in the same bed with someone who becomes, night after night, day after day, more remote. These days, even sex intensified the loneliness, leaving him washed up on some far, isolated coast. It must be the same for Julie. Was it the same for everybody? Why did no one ever say? His mind rambled: Who prays together stays together. Absurd, he thought. How about us professors? Who reads together breeds together. Not any more. Who sleeps apart weeps apart.

Yet he couldn't get away from her for a moment. Julie herself eluded him as she always had. He knew every detail of her daily routine: the children, the house, the entertaining, the mocked troop of admirers. But beyond those, behind her eyes, she lived apart. Strictly private. Trespassers will be prosecuted. So he had been careful never to intrude, knowing their differences. Yet he was obsessed by her. Or rather, not by her but by the details of her body: by the pale hollow of skin between her collar bone and her neck, the four hairs round her left nipple, her delicate wrists and the insides of her thighs, by the way her lips left her teeth wet when her mouth relaxed. He knew these details like he knew the authors he specialized in, passionately and minutely. It's not enough, he thought, staring at the moon as it sped through the trunks of another Gothic aisle of trees. I know nothing.

Why had she stayed behind? She complained continually of never getting away; his colleagues were boring, the youngsters trivial, the town's restaurants shoddy. True, all true. Yet when the chance came to get out for a few hours she said no. The au pair was in a state and couldn't cope with the children. But the au pair was always in a state – a state was her natural state – and had never properly coped. He suddenly saw Julie lying naked on their bed, her knees raised, someone else's hand on her thighs. Whose? Her tame pack was in the bus behind him, busily charming the already nostalgic foreign girls. The only absentee was Sam Green. Green? He was too young for her, too newly arrived on the scene, too naive. Surely no competition there. Anyway, he had his hands full with that swinging French girl. What was her name? Ghislaine? Gilberte? Something like that. No, hardly Sam Green. Maybe Julie just wanted to be on her own for a few hours. And he saw her again, naked on the bed with her knees raised. She had had lovers before she married him, but he knew nothing about them: a row of faceless, powerful figures. One, two, twenty? She would never tell him. Did she compare him with them in bed? *Shall I compare thee to a summer's day?* Or night?

It's just *Othello*, he thought. I'm too suggestible.

Oh thou weed, that art so lovely fair and smell'st so sweet
That the sense aches at thee. Would thou hadst ne'er been born.

The Bard always had a word for it. All the bards always had a word for it, some better than others. Quotations stifle me. *I am not Prince Hamlet, nor was meant to be.* Still less Othello. I'm too old and haven't the figure, and I live my life at second hand, through other men's writing. Maybe I should set up a quotation agency: 'A quote for every occasion. A specialist service for politicians, headmasters and after-dinner speakers. You want the best quotes. We have them.' His heart bumped heavily, his mouth tasted sour. I'm a rambling old fool, he thought. My learning's gone rancid and is contaminating my life. He looked again out of the bus window. The moon was smaller and clearer now, higher up in the sky. Through the windscreen he could see the faint orange glow of the town's lights. Not far now. Why did she stay behind?

The bus stopped in the middle of the town and Charles walked home through the echoing streets quickly, as though late for an appointment. He was relieved to see the light through the cracks of the bedroom curtains. Tonight, at least, she wasn't feigning sleep. He let himself in quietly and paused indecisively just inside the hall. Then he went into the dark kitchen and opened the refrigerator door. The jumbled light from inside threw odd shadows into the corners of the room. He took a long swig from a bottle of milk and tore a strip of meat from the debris of a roast chicken. It tasted fibry and of nothing in particular, like chewing the plastic inside the fridge itself. He took another swig of milk to clean his mouth and closed the fridge door. The shadowy presences in the corners vanished abruptly. He went slowly upstairs, paused at the bedroom door, *not yet*, and crossed to the bathroom. While the basin filled, he carefully took off his jacket and tie and rolled up his sleeves. Gratefully, he splashed his face and neck with cold water then leaned forward on stiffened arms, enjoying the coolness of the water round his wrists. A key clicked automatically in his head:

O *plunge your hands in water,*
  Plunge them in up to the wrist:
Stare, stare in the basin
  And wonder what you've missed.

He looked at himself in the mirror. You're getting old, Charley-boy. Old. His dripping image stared back at him unsympathetically, stranger to stranger, face to face. He stayed like that for about a minute, his mind drifting, then he dried himself briskly, briskly brushed his teeth, briskly crossed the landing to the bed-room.

Julie was lying propped up on the pillows, reading in the narrow lamplight. She smiled at him : 'How was it?'

'Pretty good,' he smiled back. 'Speaking as an Elizabethan theatre critic, I would say that Mr Shakespeare shows promise. He has a rare gift for the haunting phrase but should learn not to make so much hinge on a trivial incident like a lost handkerchief. Mr Burbage gave his usual vigorous performance.'

'And speaking as an Elizabeth the Second critic?'

'As I said, pretty good. Too much business, of course. But they'd have to try much harder to ruin a play as good as that.' He undressed slowly, folding his trousers carefully on to their hanger and smoothing out his jacket. 'I'm tired,' he said.

'Me too.'

'What did you do with yourself?'

'Nothing in particular. Went for a walk this afternoon on my own. Settled the children. Went for another little stroll this evening. Read. A nice quiet time.'

He looked at her and she met his eyes steadily, then went back to her book.

'Maybe you chose better than I did,' he said.

'I doubt it. I wanted to see the play but I was so tired. I thought it would be better to be on my own for a bit.'

'Did you see anyone?' he asked casually.

'Not a soul.' Her eyes, meeting his, were faintly amused. 'That's what was nice about the day. Only the kids and poor Heidi. Naturally, she has the curse again.'

'Naturally. It's a good ten days since her last, isn't it? That's late by her standards.'

They both giggled intimately. He sat down on the bed beside her and kissed her without pressure. Her mouth was unusually relaxed. His lips wandered lightly across her cheek, down her neck to the hollow where it met her collar-bone. Under the cool scent of her cologne, she smelled somehow aroused. For a moment, he again saw another man's hand on her lifted thigh, like a scene glimpsed in a flash of lightning, unmoving in the middle of movement, then lost. He kissed her mouth again. She submitted but did not respond.

The younger child began to sob next door.

'She's on cue as usual,' said Charles.

'She sounds as though she's had a bad dream. I'll go.'

'Don't worry. I'm still up. Let me try.'

He opened the nursery door softly. The nightlight made an amber gloom, without details. The boy on the top bunk slept on his back, his hair over his forehead, his mouth slightly open. On the lower bunk, the little girl sat up at once, still whimpering confusedly.

'It's all right,' said Charles, 'it's daddy.'

The child stretched out her arms. He picked her up and sat down in a chair by the bunks. The child flattened herself against his chest, her head in his neck. He held her with both arms round her small body.

'Me fright,' she said.

'What frightened you, darling?'

'Goats,' she said.

'Goats? You mean Ghosts?'

'Goats,' she repeated.

'It's all right, darling. It was a dream. Daddy's here now. The ghosts have all gone. And the goats.'

'All donn,' said the child. She lay against him unresistingly, already part way back to sleep. He rubbed his cheek against her head and began to sing quietly:

Ye banks and braes of bonny Doon,
How can ye bloom sae fresh and fair? . . .

'All donn,' murmured the child again, reassured. She lay passively, as though moulded to his chest, without bone or muscle, while Charles sang. Terrible, he was thinking. Terrible. They demand too much. And you have to respond. Excessively. There's no alternative.

... To hear the birdies tell o'er their love ...

It's not enough. In the end, they make things worse. In the end they just add to your loneliness. He went on singing, more and more quietly, to the end of the song:

But my false love, she stole the rose,
And ah, she left the thorn wi'me.

The child was already asleep. When he lay her back down in her bed she wriggled a little to get the covers over her, then lay still, arms outstretched as though gliding. The chair creaked as he stood up and the older child stirred uneasily on the upper bunk. Charles kissed his forehead. 'Go to sleep,' he said. The boy murmured something without opening his eyes. 'Night, night,' said Charles and closed the door.

He paused a moment on the landing, enjoying the silence of the house. Dependants. All these dependants. All these lives. Do I want them? He opened the bedroom door. Do they want me?

Julie looked up sleepily, her book already closed on the bedcovers. 'Thanks,' she said. 'What was the trouble?'

'Dreams. Goats, she called them. I suppose she meant ghosts.'

'I suppose so, poor little thing.'

'On the other hand,' he went on trying to sound jovial, 'she might have meant goats, after all. They exert a powerful pull on the imagination, you know. Think of *Othello*. Full of goats and other animals: *"as prime as goats, as hot as monkeys, as salt as wolves."* ' He could hear his own voice booming boastfully away, but was unable to stop. 'Then there's his cry when Iago gets to work on him: *"Goats and Monkeys!"* Not to mention Iago's *"an old black ram is tupping your white ewe"*.' He knew it all, didn't he? He stood challengingly in front of her, his attempted joviality suddenly hot and raw.

She had been looking down at her closed book during his

speech. Now she glanced up at him icily: 'You should write a paper on it. "Animal imagery in *Othello*." Another feather in your scholar's hat.'

'It's been done. More than once.' He felt weary and ridiculous. She looked at him as if he was an absurd stranger who had blundered into her on the street.

When he got into bed he took her hopefully in his arms. She lay there indifferent and unresponsive, and fell asleep almost at once. He lay awake a long time, feeling her light breathing, inhaling her scent deeply, quizzically: under the cologne, insidiously, the musky smell of arousal. He thought: She smells of sex. Why does she smell of sex? Or is it just *Othello* getting to me. *The sense aches at thee.* After all, I always respond to literature more than to life. It's just the play.

Yet in the jumble of images that came when he finally drifted off to sleep he saw her again and again in someone else's arms, although he knew she was lying quietly enough in his own.

6

The course finished and everyone drifted away; the young lecturers to their holiday cottages and trim wives, the unmarried ones south to the sun, the foreign students to their dutiful sightseeing: the cathedrals, the Lake District, Edinburgh, the Highlands, then back for the last exhausted days in London and their charter flights home.

Sam stayed on, unsinkably cheerful. Two women in one night. He was a real man at last. The French girl encouraged him by spending the last two nights of the course in his bed and persuading herself she was in love after all. 'You have the air of an adventurer. How do you say? A buccaneer.' She ran her fingertips over his big nose and boney forehead, then kissed him lingeringly, entranced by the fantasy she was spinning. When she lifted her pouting mouth from him she said, 'I think we are two of a kind,' and smiled stunningly. Sam was too flattered to laugh. They parted tenderly, exchanging telephone numbers.

Julie was irritated by his bounciness but came to the pub most lunchtimes, since she had little else to do. Now the course was over Charles buried himself again in the library from nine to five, as though in a business office. Since the night of the play both of them were depressed, watchful, distant. She was sure he suspected something, but didn't know how or what.

So she drifted, trying to keep herself apart. Charles was easier to handle than Sam. His own misery kept him at bay and his fear of what might happen to their marriage. The loneliness he gave off was a physical affliction, like bad breath. And that put her off him even more, though she felt sorry for him in a distant way. They lingered on in the almost empty town, carefully avoiding any mention of what they might do for the rest of the summer. The autumn was another world, improbable, another life they might not see. But nothing was said. She could feel, like a continual reproach, the weight, the scope, the middle-agedness of his gloom. He was like a man at the summit of some dull, cold peak: wherever he looked it was all downhill, and death was at the bottom. She felt impatient and resentful, not wanting to be dragged down with him, and also fearful. Occasionally, when he undressed at night, his face, as he watched her across the room, was black stone and his presence in bed was like a furnace, hot and heavy and demanding. But he never touched her, so she pretended not to notice, and his regular businessman's absence each day set her free. Or was it a deliberate provocation? She knew he had taken to searching the drawers of her dressing table and writing desk, looking for signs, and that he sifted the mail each morning. But she had nothing to hide, nothing like that. When letters began to arrive from the now scattered pack she made a point of reading them out to him. Their mockery was nostalgic, reminding them of an intimacy that was now slipping away.

Charles's depression was ominous, heavy with thunder, boding ill for the life they shared. But because of the routine of their marriage and the children, she could cope with it after a fashion and carry on. To her surprise, she found Sam harder to deal with. Nothing she could do would put him off. Like a bank clerk who has won the pools, he couldn't repress his cheerfulness at the sudden, disproportionate riches that had descended on him out of nowhere. Meaning her. Meaning his secret triumph over his professor and over the whole gang of older, slicker colleagues who treated him so dismissively. No matter what she said or did, nor how hangdog he tried to look, underneath he wore a perpetual silly grin. Unlike Charles, he wouldn't be refused, but kept worrying at her, like a dog with an overwhelmingly tasty bone. Each lunchtime it was the same:

'Let's go back to my place.'

'No, not today.'

'Why not?'

'I don't want to. Not today.'

'You're lying. I can see you're lying. Of course you want to.'

'I'm not. I simply don't feel like it.'

'Why not?'

'For God's sake, can't you see it's difficult.'

'I don't see why it should be.'

'You don't see much then. I'm known. I'm the professor's wife. People might see me.'

'They're all away. Anyway, I'm nobody. Why should they think anything?'

'Because they have nothing else to do. The whole town lives on gossip. Without it, it wouldn't survive. As you well know. It only needs one person to see us.'

'For Christ's sake. Since when were you so scared of what people say? I thought you didn't give a damn for any of them.'

'Stop pushing me. Can't you see how hard it is? It's not just gossip I'm risking, it's my kids, my whole life.'

Then he'd whisper ferociously, 'But I love you, I want you.' as if it were a threat. And she would give in. Day after day. Letting herself go. Why not?

Always she left the pub before Sam, trotting home to check on the children and the au pair. She would walk with them towards the park, then leave them at the gates, kissing them tenderly as though she were leaving them for good and was already a long way off. For Heidi she always had her excuses: shopping, a book from the library, tea with one of the few wives still in town. Above all, keep her quiet, feed her with information, for Julie was certain the girl was in love with Charles, in her gawping way, and was waiting a chance to make mischief. If not to Charles directly, then to the other au pairs around town, or even in letters home. Sooner or later, word would get back. It was like high diplomacy or espionage, a web of hints, allusions, inter-connecting spheres of influence and knowingness, devious and paranoid, infested with vipers.

The furtiveness excited her. The sense of exposure as she walked down the long street to Sam's lodgings, alert to the faces in passing cars and figures in the distance, ready with her excuses, ready, if necessary, to walk on past the door without hesitating. Then the long pause after she rang the doorbell while Sam came down from the top floor, the deliberately casual conversation for the benefit of the landlady in the back room, the total release as the bedroom door closed behind them. She would cling to him without speaking, without moving, her stomach full of bees, her legs butter. It made their lovemaking sharp and dangerous, like acid.

Yet why she risked it she wasn't sure. Because his body was firm and flat and his eyes lively? Because he was excitable, besotted, young? As young as she still looked, living off unearned virtues. Being with him made her forget the exhaustion of motherhood and her drab, middle-aged marriage. Yet in other ways he irritated her. Callow, endlessly callow, knowing nothing except out of the books he still read as though they mattered. He climbed mountains in his spare time – which she considered mere childishness – and talked about them passionately – which bored her. He was ignorant of expensive, older pleasures like food and drink. With his body he made her feel young again; in every other way, she felt as old as his mother. Why did she bother? Why did she take risks just for this?

Yet she did. The danger attracted her more than he did. To risk losing her children, her marriage, her security haphazardly, almost casually, worked on her like an aphrodisiac. In her violent, disrupted adolescence she had longed to be safe and well fed as poignantly as she had longed for her vanished father. Now she was both her placid life turned her stomach to ash. Charles might live another thirty years. Each time she saw herself in the mirror she wondered how she would look in her sixties, her blonde hair white, her immaculate body wrinkled and shrunk. No witchcraft could last that long. Only money could help her: money to bring in the experts with their ointments and dyes and soft fabrics. Serious money. But that wasn't Charles's world and, anyway, she had no taste for it. There was no hope.

It was the war's fault. Planes droning over night after night, the whistle and thud of bombs, booted feet in the streets and, once, at the double on the stairs, the scrounging and scheming for food and a place to sleep, the sense of everything shifting, collapsing, re-forming around her so that she might be crushed unless she remained agile and clever. A volatile, tottering world. But exciting, since she had been too young to know any better. Nothing could ever match it. Even her Russian roulette adultery seemed a thin, plastic copy of the real thing. So she went ahead, roused and appalled. For the first time since she arrived in England her life had meaning again. Is this what it meant to be in love?

She hardly knew. She had loved her grim father in his black pastor's clothes. When she was small they used to go for long walks together, visiting his parishioners. She had to trot to keep up with his stretched pace, occasionally glancing up to see if he appreciated the effort she made. But he never noticed, striding out with his jaw clenched, his blue gaze fixed on the crazy distance. When she was too tired to go further he would sweep her up wordlessly, put her on his shoulders and stride on. Now she could never see a St Christopher medallion without thinking of him – but blankly, as though he were a hole in the centre of her universe down which every feeling seeped. Her mother had died when she was a baby. She was nothing: a blur, a warm presence. Her father never spoke of her. His widowed sister kept house for them, a thin, eroded woman with a sharp nose, a sharp tongue and a cowed teenage son. They endured her without gratitude. But when the son joined the Nazi party a cloud of silence descended on the house. He reappeared only rarely in black uniform, black boots and a tinny new confidence as he worked his way slowly up through the non-commissioned ranks. Her father kept more and more to himself, striding out in the evenings to unspecified meetings, returning late after Julie was in bed. He no longer invited her along. She did what she could to show her love: ironing his clothes and laying them out for him tenderly, like sacraments, doing well at school, cooking special dishes for him. He seemed too depressed and preoccupied to notice, though he spoke to her gently, almost wistfully, as if he knew he was already lost. When they came for him she was not surprised. But she hung on for a year in the speechless house, waiting for him to come back. Her cousin swaggered in once on a forty-eight-hours leave. Beneath his uniformed bounce he seemed more cowed and furtive than ever. She wondered if he was to blame for her father's arrest. No matter, she hated him anyway. Three months later her aunt got a letter saying her son had died defending the Fatherland on the

Eastern Front. Soon after that the gaunt-faced Russian arrived. It was time to go, west, away from the invading tartar hordes to the land of Hershey bars and PX cigarettes. She left on her own but years later, when she was already married in England, a much readdressed letter arrived from her aunt, saying she was now settled in Heidelberg as housekeeper for the family of an American colonel. Well, well. Julie replied eventually and got an obsequious letter by return, hoping that her dear niece and Herr Professor would visit her when they were next in Germany. Her aunt's fantasy of the international professorial life struck Julie as funny; in those days she and Charles rarely got to London more than once a year. She didn't write again. But her father had disappeared without trace, avoiding even the book-keepers of the extermination camps. So much for love.

Charles was no father, despite their difference in age. They had a compact, an exchange between equals, need for need. But somewhere she despised his craving for her, just as she despised her own craving for security. Memories of her more dangerous, vulnerable life were mixed with memories of her lost father until risk became for her a symptom of love. She loved her two children in a hopeless way, as though they were already beyond her, but for Charles she felt a faintly contemptuous affection. She had made her choice and was resigned to it. More or less. But sometimes, when they were in bed, he frightened her. His lovemaking was headlong, grunting, agonized, like a blinded rhinoceros. It was unthinkable that he should be so desperate under his unaired *Sitzfleisch*. But usually he carried her with him to her own climax, for which she was duly grateful. Was that love, God help her? For him maybe. And at least it had been enough to keep her faithful.

Now there was Sam. His body roused her, intrigued her, reminded her of what she had missed. And the risks she took to see him roused her even more. But Sam himself, with his enthusiasms and ignorance and constant, possessive demands? No, thank you. Absolutely not. Perhaps if he had had the sense to shut up, she might relax. She might even begin to feel. But there was no sign of that. On the contrary, the more she saw of him, the more demanding he became, like an indulged child. Yet she went on seeing him. Was this love then, God help her? It didn't feel like it. There must be something more than this.

In the end, she gave up bothering. I am neither in love, nor out, she decided. I am simply living an absurd life. And always have. I must go with it. For the time being.

7

Charles and Sam used to greet each other in the library each morning over the tops of their respective piles of books. Sometimes it would be Sam's turn to smile wordlessly, but usually Charles was there first, peering up between the piled towers of learning, his chin, as always, raised too high, so that he seemed to be looking down his nose at Sam even while looking up. He greeted the younger man politely but without interest. The bluff, democratic face he put on for the summer school no longer served any purpose now the foreign students were gone. He had sweated for his present eminence. Let his subordinates know their place.

Even so, he recognized that Sam was serious. The library was almost empty, the smooth talkers dispersed. The few scholars remaining were mostly elderly, foreign and distinguished, people Charles was flattered to talk to. Yet there was Sam beavering away in their company while the sun streamed through the latticed windows in dusty columns. Charles was impressed and not at all surprised when each lunchtime Sam lugged his armloads of books back to the Reserve shelves and disappeared for the rest of the day. Late one afternoon, as he was leaving, he paused at the shelves to see what the young man was so busy at. A ticket with Sam's name on it stuck out of volume after volume of *Publications of the Modern Language Society of America, Philological Quarterly, Modern Philology.* The lad is more serious than he seems. I must encourage him.

Walking home through the clear, deep shadows, he felt obscurely pleased, like a father whose son has decided to follow him in his profession. The young seem so distant, he thought, yet maybe we influence them after all. Then he remembered Julie half a mile away, with her childish, languid body and child's face, smooth and closed as marble, preparing for another evening of silence and refusal. Home. The emptiness opened like a crevasse at his feet. Where did it go wrong?

Yet he had no real proof that anything had gone wrong. Maybe her indifference was only temporary. Maybe the veil of silence between them would be lifted as inexplicably as it had fallen. But he didn't believe it. His nose told him otherwise. Whenever he came near her in the evening, and every night when they lay in bed together, close yet separated, he thought he could smell sex on her, the roused animal juices insidiously under the scent she wore, and the showers she now took so regularly. She smelt of sex. He was certain. Yet what evidence was that? Tell that to a lawyer.

Maybe he should watch and see what she really did each afternoon, although she made a point of telling him every day, patly, casually, so that it seemed absurd to question her further on her trivial comings and goings. He didn't believe her, but what could he do? He pictured himself going off to the library, then sneaking back in the late morning – earlier she was busy in the house – and lurking somewhere to watch the front door. Lurking then following. A man of his age, for God's sake, a professor. It was unthinkable. Worse than Othello and his ravings about that paltry lost handkerchief.

Yet something was wrong. She smelt of sex.

Oh thou weed, that art so lovely, fair and smell'st so sweet
That the sense aches at thee. Would thou had'st ne'er been born.

He couldn't get the lines out of his head. It was ridiculous. He was too old now, too respected and settled, for Othello, just as he'd always been too old, even as a student, for Hamlet. But what had age to do with jealousy? Leontes was an old man: *Inch-thick, knee-deep, o'er head and ears a forked one.* Shakespeare knew it all:

... many a man there is, even at this present,
 Now, while I speak, holds his wife by the arm,
 That little thinks she has been sluiced in his absence,
 And his pond fished by his next neighbour, by
 Sir Smile, his neighbour.

49

Christ, he thought, what a memory I've got. At least that remains, even if everything else turns to dust in my mouth. He shuddered for no reason. Maybe it's all just literature. After all, none of this started until I saw *Othello*. Maybe I'm just imagining the whole thing. Maybe.

But the doubt threw everything out of balance. His passion for literature and knowledge about literature began to seem an elaborate defence against the life he led, against his own stolid dullness. He could translate every event and every feeling into other people's words so fast that nothing had time to touch him. Between himself and the world he lived in was a glimmering net of language which nothing could penetrate. He lived his life at a distance. Had he ever really seen or felt anything at first hand? He paused. The light was settling in the elms. Two pigeons drifted fussily down, looking swollen with the late sun. Somewhere, not far off, the evening traffic droned comfortingly homewards. Click:

It was a beauteous evening, calm and free.
The holy time was quiet as a nun
Breathless with adoration.

There I go again, he thought. God help me. I must change my life.

The next day he stopped Sam in the library. 'You and I seem to be the only workers left,' he said as jovially as he could manage. 'Why don't you come to dinner? Say, tomorrow night.'

He was touched that Sam should seem confused and embarrassed by the invitation. A nice lad, he thought. Modest. Knows his place.

He expected that Julie, too, would be pleased to have their monotonous silence broken for an evening. But she merely shrugged contemptuously: 'I can't see why you bother. But have him if you want.'

He could do nothing right by her.

8

That evening on the radio the weather forecaster talked confidently of a high over the Atlantic and continuing fine weather. During the night the wind swung round to the north and a cold rain set in. The next morning the same forecaster was speaking just as confidently of a low pressure system south of Iceland, showers and below average temperatures. As though yesterday and yesterday's predictions had never been. Like election promises.

The radio promised showers. All day the rain bucketed down, chill and unforgiving, hurrying the appalled tourists off the streets, flattening the flowers, bringing the leaves prematurely down from the trees. It was vicious and total. There might never have been a summer.

Sam, however, walked jauntily through the sodden evening, the collar of his raincoat up, holding a newspaper over his head to keep his hair dry. He was whistling: *I'm singing in the rain, just singing in the rain* ... The water streamed down his raised arm and seeped into his desert boots. He didn't care. The discomfort cheered him; the unspeakable weather cheered him; he was ready for battle.

The idea of dining with the man he was cuckolding, of joking with him and gossiping intimately, excited him almost as much as the infidelities. Or rather, it extended the excitement of the adultery: to be at once cosy and accepted and yet a betrayer. Is that what it means to be adult? The French girl had already given him a taste for it. His nights with her made the afternoons with Julie more poignant, just as the afternoons made the nights wilder, more inventive. Julies's eroticism was subtle and dedicated, but she had set limits on it: whatever else they did together, he must not enter her. With the French girl nothing was barred. Nothing.

For the short time it lasted, the two women were a perfect combination.

But now the French girl was back in Paris and he had Julie to himself. Literally so. He believed her when she told him she hadn't made love to Charles since their affair began. But he couldn't tell whether this was because their afternoons together had made her husband distasteful to her, or because she was being, in a demented way, faithful to her lover. As if that cancelled out her other infidelity. He didn't know and he didn't care. All that mattered was, he had her to himself. Her and, through her, the world of experience with its improbable virtues of silence, delay, stillness. It seemed to him now that all his previous lovemaking had been somehow wrong: too hectic and too excited, with too many thin orgasms and too frantic a need to try out all the positions he had read about in books or dreamed up in his head. Without even letting him inside her, Julie introduced him to another form of sensuality, slower, deeper, more selective, involving not just their genitals but their whole bodies. He began to learn her from her pale hair with its faint, far, animal scent to the polished insteps of her feet. He studied her body in those long afternoons like a guerilla fighter learning the countryside, discovering the varying tastes and smells and textures of each part of her, and how every curve, plane, hollow and cleft differed from the others and interconnected, like veins of colour in a block of marble. It was a new world of knowledge and there were no books on the subject; the libraries couldn't help him. So he looked at her with awe, as though she were unique, a wonder, a purveyor of mysteries he had never guessed at. He was like a man suddenly able to hear without a radio all the music and voices the air is constantly full of. For everyone else the world went on as always: a plane boomed over, the traffic snored and hooted, dogs barked, children cried, people talked and shouted and strolled by with transistors pouring music. For them everything was moderate, casual, ordinary, while for him there were symphonies in the head, newscasts in unknown languages, urgent calls for police, ambulances, firemen. All at the same time. He had never imagined there was such depth to the world. Even the rain gave him pleasure: its weight on the dripping trees, the way it soaked down the facades of the colleges, darkening their colour, its soft persistent sound.

Charles opened the door to him. 'Vile weather,' he said feelingly.

'Oh, I don't know,' Sam said, 'this summer rain is rather nice.'

'But cold.'

'Yes, cooler.'

Charles took his coat from him and hung it carefully apart to drip on the parquet in isolation. There was a pile of unopened letters and packets on the hall table. Sam glanced at it admiringly. He always opened every last bit of junk mail immediately in the hope of something unexpected, some communication from God knows where which might change his life. That's maturity, he thought, looking at the heaped circulars and packages bearing publishers' labels. He followed Charles's heavy figure enviously in to the drawing-room.

The furniture was dull and weighty, like Charles, but the walls were lined with books and paintings, and there were vases of flowers nodding in the subdued light. Julie came in from the kitchen, wiping her hands on her apron.

'Good evening, Mrs Stone.'

'For heaven's sake. This isn't a committee meeting, Sam. My name's Julie. Charles is Charles.' Then she added icily, 'But not Charlie.'

There was going to be no help from her.

When Sam told her of the invitation in the pub the day before she had been furious. 'Why didn't he ask me first? I could have got us out of it.' (Us, thought Sam, us.) 'I hate this kind of hypocrisy,' she said, 'I don't know why you go along with it.'

'What else could I do? How could I have refused in cold blood?'

'You could have found an excuse.'

'He took me by surprise. I couldn't think of anything on the spur of the moment.'

'Maybe you think it'll be good for your career.'

'I don't have a career here, not any more.' He had never thought of that before. So that's what he was doing. 'And even if I did, I can't think of anything worse for it than what we're up to.'

She had no answer to that. But she refused to go back with him to his rooms and the next day, for the first time in weeks, had not turned up at the pub.

'Quite right,' said Charles. 'No one ever calls me Charlie. I wonder why.'

'Respect for your eminence,' said Sam.

'No. They never have. Not even when I was a little boy.'

'It's hard to think of you as a child,' said Julie, still icy.

Charles was unperturbed. 'It's hard to think of myself. Yet sometimes it feels quite close. I can remember all sorts of inconsequential details about my childhood – things like the pattern on the water jug in my bedroom, or the feel of my mother's apron when I sat on her lap after a bath. Strange that. I must have been tiny. But my twenties now, they're just a vague blur. Absurd the tricks memory plays.'

'I can remember every detail of my teens but nothing at all of my childhood,' said Sam.

'But you're still in your early twenties. As you get older, your adult years don't seem to matter much. More a source of embarrassment than anything else. Don't you agree, dear?' He turned to Julie. 'Can you remember your childhood?'

'Oh I can remember it, all right. But I prefer not to.' She went back into the kitchen. The two men sat in silence for a moment, registering her contempt, then Charles began to question Sam about his work in the library. To be back with his own certainties again gradually lifted his gloom. By the time Julie called them to dinner, he was positively jovial.

It was an elaborate meal: homemade pâté, veal baked with ham and cheese, *crème brulée*.

'I didn't know you were going to put yourself out like this,' Charles said. 'I hope the wines don't let the food down.' They didn't.

Sam sat like an umpire at a tennis match while they competed with each other through him. He felt flattered and surreptitiously powerful. But because Julie held off as if brooding on some obscure insult, he found himself siding with Charles, man to man, against this troublesome, offended woman. Eventually, they began to talk shop and Julie lapsed into silence, creating a frozen pool of distaste at her end of the table.

'What about the washing up?' Sam asked when the meal was finished at last. It seemed to him they had been eating for hours. The wine made him want to giggle. He looked at Charles, thinking, If only you knew.

'Don't worry,' said Julie in her chill voice, 'the au pair will do it.'

'At least let me help you clear away.'

Charles pushed his chair back from the table and said, 'It's not really necessary.' He was damned if he would placate her. He got up slowly and went into the drawing-room. If she wanted to be offended for her perverse reasons, let her get on with it. After all, the lad was surprisingly pleasant company. No reason to apologize for him. Better than most.

Sam and Julie piled the dishes in silence, moving between the dining-room and the kitchen, not looking at each other. Finally, they came together at the sink. Sam pressed his thigh against hers and she leaned briefly against him in return. He ran his hand over the curve of her buttocks. She smiled down into the sink and didn't look at him. They went back together into the drawing-room.

Charles was standing at one of the overweight tables pouring brandy. He handed them each a drink and then stood in front of the cold hearth spinning his glass so that the amber liquid spread delicately up round the balloon. He sniffed it deeply and sipped. He seemed truculently set on enjoying himself.

'That was a triumphant meal, my dear,' he boomed. 'I think we need cigars to complete it.' He rummaged unsuccessfully in a cupboard under a solemnly ticking clock. 'They must be up in my study.'

'It doesn't matter,' said Sam. 'A cigarette will be fine.'

'But it does, it does.' Charles was determined the evening should be complete, determined that Julie shouldn't spoil it. She's like a surly child, he thought as he climbed the stairs, having her tantrum in public. It won't do. He opened his study door. His world: orderly papers on his desk, four walls of books broken only by the door and window, peace. I'm happy here, he thought, then added out loud to the listening books, 'I thought it would please her to have someone young in for dinner.' She didn't make sense any more. He had lost control. Yet a dinner like that must have taken her the whole day to prepare. She didn't make sense.

He sat down at the desk and glanced at an unfinished page of his small, neat writing. Not bad. Not bad at all. Let them pay attention. Then he opened the bottom drawer of the desk and brought out a box of cigars. *Romeo y Julietta*. He smiled, thinking, A Juliet is only a Juliet, but a good cigar is a smoke. Even for Romeo. He went back to the door and turned to look at the room. By lamplight the shadowy walls seemed to crowd closer round the desk. This was his real love. He switched off the light, closed the door quietly and quietly went downstairs.

Halfway down he paused. The drawing-room door was open and he could see Sam and Julie standing silently on each side of the fireplace. A charming tableau. Innocence and maturity modern-style: the young graduate student, too shy and inept to make conversation, and his tolerant professor's wife, politely bored by his gaucheness. He smiled condescendingly. Yet somehow they didn't look constricted by the silence. And suddenly he realized that they were perfectly at ease in this hiatus, as though they knew each other too well to need to talk.

Sam was looking at her quizzically. Her face was turned away, her eyes on the carpet. As Charles watched, the young man murmured something inaudible. Julie glanced up, gave him a quick smile and nodded. Her closed, marble look was gone. Her eyes were soft, her face naked. Then she looked down again and the scene was over as if the door had slammed shut.

So it's him, thought Charles. Who else could it have been? He saw the young man's heavy head, now half turned towards the door, with its slightly histrionic forehead, slightly narrow-set eyes and slightly sardonic mouth. Something else struck him: He's a Jew, he thought. They all are. Though who 'they' were he wasn't sure.

He bustled purposefully into the room with his box of cigars. Sam took one admiringly and said, 'That's regal.'

'Merely appropriate to the cooking,' Charles replied. It gave him pleasure to see how ineptly the younger man mangled his cigar's sleek end with the cutter. Young upstart. Not used to these things. He settled comfortably into his armchair.

'Where are you from?' he asked.

'London.'

'I mean originally.'

'London,' Sam repeated. 'My parents were born there. And my grandparents.'

'Oh really. I rather thought . . .'

Sam blushed. 'If you mean, am I Jewish, the answer is yes. But that doesn't mean I'm a refugee from anywhere. There are an awful lot of English Jews.'

'Of course. Of course. And they have made a most valuable contribution to the culture. Some of the finest scholars . . . Shapiro, for instance.'

'And some of them are your best friends,' Julie put in icily. 'I always thought you liked refugees.'

'You know how much, dear,' he said as jovially as he could. There was no way he could move without blundering up against her. He turned morosely to Sam. 'Is your father a literary man?'

'God, no. He's in the rag trade. But his real passion is music.'

'Ah, yes.' Charles made a flowery gesture. 'A musician. So many are. Extraordinary. What instrument does he play?'

'The gramophone. But with feeling.' Sam giggled, then shrugged apologetically. The cigar made him feel giddy. 'He reads travel books, too. They're like the records, a way of getting out without having to move. He's the world's worst businessman. A one-man disaster area.'

Julie said, 'You sound fond of him. That's a change.'

'I am. He's a nice man. A bit excitable, but nice. What about yours?'

'I was fond of him, too. But he's dead.'

'I'm sorry.'

'It's not your fault, is it?'

There was a silence. Charles stirred uneasily, puffing his cigar. *Inch-thick, knee-deep.* Finally, he said, 'Did you go to boarding school?'

'Afraid so.'

'Wasn't that rather difficult? I mean, with your dietary laws and all.'

'They're not my dietary laws. Nor my parents'. In fact, I doubt if I've been to a synagogue more than half a dozen times in my life. Just for weddings and funerals. My parents don't believe in it.'

'What do they believe in, then?'

'Nothing in particular. Neither do I.'

'Then you're hardly Jewish are you?' Charles sounded as though he were reassuring Sam that he didn't, after all, have a club foot.

'Not eating bacon or believing in God hasn't anything to do with it. Like it doesn't matter how long my family has been here. In England a Jew's a foreigner and that's that.'

Charles sipped his brandy and boomed, 'Come now, that's hardly fair. There's very little prejudice in this country.'

'Oh, nothing obvious, sure. Maybe it would be easier if it were, I mean, if you see "Jews out" painted all over the walls, at least you know where you are. Here it's a social thing. It's just not done to be Jewish. You're pigeon-holed just as surely as if you dropped your aitches. Gentlemen aren't Jews.'

Julie said: 'It's the same being German. So far as the English are concerned I'm just some sort of blonde, blue-eyed wog. For a foreigner to be accepted here, he's got to be very famous or very rich. Otherwise they condescend to you.'

'But I'm not a foreigner,' said Sam, 'at least not in any normal sense of the word.'

'The Germans aren't exactly famous for their love of the Jews,' said Charles. The bitch. First, she cuckolded him; now she was making a fool of him in front of her student-lover.

'You can't blame me for that. I was only a child.'

'Then why blame the English?'

'I wasn't blaming them. I was just pointing out that they're insufferably superior. They want everyone else down. Right down. But very politely, of course. Nothing you could make a fuss about.'

'England has always been a haven for the persecuted.' Annoyance made Charles slip automatically into his lecturer's manner.

'Think of all the political refugees who came here in the last century: Marx, Engels, Herzen, Bakunin.'

'They took them in because they didn't really notice them. It might as well have been an invasion of ants,' said Julie. 'They didn't give a damn. They thought the refugees ridiculous with their politics and their passions. Just so much absurdity. It confirmed them in their comfortable, middle-class Philistinism.'

'My God you sound like all those people who fled from Hitler before the war and then complained that the music was so bad over here.'

Sam watched them fascinated, screwing up his eyes to keep them focused. He wasn't used to so much drink. Whenever he relaxed everything doubled: two brandy glasses, two Julies, two professors. They were quarrelling about something else, something more intimate which neither of them would mention. He wondered if Charles suspected. He almost felt sorry for this greying, angry man who puffed at his cigar and glared down his nose while his young wife leaned back in her chair and baited him coolly. The rhino and the cheetah. Let them get on with it. It seemed to him somehow contemptible that they should be so much at each other's mercy, so maliciously and inextricably joined. Thank God he wasn't married.

He got up. 'It's getting late. I ought to be off, otherwise I'll never make it to the library tomorrow.'

'You seem to be working very diligently,' said Charles.

'Well, if I don't get my thesis written now, while there are no distractions, I never will.'

'That's the way,' said Charles avuncularly, 'that's the only way. Keep at it.'

Sam shook Julie's hand. 'It's been a lovely evening and a beautiful meal. Thank you so much.'

'I enjoyed it, too. We must meet again soon.' The last word was faintly inflected. She squeezed his hand privately and turned away.

He walked with relief into the streaming rain. The wind had got up and the branches of the trees lashed wildly in the lamplight as if trying to pull free. He huddled into his raincoat, walking fast, enjoying the cold rain on his face. It washed away the evening's heaviness : the rich food, the wines and brandy, the clinging smell of cigars and married rancour. He was in far enough. Time to pull out. Yet he wasn't altogether free. He remembered the pressure of Julie's thigh against his, the curve of her buttock, the suddenly naked look on her face when they were alone, and the quick, secret sign she had given him as he left. The game wasn't over yet.

9

Charles stood with his back to the cold fireplace watching his wife as she moved silently about the room, collecting coffee cups, glasses and filled ashtrays. His wife: sleek gold head, closed face, supple body. What had he to do with her? After all these years, they hardly knew each other. *Oh, thou weed.*

'It scarcely seems necessary,' he boomed, wondering why anger always made him sound pompous, 'to accuse me of antisemitism in front of a graduate student. A Jewish graduate student.'

'I didn't accuse you.' There was no interest in her voice. She might have been giving an order to the grocer. 'You started it. All that business about "Where do you come from?" and "How about the dietary laws?" Anyone would have thought he'd just arrived from Odessa. I don't know what possessed you. He's as English as you are.'

'That's a matter of opinion. Anyway he understood what I meant. It was you who turned it into an issue.'

'Rubbish. The issue was that you wanted to be offensive and condescending at the same time. I don't know why you invited him. Surely that's not how an English gentleman behaves to his guest?'

'I never knew you hated this country so much. You were glad enough to come here.'

'I didn't know what a seething cauldron of snobbery and pomposity I was getting into.' She went out into the kitchen carrying a loaded tray. Charles collected the bottles and put them back in the cupboard, then followed her, pausing uncertainly in the doorway. She took no notice of him, but went on piling things in the sink.

'Have you been seeing him?' His voice wasn't quite steady.

'Seeing who?'

'Whom.'

'Seeing *whom*,' she echoed sarcastically. 'I'm so sorry.'

'Sam, of course.'

'Don't be ridiculous. Why should I?'

'I don't know. You tell me.'

'I'd hardly have the chance, would I? I gather he works in the library all day. No doubt under your watchful, avuncular eye.'

'He only spends the mornings there.'

'Thanks for telling me. Now I'll know. But I'm afraid I'm not a cradle-snatcher.'

'You seemed very easy together.'

'Maybe that's because we're both foreigners, as you would say.'

'Don't be cheap. It's not becoming.'

'Neither is your suspicion. Do you think I'm having it off with him, or something?'

'God, where do you learn these phrases? I didn't say that.'

'You were implying it.'

'All I said was you seemed very much at ease together.'

'Why shouldn't we be? I saw him during the summer course, along with all your other clever young men. I thought that was supposed to be my role : keep them happy, string them along a little, make sure they stay interested in you. I was just being the loyal little wife, helping her hubby's career.'

Charles stared at her dumbly. He had never dreamed she hated him so much.

She wiped her hands on her apron, took it off and hung it up. Then she crossed to the door where he stood. 'I'm tired,' she said, 'I want to go to bed, if you've finished the cross-examination.'

He reached both hands towards her shoulders. 'Darling, for Christ's sake let's stop this. It's intolerable.' And Othello's voice echoed in his ears, *Oh insupportable.*

She swayed back out of his reach like an agile boxer and looked at him, her mouth tight, her eyes blue slits.

'You make me sick,' she said.

She stepped round him and went upstairs. Charles wandered back into the drawing-room and sat looking at the fireless hearth. He listened to the water running in the bathroom above, then her steps across the landing and the click as she closed the bedroom door quietly to avoid waking the children. To avoid waking the children. What a laugh. He stared blankly at the grate, hearing the steady tick of the clock and the rain pattering against the windows. There was nowhere to go.

Finally, he got up, draped his mackintosh round his shoulders and went out into the street. The rain drummed down, streaming across his face like tears. He ducked his head and made a dash across the road to where his old Jaguar was parked. He got in, started the motor and switched on the lights. The dull, deep note of the engine and the row of glowing dials were obscurely comforting. He let the clutch in gently, not thinking of anything in particular, simply wanting to move. At the end of the road he paused, looking at the heaving trees picked out by the headlights in the park opposite. Where would he go? 'West,' said the sun, 'for enterprise.' The quotation came pat as ever. So he turned left, driving carefully down the florid Victorian streets. He felt perfectly sober, but technically he was far over the legal alcohol limit. He didn't want to risk provoking some bored patrolling policeman.

Where the houses ended at a roundabout, he swung left again onto the deserted main road. Ahead of him the western rim of the sky was still pale beyond the veils of rain and the drenched hedges. He leaned back, watching the needles of the rev counter and speedometer climb in unison. When the right-hand needle reached 85 he held it there, enjoying the roar of the wind and the monotonous swish-swish of the windscreen wipers. Going nowhere. Usually, he was a cautious driver. Speed frightened him. He thought it frivolous and unbecoming to the serious figure he cut in the world. He had not realized how soothing it could be, this mindless concentration. Everything dropped away behind him, swallowed up by the wind and the rain and the droning engine.

The sign said SLOW. ROUNDABOUT AHEAD. He eased off dutifully remembering his responsibilities. Even so, the great white arrow pointing left came towards him terribly fast. He jabbed the brakes and the tail of the car broke heavily away on the wet surface. He heaved at the wheel, still braking, and the car began to swing inexorably round, all the wheels sliding as though on glass. The rear of the car thumped against the curb on the inside of the roundabout then bounced back into the middle of the road, pointing him, despite himself, in the right direction. He laboured at the steering wheel panic-striken, and the car began to turn back to the left, sweeping over onto the wrong side of the road. Half a ton of metal with a will of its own, sliding in a blurred landscape, nothing where it should be. Then the car slowed and the world reassembled itself while the rain pelted down. He braked again gingerly and stopped. He was trembling and sweating like a man with fever. 'Jesus Christ,' he said out loud. He rested with his damp forehead against the steering wheel, his whole body shaking. Finally, he put his raincoat over his head and climbed out of the car. It was too dark to see much, but when he ran his finger round the rim of the rear wheel he felt two angry welts in the metal. 'Jesus Christ,' he repeated. He probed the rough groove carefully and a sliver of metal stuck in his finger-tip. He stood up, angry and almost in tears, sucking his bleeding finger. The rain was cold against his face. He got back into the car and sat quietly, listening to the throb of the idling engine and the swish of the wipers. It's a good car, he thought, solid. Somehow this reassured him. He drove slowly on.

After a few miles the road joined the main trunk route. He took it, heading north towards the midlands, where he had been born, driving slowly in the inside lane. Occasionally a lorry thundered past, its plume of spray momentarily blinding him, its back-draught buffeting his car sideways towards the shoulder of the road. He glared resentfully at each set of receding lights, feeling humiliated.

A long way ahead he saw a red neon sign flashing on and off. *Like a good deed in a naughty world*, he thought automatically. 'Bill's Cafe,' 'Bill's Cafe,' 'Bill's Cafe,' said the sign. Behind it was a cinder parking area and a long, low building with a white stucco front, one end lit, the other dark. He drove in between the shadowy, stranded hulks of long-distance lorries and parked near the door by a clutch of bulging motor bikes. The dining-room was hot and steamy ; it smelled of rancid frying oil and wet clothes. A juke box was throbbing in one corner. Four youths sat in front of it, lean, pinched figures in dank leather and black boots. Their red and yellow helmets lay on the table among mugs of tea and unfinished plates of food. Their hair was shoulder length and as greasy as the plates in front of them, their leather backs glinted with ornamental patterns of studs surrounding the words, 'The Outcasts'. Charles began reciting silently to himself. *They that have power to hurt, and will do none.* He felt foolish standing at the high counter in his dark suit, sober tie and paunch. The two youths facing him looked at him contemptuously and muttered something to their friends who also turned and looked.

That do not do the thing they most do show,
Who moving others, are themselves as stone,
Unmoved, cold, and to temptation slow . . .

The eyes of all four were flat and blank, as though not yet awakened into a world where people have feelings. The youths laughed together and one of them shrugged. Then they went back to their inaudible conversation.

'A cup of tea, please,' said Charles to the woman behind the counter.

'With or without?' Her face was greyish; she had bony wrists.

'Without.'

'Anything else?'

Charles eyed the wilted chips in the panniers behind her and the glass case of curling sandwiches on the counter. 'Just tea, thanks.'

He sat down at an empty table, his back to the leather clad spectres, and stared at the steam rising from his cup. I might have killed myself, he thought. When he lifted the cup to his mouth his hands were still trembling.

The summer's flower is to the summer sweet,
Though to itself it only live and die . . .

Behind him the juke box blared away remorselessly: *I can't get no satisfaction. I can't get no . . .* The lorry drivers at the other tables seemed not to notice, shovelling away their platefuls of eggs and bacon, chips and baked beans. Bitch, he thought. Bitch, bitch, bitch. *For sweetest things turn sourest by their deeds, Lillies that fester smell far worse than weeds.*

The door opened and a big, red-faced man came in. His overalls were dirty and wet, his hair iron grey. He wiped the rain off his face with a hand like a porterhouse steak. He seemed to bring the weather in with him.

'Evening, Flo,' he said loudly to the woman behind the counter. 'Cheerful as ever?'

'None of your sauce.' She managed a ghoulish smile. 'What d'you fancy?'

'Two bacon butties and a cuppa char. Lots of sugar.'

He leaned against the counter and looked round the room confidently. The leather boys glanced at him quickly and then went on with their conversation. 'Mixed bag tonight, Flo,' he said loudly. 'Still, I suppose beggars can't be choosers, can you, love?'

The woman put a plate and a cup on the counter. 'Get on with you,' she said gloomily.

The man picked up his food and walked across to Charles's table. 'Evening,' he said.

'Rotten night, isn't it?'

'Bluddy awful.' That accent: at once intimidating and comfortable. For a moment Charles was back in the asphalt playground, his back against the high brick wall, watching the yelling, frightening, exclusive children, yearning to join in. They seemed sturdier and more knowledgeable than he ever dreamed of being.

'You're from Derby,' he said.

'That's reet. How d'yer know?'

'I'm from Derby myself.'

'Yer don't sound it.'

'I left a long time ago.'

'It's not a bad place still,' said the driver, 'despite what they've done to it.' He eased his heavy shoulders as though settling into an armchair. Innocent blue eyes, grizzled hair, forearms like pine logs. There but for the grace of God, thought Charles.

No, why give God the credit? It was Mr Rotherham who did the work, picking him out, encouraging him, pushing him on through exam after dreary exam, determined to make this child into the success he himself had never been. A fierce little man. 'My name's Rotherham and I come from Rotherham. We work up there and don't you forget it.'

He was still at the school, greyer and more ferocious than ever.

when Charles returned in triumph years later to show off his first, his doctorate, his new lectureship at a good provincial university, the only boy from the school ever to make it in the dubious world of academic honours. He had been surprised how small the place was and how shabby, the air thick with chalk dust, the noise intolerable. The children were less pinched and badly dressed than in his day, but no less bored. When the lunch bell sounded Mr Rotherham took him down to the staff dining-hall, a disused classroom, its walls lined with benches and broken desks. The other teachers waited hungrily round a bare trestle-table. Their suits were polished and smudged with chalk. At the centre of the table were three aluminium canisters containing fish fingers soggy carrots and grey mashed potatoes.

'This is Charles Stone,' Mr Rotherham barked, 'our most distinguished old boy.'

They looked at him without interest. One of them peered into the canister of fish. 'Nobody told the kitchen there was an extra person for lunch,' he said querulously.

'That's all right,' Charles said to Mr Rotherham, 'I wanted to buy you a meal, anyway. Now's my chance.' He tried to sound jovial but the canisters of institutional food made him uneasy, as if he had somehow betrayed the old man by his success.

At the local hotel he ordered the best steaks on the menu and a bottle of good burgundy. Mr Rotherham ate and drank with relish. 'I used to come here with my wife,' he said between mouthfuls, 'on our anniversary.'

'How is she?'

'She died six years ago.' Then he added, 'A pity we never had a child. But there you are.'

They ate for a while in silence, then Mr Rotherham said, 'You know, you're the only boy who ever turned out right.'

Charles mumbled self-deprecatingly, feeling pleased.

'Oh, lots of them have been successful. Made pots of money, did research for ICI, and the rest. One even became an MP, God help him. Or us. But you're the only one who really cared about the things I care about. In forty years. Think of that. Forty bloody years. I'm retiring at the end of the summer.'

I don't want to know about your failure, Charles was thinking.

Don't tell me. I've got a career to consider. Aloud he said, 'The place won't be the same without you.'

'Don't you believe it. But I won't be the same without it.'

'What will you do?'

'God knows. I can't bring myself to think about it. Go and live with my sister, I suppose. She's widowed, too.'

Charles ordered brandy and then the two men walked muzzily back to the school. They parted outside the playground where the children milled and shrieked.

'You've made me tiddly,' said Mr Rotherham.

'I'm glad.' He watched the old man plough abruptly through the uproar. *Goodbye-eee, don't cry-eee . . .*

Two years later Charles's last surviving relative, an ancient, gossipy aunt, wrote to tell him that Mr Rotherham was dead. Of cancer. Dead like his own father and mother. Dead like the authors he loved. Dead despite his fierceness. He should never have retired. How lonely the dead must be, and the living they leave behind.

He hadn't been back since, not even when he was invited as guest of honour for the opening of the new school buildings. The grim red brick had been torn down. In its place was glass, steel and washable coloured walls, a gleaming gymnasium and a proper football pitch. But no Mr Rotherham. Professor Stone regrets he is unable to accept the kind invitation owing to a prior engagement.

The lorry driver looked at Charles's careful suit and tie. 'You commercial?'

'No, I'm a teacher.'

'I couldn't do that, even if I had the learning. Which I didn't. No more than I could do a job in an office. I don't like being cooped up.'

'It doesn't always feel like that.'

'It would to me. I like being on the move.'

'But that can't be easy either,' Charles said. 'How does your wife take it?'

'She doesn't mind. She knows it makes me happy and the money's good. She doesn't want for anything.'

Charles wanted to ask, 'How do you keep her faithful?' But the other man's heavy muscles and childish, cheerful eyes answered him. When he took another sip of tea his hands were still shaking.

'Anything wrong?' asked the lorry driver.

'I had a bad skid. Lost it on a roundabout and hit the curb.'

'That your Jag outside?'

Charles nodded.

'Brute of a car in the wet,' said the other man sympathetically.

He feels sorry for me, Charles thought. Me with my distinguished career, my professorship at a famous university, my fame in certain circles. A forty quid a week lorry driver who left school when he was fourteen and has a council house within a mile of where he was born. What am I coming to?

'It was my fault,' he said. 'I overdid it a bit.'

'Happens to the best of us.' The lorry driver opened his sandwich and upended a bottle of brown sauce over the bacon. He picked up the soggy bread in both hands and took a large bite. 'They do a good bacon butty here,' he said, chewing. 'About all they do.'

'The tea's all right,' said Charles.

The other man looked over at the motor cycle boys. 'Scum,' he said loudly. 'If it weren't for their leather gear, you'd think they were girls, with their hair down on their shoulders like that. If I was their dad, I'd take a strap to them.'

Charles twisted in his chair and looked at the table behind him. Two of the youths had also turned and all four were watching him venomously, their blank faces suddenly ignited as though with burning petrol. 'They may not be so bad,' he said in a low voice. 'They'll probably get over it.'

'Get over it!' said the lorry driver more loudly than ever. 'I'd get 'em over it real quick if I had half a chance.'

'Maybe their parents are as much to blame,' said Charles, remembering all the arguments he had swopped comfortably at home with his colleagues: broken homes, urbanization, childhood deprivation, lack of proper social care, the unconscious delinquency of drunken, bullying parents. He had them all off pat. But seeing the shallow, malignant fire flickering on the young men's faces, he was not convinced. Evil is evil. He turned his back.

The lorry driver attacked his second sandwich. 'Bollocks,' he said. 'The only thing they're to blame for is not giving them a good thrashing in time.'

'Perhaps they thrashed them too much.' Charles went on mouthing his liberal platitudes out of a sense of duty. How long had he believed that one must spread the word, enlighten where one can, every little helps? All balls. So much hypocrisy. The lorry driver was right and he was angry with himself for not admitting it out loud. Julie, Sam, these louts in their menacing leather: they didn't belong. Better to cast them out and have done. Why couldn't he come out and say so? He finished his tea and got up.

'I'd better be going. It's late. Time to go home.' Home. Home to what? Black ice. 'It's been nice talking to you.'

'Ay,' said the other man, 'it has that. You never know, maybe I'll see you in Derby one of these days.'

'You never know. But I haven't been back for years.' He realized that he sounded as if he was apologizing.

The lorry driver grinned. 'I'm not there much myself. Maybe that's why I'm still fond of the place.'

Outside the rain had eased to a drizzle and the wind was warmer. Charles drove slowly across the parking lot, the car sending up spouts of dark water as it thumped through the puddles. The main road was empty. He nosed across it cautiously and turned in the direction of home, going quietly, lulled by the swish of the wipers and the spray hissing from the wheels. What would he do if she left him? He pictured the carefully sympathetic faces of his colleagues, the sudden flood of invitations to tactful dinners, the mockery behind his back, the delighted malice of the pack. At last they would really have something to gossip about. He felt foolish and impotent. She had no right to expose him in this way.

The drink had worn off, and the fright. He drove slowly, brooding on his revenge. She would lose the children, he'd make sure of that. No court was going to give her custody if she went off with a penniless student – who'd stay penniless if he wanted a university job. He'd make sure of that, too. *Revenge is a kind of wild justice.* Too true. The road stretched monotonously in front of him. He began to feel sleepy and screwed up his eyes to make himself concentrate. How would he explain it to the children? His daughter would be all right. She would grieve for a while and then be triumphant, having him to herself at last. But the boy? He was already more intimate with his mother than Charles had ever been. They had private jokes and rituals from which everyone was excluded, his sister as much as his father. How would he survive? She had no right.

Then he remembered she hadn't gone yet. Maybe it would be easier if she had. To have done once and for all. No more uncertainty, no more suspense. He saw himself strangling slowly through the long black months, going under, having to put up a front. It wasn't fair. All he had wanted when he married her was to have his youth, belatedly, before it was too late. He thought he could postpone death through her slippery body and subtle hands, the taste of her saliva and her cunt. Wrong. In the end, she had only made him understand how old he was, how fat and distasteful. *Weary, stale, flat and unprofitable. Crammed with distressful bread.* And so on. What kind of future had he now? Maybe he should go to America for a year. They were always asking him. *Silence, exile and cunning*, a good formula. I'd rather have silence, exile and cunnilingus, he thought and laughed out loud. James Joyce himself would have appreciated that.

The headlights, appearing suddenly in his driving mirror, dazzled him : four unblinking eyes coming up on him fast. 'Selfish bastards,' he said, 'why don't they dip the things?' He squinted through the windscreen and slowed down, waiting for them to pass. Two cars in a hurry, he thought, young fools dicing home after a party. The young again. They had to be young. He couldn't get away from them.

But the lights didn't pass. Instead, they settled down behind him, just out of reach of his spray. Four searing beams illuminating the inside of his car until he felt like an actor exposed alone on a blank white stage. The road in front of him became blurred and indeterminate in the glare. He put up his hand and tried to cover the driving mirror, cursing the time he'd taken off the small anti-dazzle mirror and replaced it with this great cinemascope affair. So much safer, he'd explained to Julie; you don't have any blind spots. He could use a blind spot or two now. A car coming from the opposite direction flashed its lights angrily, but the hard blaze behind him did not wink. Why me? Why pick on me? He put his foot down viciously and the Jaguar heaved forward. Behind him the other cars accelerated in unison, dropping back a little to be clear of his spray. At the first tight curve he braked only slightly and then accelerated hard. The bulky car wallowed like a ship in heavy weather but the wheels, miraculously, stayed where they should. When he straightened up the headlights were at the same distance as before, two and two, as though towed along by him on a rope.

He said, 'For God's sake,' and stamped on the brakes. Suddenly the two cars became four separate headlights. Two motor cyclists shot past and then pulled in ten yards in front of him. One remained behind, keeping him transfixed, like an insect, on its beam. The fourth bike slid up alongside until it was on a level with Charles. The rider turned and looked at him. The face under the red and yellow helmet was featureless: a white silk scarf tight over the nose and chin, like a mummy's shroud, then the flat stare of goggles. The helmets of the riders in front were also red and yellow and the inscriptions on their backs glinted in his headlights: 'The Outcasts'. Like robots, thought Charles, four robots loose on the public highway. They slowed to a walking pace and Charles slowed with them, the Jaguar's bumpers inches from their rear wheels. Behind him the headlights from the following bike seemed to be coming right in through the window. The rider at his side stared blankly in. They moved for a few hundred yards, the five machines locked together like a liner attended by tugs, then stopped. Charles glanced nervously at the car door: it was safely locked, the window closed. Then he sat holding the wheel, staring straight ahead, listening to the engine of his car quietly ticking over and the looser, noisier clatter of the idling bikes.

The two robots in front dismounted stiffly and pulled their bikes up on to their rests, leaving the engines running. They walked slowly to join their companion at Charles's side. One of them trailed his gauntleted hand idly along the bonnet of the Jaguar, flicking the wing mirror back to front as he passed. Out of the corner of his eye Charles was aware of their shrouded faces and insect goggle eyes watching him. One of the riders drew off his heavy gauntlet and slapped it down loudly on the car roof immediately above Charles's head. He jumped and glanced round at the staring trio. The youth unzipped a pocket in his leather armour and pulled out a packet of cigarettes. He waved it at the other two who shook their heads, eased down his scarf and began to smoke. His face, below the goggles, was pinched and sallow, as though nourished by a lifetime of greasy chips. He had a thick, long underlip balanced by a Mexican moustache. On his right cheek was a single, angry spot, the last stigma of adolescence.

One of his shrouded companions tapped the window. 'Open up. We want to talk to you.' His voice, muffled by his scarf and the glass, seemed to come from a long way off.

Charles shook his head.

'I say,' said the youth in a mock posh accent, 'I call that unfair, don't cher know. First he jeers at us in the caff, then he won't speak to us. Not cricket, what?'

'I didn't jeer at you. In fact, I defended you.'

The youth cupped his hand to his ear. 'No use. Can't 'ear. You gotter let down the winder.'

Charles didn't move.

'Now be reasonable, mister.' His voice was wheedling. 'You insulted us back there. We want t'ear yer say yer sorry.'

Charles lowered the window half an inch and boomed in his professorial voice, 'I didn't insult you. I defended you. I said it wasn't your fault.'

'What wasn't, mister? What wasn't?' He turned to his companions. 'Know what? He's a fucking do-gooder. Fucking social worker.' He went into his posh accent again. 'We mustn't blame the children. We *reelly* mustn't. It's their backgrounds.' He turned to the youth who was smoking. 'Right, Johnny? Our fucking backgrounds.'

Johnny took his cigarette out of his mouth and spat. 'Jesus fucking Christ,' he said. He slid his cigarette through the crack in the car window and tapped the ash on to Charles's shoulder.

'I've got news for you, mister,' the other lad went on. 'Fuck the background. We like it this way.'

Charles flipped the engine of his car. 'Get out of my way,' he said, 'I'm going.' He put the car into gear.

'I wouldn't do that, mister, not if I was you. You might fuck our bikes up and we wouldn't like that. We really fucking wouldn't.'

I'm dreaming this, thought Charles. Any moment I'll wake up. But he could feel the steering wheel slippery with his sweat and hear the churr of the five engines. All real, like the four adolescents out there in their menacing uniforms. He felt less frightened than amazed. There was no end to the treachery and malice of the young. I'm still in my fifties, he thought. How could I have outlived my usefulness already? Depression was like a weight on his back, bowing him over the steering wheel.

'If it's money you want,' he said, 'you can have what's in my wallet.'

The spokesman turned to his companions: 'He's insulting us again. Some bleeders don't know when to stop.'

'Then what do you want?'

'We want yer to say yer sorry.'

Charles stared dumbly through the smeared windscreen. In another place they would have been negligible creatures, younger than his students and too stupid to notice. The world was crumbling around him.

'I'm sorry,' he said.

'And you won't do it again.'

'I won't do it again.' His tongue felt thick and tasted brassy from the strong tea he had drunk. 'Now will you get out of the way?'

The taunting voice replied, 'What's yer 'urry?'

The bikes in front of him were too heavy and too close. If he went forward and knocked them down, they'd be too bulky to drive over. He'd be stuck, at the mercy of their senseless fury. And the scholar echoed in his idiot voice, *Motiveless malignity*. But if he backed suddenly, knocked over the bike behind and then swerved outward? Perhaps he might get away, but they'd be after him immediately, this time with an excuse. It was twenty miles back to town, on wet roads through darkened, silent villages. He'd never be able to outdrive these robots on their massive, glittering machines. He flipped the accelerator again and the youth at his side, still astride his bike, revved his engine in response, as though reading his thoughts. He'd never lose them.

With his cigarette hanging damply from his mouth, Johnny walked towards the front of the car and suddenly jerked the wing mirror. It resisted for a moment and then came away in his hand. 'Hey,' he said, 'look what I've got here. A fucking vanity mirror.'

'Show us.'

Johnny tossed the mirror to the youth who had done the talking. He held it by the stalk to his swathed face and began to primp. He turned his head from side to side, admired his muffled profile and pushed at the long hair hanging below his helmet, clicking his tongue and saying in a mincing voice, 'I just can't seem to do a thing with it.' Then he shoved the mirror against the car window. 'Want to admire yerself, beautiful?'

Charles saw deep lines bracketing a down-turned mouth, like a Greek mask, and crow's feet round staring eyes. Too old, too frightened; outlived your usefulness. He looked away.

'He fucking agrees with us,' said the youth. 'He don't like his fat face either.'

They began to throw the mirror around like children. Johnny in front bounced it off the car roof to the unseen youth behind. He bounced it back and it fell, shattering on the wet road. Johnny kicked at it, another of the riders tackled him, the one still astride his bike flailed at it with his great boot. For a moment, they had forgotten Charles.

Now's my chance, he thought, but sat still, unable to move. The enormity of the risk paralyzed him. Too old, said the voice in his head accusingly.

The football game ended as quickly as it had begun. The four zombies paused, almost in mid-movement, suddenly at a loss. 'Let's get on with it,' said the leader and pulled off his gauntlet. Johnny caught his eye and smiled for the first time with real pleasure. Charles noticed that his teeth were long and uneven. He wondered inconsequentially if he ever brushed them and had a brief image of his own small son perched over the basin, intently scrubbing away.

The two youths fumbled in their stiff pockets and brought out what looked like cigars. They held them delicately on their open palms and touched them with their thumbs. There was a sudden glimmer of light, like fish moving out of shadows, and two blades were in their hands, thin and tapered on one side. Johnny ran the tip of his knife along the wing of the Jaguar and carefully prised up fragments of paint.

Charles shouted 'Stop that' and started to open the car door. Then he halted abruptly, realizing that this was what they were after. Rage and impotence were bringing him to the edge of tears. There seemed no end to his shame.

The youths watched him, gently hefting their knives. Johnny's ragged mouth was stretched in an empty grin, the swathed faces of the other two creased derisively. Johnny moved towards the front tyre, his knife poised, while Charles sat helplessly, thinking, This is what the Day of Judgment will be like. He heard Mr Rotherham's voice booming the morning prayers from forty years before: 'We have left undone those things we ought to have done and have done those things we ought not to have done. And there is no health in us.' Better even the old man's cancer than this terror.

The knife made a silver arc against the headlights. There was a sudden hiss and the car knelt forward to one side like an obedient elephant. Johnny straightened up, his grin triumphant and more ragged than ever. The other youths cheered sardonically from behind their masks.

Then, without any warning, they began to move towards their bikes. Slowly, stupid with misery, Charles became aware of another brightness in the glare behind him and the drone of a heavy engine. The great oblong mass of a container lorry heaved past, sending up dirty spray. With a sudden squeal and pneumatic hiss of brakes, it came to rest thirty yards up the road. Its back was festooned with red lights. There was a moment of stillness, then the lorry driver from the café climbed out holding a tyre lever. He stood blinking in the blaze of the clustered headlights and then walked towards them, bouncing the flat iron bar almost tenderly against the palm of his left hand.

Charles flung open the car door as though released from a trap. The engines of the motor cycles were blaring hysterically. He made a grab for the rider at his side and caught an arm as it lashed at him. The gauntleted fist thumped heavily against his chest but he hung on, driven by rage beyond pain and shock, while the bike surged forward, dragging him with it. He ran a few steps, still hanging on and pulling, and then began to lose his balance. He let go and stumbled forward onto the ground while the rider from behind the car swerved deafeningly past. When he picked himself up the other two youths were still struggling to get their bikes off their rests while the lorry driver walked steadily towards them like fate. As Charles jumped at the nearest rider, both machines leaped forward, rear tyres spinning and sliding, front wheels almost clear of the ground. He saw the lorry driver swing at Johnny and the metal bar thud home. Then there were only four red lights going away into the night and the fading yell of the engines.

'Did you get their numbers?' said the lorry driver.

Charles shook his head.

'Scum,' said the other man, 'bluddy scum.' He looked angrily at Charles. 'You didn't believe me, did you? I've seen too many of that kind before. I know about them.'

Charles stared into the darkness where the lights had vanished and said nothing. The drizzle had stopped and the damp wind soothed his sweating face. He loosened his collar and tie, mumbling, 'I don't know how to thank you?'

'Don't. It was a pleasure, a reet pleasure.'

'I wonder if you hurt the one you hit.'

'You worried?'

'Hopeful. I'd have killed them if I could.'

The other man looked at him ironically. 'You know, I think you mean it. Fuck me, I think you mean it.' When Charles smiled sheepishly he added, 'That's a start, any road.'

'A start of what?'

'Of knowing what's what.' He walked over to the Jaguar. 'We'd better change that wheel.' Charles opened the boot and began fumbling in the darkness, but the other man shouldered him gently aside: 'I'll do it. You've had enough for one night.'

Charles didn't resist. He leaned against the car, feeling empty and powerless, near to tears, while the other man worked efficiently away. Finally, he stood up, wiping his hands on his overalls:

'The name's Arthur Clegg. You'd better have my address if you want to go to the police.'

'I suppose I'd better. At least I know the name of the gang. And one of them's called Johnny.'

'That's not much. What make of bike's were they?' Charles shrugged dumbly and Clegg said, 'You didn't notice much, did you?'

'I'm sorry.'

'Don't apologize to me. It's you I'm thinking of. Any road, the police will check up at the caff. Maybe Flo knows them.'

He took Charles's diary and carefully printed his name and address at the back. Charles gave him a card.

'Professor, eh? Bugger me.'

'We're both Derby men.'

'Aye. It takes all kinds.'

They shook hands.

'I'll tell you what,' said Clegg. 'In case the little sods are still around, I'll follow you in. It makes no difference to me to take the bypass. Probably quicker at this time of night.'

'You're very kind.'

'Pleased to help.'

Though they passed nobody on the drying roads, Charles was grateful for the dark mass of the lorry rumbling behind him like a battleship, with dipped lights. Same birthplace, same generation. At least that was a comfort. The wheel under his hands was still slippery with sweat; his shirt and jacket were soaked. When he eased his shoulders he could feel his coat unsticking itself from the seat like a Band Aid.

At the roundabout into town he lowered the window and waved. The lights behind him flashed twice. He turned right, then slowed to watch the massive, comforting shape with its carnival string of lights booming off down the bypass.

10

From the bottom, the stairs looked as long and steep as the Eiger. He toiled up painfully, pausing twice in a weariness that had come down on him like a hammer blow as he closed the front door. When he turned on the bedroom light Julie sat up immediately, as though controlled by the same switch.

'What's the time?' Her eyes were still empty with sleep.

Charles looked at his watch. 'Half past three.' He had forgotten all about her, forgotten why he had gone.

'Half past three?' she repeated in a puzzled voice. She sank back into the pillows, then focused on him, suddenly awake, and sat up again. 'God almighty, what's happened to you? Where have you been?'

Charles looked at himself in the mirror. His face was drawn and greenish with fatigue, his thin hair rumpled, his collar gaping and filthy, his tie askew. The ash from Johnny's cigarette was still smeared on his jacket shoulder. He sat down on his side of the bed and eased off his shoes gratefully.

'I've had some trouble.'

'God almighty,' she repeated, 'what happened?'

He told her as briefly and blankly as he could. She was one of them, not to be trusted.

When he had done she said, 'Poor darling,' as if she meant it. She knelt on the bed beside him and pulled off his jacket and tie, peeled off his soaked shirt, unzipped his trousers and pulled them down, and finally went down on her knees and took off his socks. He sat passively, unresisting, like a child miserable beyond complaint, with creased stomach and creased face. It was her fault.

For some reason the pungent, stale smell of his sweat aroused her. She kissed him on the mouth. He moved his head aside.

'I must wash. I stink.'

'It's all right. I like it.'

He shook his head and repeated, 'I stink.'

'Stay where you are.' She went out, leaving him staring unblinkingly at the bedroom wall, then returned a minute later with a cool, damp flannel. Gently she wiped his face, chest, back. She raised his arms like a baby's and sponged his armpits. He neither helped nor resisted and when she kissed him again he did not respond. He seemed to be looking past her, past the walls of the bedroom, back into the violent night.

Usually it was he who made the advances, she who held off in distaste or fatigue. Now his dulled and obstinate passivity puzzled her and frightened her a little. And that, in turn, was vaguely exciting. She knelt down by the bed, pulled off his underpants and put his limp cock into her mouth, inhaling the musky, private smell. He didn't move. She worked deftly away on him, licking, sucking, fingering, until he gradually began to harden.

Got him, she thought. All's well with the world again.

Then, without warning, he locked both hands into her hair and jerked her up by it onto the bed. She yelped like a puppy in pain and surprise. He flattened her on the bed, arms and legs outstretched like some Aztec sacrifice, and leaned above her, hands round her throat, his arms stiff, staring blankly into her astonished face.

'Don't,' she whimpered. 'You're hurting me. For God's sake.'

He tightened his hands round her throat experimentally, as though he were testing the ripeness of a melon, while she shook her head frantically from side to side. What frightened her most was his blankness. He seemed simply curious about the expression on her face and the sensations that flowed in from the ring of skin and bone, tendon and muscle with which he encircled her throat. Then, without shifting his hands, he entered her and began to pump brutally, still leaning above her stiff-armed and staring. So this is what he had been holding back through all those long years of domesticity. She twisted her legs up and locked them together behind his steadily shoving buttocks, then went with him, the lower part of her body heaving and shuddering, hanging from him clear off the bed. Nothing mattered beyond this. Why had he kept it hidden? He hates me, she thought.

They laboured together, all their old skills and familiarity suddenly transformed by this violence, like two professional wrestlers thrust unexpectedly into a battle to the death. Julie heard herself shouting gutterally and in German, while Charles grunted like an ox between clenched teeth. When they came at last and simultaneously, it was like a suicide pact: down, down together. He rolled off her abruptly.

'I love you.' When had she last said that? In another age. He didn't reply. She looked sideways at him. He was staring up at the ceiling in slabby profile, his mouth loose but his eyes still stoney. When she touched the side of his jaw with her fingers he didn't respond. She sat up and leaned over him, interposing her immaculate, madonna face between him and the ceiling. He focused on her slowly, indifferently. She was surprised how lined the skin was round his eyes. Like shattered rock. He seemed to read her thoughts.

'You think you've got me because I'm old. You think I haven't the energy or the guts to change my life now. Think again.'

She pretended not to understand: 'What's wrong, darling? Wasn't it all right for you?'

'Give him up.'

'There's no one to give up. It's you I love.' For the moment she believed what she was saying. For the moment her body had had everything it needed. Nothing else seemed important.

'I learned something tonight, something I'd never thought of in all those years of teaching.' He spoke slowly, in a flat voice. 'There's a war on between the new generation and mine. You've got to choose which side you're on.'

'Those vicious little swine upset you. You need sleep.'

'You've got to choose,' he repeated.

'They were psychopaths. Gangsters. The police will deal with them.'

'You're all psychopaths. The only difference is in style.'

She got up and put on her nightdress. 'You're upset. Go to sleep.' She was too vulnerable and he was too angry. She couldn't cope. She switched off the light and opened the curtains on the grey morning sky. Then she lay down beside him and put her head on his shoulder. Automatically, he took her in his arms, lying

81

there naked, heavy and miserable, still staring at the ceiling, pale now in the oyster light of dawn. Outside the birds began to rustle and chirp, tuning up for the day.

'Give him up,' he repeated.

A moment later, they were both asleep.

I I

Sam was bored. He stared over the piles of books on the desk in front of him and the scattered, silent heads, bowed in worship. The walls were books, there were books in the rooms above supporting the roof, books in the basement supporting the building, standing armies of books stretching in every direction, above, below, around, lifeworks, monuments to ambition and defiance, an expanding galaxy of words, an infinite weariness of the flesh. Fragments of torn cloud moved slowly across the windows, the sun coming and going between them. He stirred irritably, shifting from buttock to buttock in his seat. He rubbed the thumb of his left hand against the tips of his fingers, then scratched his bony forehead. His right hand was still, the pen in it poised over a blank sheet of paper like the dagger of a hired assassin. Bored.

An elderly American, broad shouldered and pot bellied, with the smooth, benevolent expression and beady eyes of a department head, swayed reverently down the aisle under an armload of books. His tweed jacket was neat, unfashionable and new; loot, thought Sam, from some lush research foundation, each stitch paid for in impenetrable footnotes. The wandering scholars: filing primly off the transatlantic jets with their corseted wives in linen suits and adolescent gipsy children, avid for two months of European culture at a favourable rate of exchange, then back to their placid, managerial routines at the great educational factories somewhere in the interior. Executives in the academic industry; perhaps not as lucrative as other forms of business, but the perks were similar and the prestige greater. His mother would like it if he went that way; it would compensate her for her husband's failure to make money, for all that bitterness and all those years of waiting. Well, it was a gratification she would be spared, as she had been spared most other gratifications.

Sam put down his pen and picked up a red felt-tip he used, in obsessional moments, for underlining headings and important points. He drew a large X from corner to corner of the virgin sheet of paper in front of him. Henceforth his academic future was cancelled. Then he drew a series of heavy lines vertically down the page, changed pens and sketched in a face with wild black eyes staring out from behind the red bars. He made the mouth into a ferocious, gap-toothed grin; he added sprigs of hair to the ears and upper lip. Across the bottom he printed in large letters:

'Tis well an old age is out,
And time to begin a new.

More words. He might end up like Charles, living his life through quotations among the orderly buildings and beautiful gardens, putting on weight and putting on words while he prosed on to his students about 'moral seriousness' and 'the quality of felt life'. Strange, strange: the more passionately they went on about morality and 'felt life', the more rancorously they squabbled with their colleagues, as if the fine-sounding phrases somehow justified their paranoia and malice. They were all the same: culture bearers in their fantasies, but in reality politicians scrabbling for power and influence in a society of adolescents. His mother might be pleased, but his father was not so easily fooled.

Last night after the dinner party he had dreamed about the old man. They were together on the staircase of a large bookshop. Sam had been searching the upper floors for a volume of anthropology and now they were leaving. He was in a hurry to get back to work and very sure of himself. This was his territory. But his father dawdled on the shelf-lined stairs, peering at books Sam knew he would never read, asking pointless questions, unable to make up his mind. Sam began to nag him impatiently and was just getting his way when the old man turned to him with surprising dignity and said, 'Give me time. I may not know about these things like you do, but I'm interested. I want to try. Give me time. I'm an old man. Don't put me down.' His eyes were watery, his hair thin and white. But he's not that old, Sam thought and began to weep, saying, 'I'm sorry. I'm so sorry,' tears streaming down his face is if his father were already dead and he were to blame. He had woken in a panic. The dream faded, but all morning he felt uneasy. He had done something wrong and couldn't remember what. Now he stared at the dusty columns of light and heard his father say again, quite clearly, in his ear, 'Don't put me down.' He shivered, wondering why it wasn't possible to get on without trampling on other people.

The grinning face behind red bars stared up at him from his notebook. He picked up his pen again and converted one eye into a wink, then added a Jewish bump to the bridge of the nose. Not that they were exactly falling over themselves to offer him jobs. But he'd get one sure enough, here or somewhere similar, if he hung around long enough, ground out an appropriately dull thesis and kissed enough backsides. Yet the truth was, the only backside he wanted to kiss, or bite, was Julie's, and the only reason he was still here was those sharp, brief afternoons in bed with her. She was a part of the scene, yet she had made the scene impossible for him. In a way, she belonged to the place even less than he did: more of an outsider, being foreign, more sceptical, more erotic – though he was learning. She had materialized like an apparition from another world; she had had children and been hungry; she said she had seen people die; she was impatient with his grand protestations of feeling. And gradually that impatience had rubbed off on him. Maybe she was a witch. He was sure she wanted something of him, something serious and apart. But she was searching for it only in his body. His mind and its lumber-rooms of books she left strictly alone. Am I in love with her? he thought. What else could this be? She has set me free.

He closed his notebook and got up. It usually took him two journeys to return all his books, but this time he gathered them into a double tottering pile, higher than his head, and staggered blindly to the librarian's desk. Instead of arranging them neatly on the Reserve shelves, he dumped them onto the table from where they would be returned to their silent vigil in the library's cavernous stacks. As he walked back to his desk, his arms were so light after the strain that he could no longer feel them. His head, too, felt light. *Finis, finis, finis.* He picked up the drawing of the prisoner and began to tear it out, then changed his mind, closed the notebook and tucked it under his arm. He wondered if he should simply leave the thing where it was but hadn't the courage to abandon so many months of labour. He was closing the door on his past. But not quite. He hadn't the nerve.

Downstairs, the wind swept round the corner of the library, blowing up dust from the flagstones of the great courtyard. He blinked his eyes against the boisterous sunlight. A clock struck eleven and all across town other bells took up the note, one after the other, each in its own way, as though greeting his decision: 'time to begin a new', 'time to begin a new', 'a new, new, new . . .'

His lodging house was one of a crumbling row of eighteenth-century slums under what had once been the city wall. He let himself in with a massive gaolers' key, closing the door gratefully on the fuming traffic. The passage was dark and lined with framed photographs of college groups. The indolent, confident faces stared at him disapprovingly, jaundice coloured with age, their owners long dead. 'Sneer away,' he muttered, 'see if I care,' walking towards the sunlit glare of garden at the end of the corridor.

His landlady was sitting, as usual, in her outhouse kitchen, sipping Guinness and contemplating the pile of greasy plates in the sink. She was a little gnome of a woman with a child's rosy face under a surprising halo of white hair. 'Not working today, Mr Green? Was the nice weather too much for you?' She ducked her head sideways apologetically when she spoke, as though still wincing away from the iron aunt who had terrorized her for three long decades after she became an orphan. 'Auntie' had been underground for more than twenty years, although Elsie still didn't believe it. So she kept her head cocked alertly, listening for that careful, steely voice, waiting for her gaunt figure to reappear from wherever it was it had been biding its time. She hardly even dared to change the prices, which meant that Sam and the other lodger lived absurdly cheap but had to chip in each quarter when the bills came in. Meanwhile, Elsie served up three-course Edwardian breakfasts and waited in her kitchen, drinking Guinness and expecting the worst.

'Too much for you, too?'

She giggled and ducked her head sideways, a sixty-year-old naughty child.

The garden, boxed in between high walls, was narrow, windless and overgrown. It smelt green. At its end, under the crumbling medieval wall, was a loo festooned with creepers. An overdressed girl advertising Pears Soap watched Sam coyly while he peed. He winked at her. He had the whole day before him. He could sit in his room and stare at the moving tree tops, doing nothing, or read a book he didn't have to, without a pencil ready in his hand to make notes. Later, perhaps, he would go swimming, then lie in the sun and sleep.

The carpet on the stairs up to his room was shredded, the wallpaper roses dark with age. He was halfway up when he heard a rattle at the letter box. There wouldn't be any mail for him; there never was; but he went down, anyway. A blue, unstamped envelope lay on the mat, his name written on it in large, round letters. He opened the door and saw Julie hurrying off down the street. When he shouted her name she stopped but didn't look round. He ran after her. In her sleeveless dress her arms looked unnaturally thin and her shoulder-blades stuck out like a child's. But when he came close he saw how smooth her skin was. There were fine beads of sweat at the top of her spine, where it disappeared into her dress. He felt suddenly private with her, as if they were alone in his bedroom, despite the traffic blaring past.

'Heh, what's up?'

'I didn't think you'd be in.' Her face was flushed and anxious.

'Well, I am.'

'You should be in the library,' she said irritably.

'I've had enough of the library. I've decided to jack it in.' When she didn't reply he waved the envelope vaguely at her. 'What's this about?'

'You'd better read it and find out.'

'Why not come back and have a coffee and tell me?' His pleasure at seeing her unexpectedly made him imperturbably good humoured.

'I don't think that's a good idea,' she said uneasily.

'Now you tell me.' He remained impervious, all smiles.

She shrugged and followed him back to the leaning, ramshackle house, up the tattered stairs, into his room. He closed the door with relief and leaned against it for a moment, looking at her, then crossed to where she waited nervously in the middle of the room and tried to kiss her. She shook her head and moved away.

'What's the matter?'

She shook her head again and said, 'He knows.'

'Who knows?'

'Charles.'

'About what?'

'Us.'

Sam was silent. He could feel bees crawling in his stomach. Finally he said, 'Did you tell him?'

'Don't be stupid.'

'Then how the hell did he find out?'

'How should I know? He wasn't saying. But he's not a fool. I suppose he noticed something.'

Sam grinned. 'So that's what it was all about. I just thought he didn't like the Jews. It's me he doesn't like. That makes me feel better about him.'

'I'm glad you think it's funny.'

'Take it easy. I don't think anything, except that it's probably not as bad as you imagine. What did he say?'

'After you'd gone, he asked me if I'd been seeing you. Of course I said no.' She paused. 'And you know something? In some curious way, I almost believed it myself. I was outraged. Isn't that odd?' Her face was as pure and delicate as a Sienese Virgin: exquisite nostrils, blue almond-shaped eyes, calm mouth framed by the gold-leaf of her hair. Sam watched her uneasily, thinking, Women, for Christ's sake.

'Anyway,' she went on, 'we had a kind of flare-up, then I went to bed. For some weird reason he decided to go for a drive. And on the way back he got involved with some thugs on motor bikes.'

'*Charles?*' Sam laughed unbelievingly.

'Honestly. They stuck a flick knife in his tyre. I think they'd have stuck one in him, too, if a lorry driver hadn't stopped.'

'He's making it up.'

'I don't think so. He was in a terrible state. I've never seen him like it. And he had the name and address of the lorry driver. He says he's going to the police.'

'I don't believe it. He's having a breakdown.'

'He may be, but I'm sure it's true. He nearly killed me when he came back.'

'*Charles?*' Sam repeated incredulously. 'You're joking.'

'I wish I was. He got his hands round my throat. I thought he was going to strangle me. Look at the marks.'

She pointed at her neck and Sam leaned forward. Under the skin on each side of her throat were faint, bluish marks. He kissed them, saying 'Jesus Christ', inhaling her subtle smell. She moved away from him.

'What happened?'

'Oh, I managed to calm him down.' She looked quickly away and ran her fingers over a book on the green baize tablecloth. Sam felt a squirt of jealousy. 'I bet you did,' he muttered.

Julie went on : 'In some queer way, he thinks we're to blame.'

'Us? For God's sake, why?'

'Because we're young. You're young, I'm younger than he is, the motor bike boys were young. He thinks all the young are against him.'

'Isn't that what they call paranoia? You should get him to see a shrink.'

'It's not funny. I don't know what to do.'

'Where is he now? He wasn't in the library.'

'He's in bed. He didn't wake up this morning. I've never known that before. He must be feeling awful.'

'And he's there now?'

'I hope so.' She went to the window and peered out into the racketty street. Sam followed her and put his arms round her waist, pressing her against the curtain. She shook her head from side to side.

'Go away. Please go away. I don't want to go on any more. I want to stop.'

'Is that what's in the letter?'

She nodded. Sam took the envelope from his pocket, tore it through without opening it and threw the pieces in the waste-paper basket. 'Fuck the letter.'

Julie still stood pressed to the curtain, watching the street outside and shaking her head. 'Go away,' she repeated. 'Just go away and leave me be.'

'Too late. I'm in too deep. Anyway, things have changed. I'm going to jack all this in and clear out.'

'Clear out then. That's what I want.'

'No, not while you're still here. Just out of all this airless mess.' He made a gesture with his hand which took in the books on his shelves, the distant library and the college garden opposite with its sleeping trees.

'Bully for you,' she said wearily, 'but what's that got to do with me?'

'Everything. It's because of you I've decided I don't want this any more.'

'You talk such rubbish. Why blame me because you've started to grow up? God knows, it's high time.'

'Because I love you.'

'I love you,' she mimicked. 'That's kids' stuff. It doesn't mean a thing. You've taken a decision, now be responsible for it. Don't push it onto me.'

'You're a hard girl.'

'I'm not a girl. I'm a married woman with two children. I've got enough on my back already.' She glared at him angrily, then returned to her watch on the street, rubbing the palm of her hand on the curtain behind her as if she was trying to get it clean.

Sam said, 'It's not that easy,' and walked back to her, pressing her as before against the curtain. When he tried to kiss her she twisted her head away as though determined not to give up her vigil on the world outside. He took her face in his hand and pulled it round until he could kiss her mouth. 'Enough's enough,' he muttered. 'Now it's my turn.' He slipped his other hand behind her buttocks, forcing her against him. She struggled for a while, whimpering 'No, no, no, no,' then slowly relaxed. When she finally began to respond, he undid his trousers with one hand and eased them down. She went on kissing and whimpering as if she hadn't noticed and tears began to ooze down her face. Without warning, still holding her face to his, he shifted his other hand, slid it up under her dress and tried to pull down her pants. They stuck at the top of her thighs and when he tugged at them clumsily they ripped. He levered her legs open with his knee and slid inside her. For the first time, he thought. Dear God. She went on whimpering, 'No, no, no, no,' while she heaved and shuddered with him.

They finished up on the floor beneath the window, streaming sweat, their faces and thighs as slippery as Roman wrestlers'. Julie wept like a child, without restraint or pride. 'I can't,' she kept repeating. 'No, I can't, no.'

Sam kissed her eyes: 'But you have. You can't leave me now.'

She wailed 'O-o-o-oh' and began to cry more desolately than ever.

He stroked her patiently and absent-mindedly kissed her hair, aware again of the noise of the traffic coming in through the open window. 'Come on,' he said gently, 'it's not all that bad.'

'What am I . . . hk . . .', grief made her hiccup, 'going to do?'

'It's all right. After everything we'd done before, this had to happen sooner or later. What does it matter? What's the difference?'

'Don't you . . . hk . . . see?' Another spasm of grief went over her. 'It's changed . . . hk . . . everything.'

'Don't be stupid. How?'

'You don't understand. You never went . . . hk . . . inside me, so you weren't really my . . . hk . . . lover. That's why I could handle Charles. You weren't really my lover. Hk. Now what will I do?'

Sam looked at her weeping face with amazement. She really believed it. One minute she was carved out of black ice, the next she was carrying on like a teenager with a whole contorted system of private rules and ceremonies to prove that she was always in the right. This was the girl who had convinced him that, through her, he had graduated into the adult world. What set of rules had she used for that trick? He stood up, pulled on his trousers and said, 'Would you like a drink?'

She shook her head and got to her feet, smoothing down her dress. 'I want to wash my face.' She picked up her torn pants. 'Have you got a pin or a needle and thread?'

'In the bedroom on my dressing-table,' said Sam. 'There's a towel by the basin. I think it's pretty clean.'

He opened the door for her politely, as if they had just met, and she went across the landing to his bedroom, closing the door behind her. Also like a stranger. He went back to the window and peered out. The traffic rumbled on unforgivingly. There was no sign of Charles. Her nervousness was contagious. He had a mistress, a real mistress, with a husband and two children. Then he realized that he had lapsed into Julie's demented way of thinking and caught himself: I've had one for weeks. Nothing has changed.

A wind had got up, bringing in towering clouds, gunmetal, silver and white, rifted with blue. The stately trees opposite began to toss backwards and forwards as though overcome, their leaves shivering excitably. He switched on the radio and the room was suddenly full of drama, a Beethoven sonata boiling away over the perpetual din of the traffic, as thick and rich and emotional as the heaving trees. He lit a cigarette and settled into his tatty armchair, letting the music seethe over him. The shelves of books each side of the fireplace filled him with distaste. *Time to begin a new.* He thought of Julie in the other room, sponging her face and her crutch, trying to put the pieces back together again. She too. Mad as a hatter under all that subtlety. Was he any saner? The bland world of reasonableness was an illusion. I am what I am, he thought. Can't change now. Much too late. But why did she have to cry like that? It turned him to ice. Maybe he should have stuck with the French girl. With her at least he knew where he was: two closed systems touching for their mutual gratification, no questions asked or demands made. Yet that, too, had been a form of play-acting. He didn't know what he wanted, only that there was a little dynamo whirring obscurely away inside him. He was ambitious for something. Not for the ambiguous glories of a university career. Not any more. He was clear about that. For life, then, as adults lead it: difficult, sophisticated, adulterous? Am I still such a little boy? he thought.

Julie came back into the room, washed and cool, as though nothing had happened. Sam smiled at her cheerfully, taking his cue: 'How are the knickers?'

'They'll do for the moment. I'll go and buy some more on the way home.' She crossed to where he sat, leaned down and kissed him on the mouth. 'What lovely music.' She kissed him again. 'It'll be all right.' He couldn't tell whether she was reassuring him or herself.

'Of course,' he replied, 'of course.'

'But we must be careful. I don't know what's going to happen.'

'Don't worry. Everything'll be fine. Promise you. But you must let me know how it works out with Charles. I'll be in the pub tomorrow. Will you come?'

'I'll try. But I don't know. Don't crowd me. If things go wrong, I'll drop you a note.' She kissed him again and left.

He listened to her steps going downstairs and the sound of the front door closing. Then he leaned out of the window and watched her walk off down the street, her blonde hair swaying on her shoulders. Just short of the corner she passed two workmen in overalls on their way to lunch. They turned and gawped at her demure, untouchable back. One of them whistled. What would they think if they'd seen her twenty minutes before, Sam wondered, her pants ripped off, her elegant body squirming and shuddering, suspended on him, tears streaming down her face. Unseen, he grinned down at them in triumph. In the garden opposite a blackbird was singing elatedly in the bucking trees.

12

His bones ached down to the marrow and his head was filled with hot iron. Every time he drifted up from sleep he felt the weight and heat of his body thrusting him back down. There seemed no point in fighting it. He lapsed back into darkness. At half past seven the children had come in as usual, but seeing their father's grey, emptied face on the pillow had crept out again in awe, with exaggerated quietness. Vaguely through his sleep he heard Julie shushing them in the next room as she got them dressed, then blackness swallowed him again. Some time later he heard her come back into the room while the children whispered excitedly on the landing. Then the front door closed and he slept. When he woke an hour later he saw a cup of coffee on his bedside table, but it was cold. He lay listening to the sounds of the morning: footsteps in the street and occasional cars, the radio playing pop music somewhere downstairs while the au pair sulked at her chores. Again he slept and when he woke the heat and heaviness had drained away, leaving him empty, like an abandoned hulk on the seashore. It seemed to him that his ribs must show through, despite the layers of comfortable fat encasing them.

Julie opened the door quietly. When she saw he was awake she came and sat beside him on the edge of the bed and kissed him gently. 'How are you feeling?'

The same old spasm of jealousy took him and made him shiver: that smell. Then he remembered that it was his sex she smelt of. He relaxed and smiled back at her. 'Better,' he said, 'but still a bit washed out. What's the time?'

'Quarter past one. I'm just giving the children their lunch. Do you want some?'

He sat up in bed. 'Yes. I'd better get up. I've wasted a whole morning.'

'What does a morning matter? You're not well. Stay in bed and I'll bring you something up.'

'I'm perfectly all right. I was just exhausted, that's all.' But when he tried to get out of bed he felt as thin and fragile as tissue paper. Julie pushed him gently back down onto the pillows.

'I ought to go to the police,' he insisted, but without conviction.

'They can wait. You rest. I'll get you some lunch.' She started to get up, but he put her hands on her hips and held her where she was, looking anxiously into her face. Was she an enemy? Her smooth, virginal features made him aware of the pouches below his eyes and the weariness in his bones. Had she opened her legs to anyone else? He shied away from the thought, reached up tentatively and ran his fingers over her eyes and mouth, then down to the smooth skin where her breasts divided above her summer frock. She stiffened for an instant and her face went blank, then she smiled again, registering appropriate concern. She took his hand and kissed the tips of his fingers. 'I'll get you some lunch.' She closed the door quietly as though she were in a hospital.

He lay considering his body: as heavy as pig-iron and as impermeable. The thugs last night had been banking on his sagging belly and thin grey hair; Julie too, in her different way, and her lover. If she had a lover. For a moment he understood their contempt and the excuse it gave them. Youth deserved youth and had its own special rights. Anger stirred him sluggishly, like a wintering animal. He wasn't that old. Why should he be boxed into this moribund corner? He watched the light shift in the trees outside his window and the leaves shivering together. They made a shimmering sound like silk dresses, like the beginning of rain. They had never seemed so beautiful. It was as if he was seeing them for the last time, saying good-bye. But why should he accept this role? He wasn't ready to bow out.

If I lie here, I'm lost, he thought and swung his legs out from under the sheets. When he stood up the room tilted twice, then steadied. I must stand on my own two feet like a big boy. And the padded, sagging figure in the mirror echoed him derisively, Big boy. He stretched his arms out wide to ease his aching shoulders, then went into the bathroom and stood under the shower for a long time, letting the water wash away last night's nightmare. The after-shave lotion stung his face into a semblance of real life.

By the time he got downstairs his son had already finished his lunch. 'I want to watch telly,' he complained. His grey flannel school uniform made him look like a midget businessman.

'There's nothing on except the Test Match and you don't like that,' said Julie. 'Anyway, it's almost time to go back to school.'

The child turned his large, serious eyes on Charles. 'Can't I see "Watch With Mother"?'

'It's finished. Why don't you go into the garden and get some air before they lock you up again in that stuffy classroom?'

'I'd rather see "Watch With Mother".'

'It's finished,' Charles repeated.

The younger child was chasing a lump of ice-cream round her dish with a spoon. When she finally trapped it she tilted the spoon on the way to her mouth and the ice-cream slid down her bib. Charles waggled his finger at her stomach and she gave a yelp of pleasure.

'You shouldn't be up,' Julie said to him.

'I'm all right. But I'd like a cup of coffee.' He felt suddenly hungry and cut himself a slice of bread and some cheese. But it tasted dank and heavy in his mouth, like a chunk of old putty. He made an effort to swallow it, then sat reading the paper and ate no more. His son came and sat on his lap, looking anxiously into his face. 'Look,' he said, 'I've lost another tooth.'

'You look like a Hallowe'en pumpkin. All you need is a candle in your mouth.'

The boy jumped down, grimacing, his hands lifted like claws. 'I'm a monster,' he cried, advancing on his sister who began to cry.

'Time to go back to school,' said Julie.

Charles took his coffee into the garden and stretched out in a deckchair, staring up into the trees. Their beauty offended him: effortless, mindless, not of their own doing. For more than half a century he had moved among them obliviously, going about his overwhelming business, knowing them, at best, only through his beloved poets and novelists. *Oh chestnut tree, great rooted blossomer.* That was enough for him, more than enough. So he had never bothered to look. Now he was seeing them as they were for the first time, a condemnation of his whole way of life: no texts, no footnotes, no brilliant insights or witty put-downs. Just beautiful. Like his wife. Well, he had time on his side. Sooner or later the taut curve of her cheeks would begin to sag, the bones would show through and wrinkles spread like spiders' webs. *Vengeance is mine, saith the Lord.* In time, in time. Her invulnerability would crack and she would become absurd like him, a ghoul at her own feast, desperate for younger and younger admirers. He just had to hang on. He stared up at the trees, aware of the aches and reluctance of his own padded, baggy skeleton. I must conserve my strength, he thought, I must get better. Despite the coffee, his mouth tasted foul. The sun, emerging from behind a cloud, dazzled him. When he closed his eyes he saw, in the red glare, Johnny's drooping lower lip and ruined teeth. A slow wave of anger rolled over him, then he drifted off to sleep.

When he woke Heidi was lying in a deckchair a few feet from him, her eyes closed, her skirt drawn up her thighs, and her blouse eased off her shoulders to receive the sun. She was a slow, heavy girl with a sulky face surrounded by a sweep of auburn hair. The flesh on her shoulders and neck glowed with the sun. When Charles stirred she sat up apologetically. 'You do not mind, please? I have finished my work.'

'Of course I don't mind. Enjoy the sun while it's out.' He peered, as usual, down his nose at her but smiled pleasantly. She smiled back.

'So long as I do not disturb.'

'You do not disturb.'

She remained sitting up, looking at him devotedly. 'I am very sorry you are ill.' Her voice was solicitous. 'You feel perhaps a little better now?'

'I'm not ill, just tired. And I'm feeling much better.'

'Mrs Stone told me you have trouble last night with some – how do you say? – hoodlums. That is not good. In Germany we do not have such people very much.' She was hot with indignation and concern.

'Germany is a very well-ordered country these days.'

'It is not right.' When Charles said nothing she asked, 'You go to the police?'

'Perhaps. But I don't suppose there's much they can do.'

'It is not right,' the girl repeated. 'Such people should be punished. They should be locked away.'

'I wish it were that easy.' He smiled at her wistfully, enjoying his martyred role and her outraged devotion to him. She was a big girl, but her hair was beautiful and she had splendid Wagnerian breasts. Her shoulders were dimpled and rosy with the beginning of sunburn, as succulent as a country ham. She saw him eyeing her and her face, already flushed with indignation, became redder.

'You should . . .' she fumbled for the right word, 'pursue them. They should not be allowed to escape with such things.'

'Your English is becoming very fluent,' said Charles benignly. The girl flushed again, this time with pleasure. 'Where's Mrs Stone gone?'

'She is in the park with Tanya, I think. That is where she usually goes when she takes her out.'

'Doesn't she usually?'

'Oh no. When Peter has lunch at school Mrs Stone goes out about half twelve and I take Tanya for her walk.' The girl's voice was heavy with intent. She seemed to be saying, 'Didn't you know?'

'Oh,' said Charles, thinking So that's when they meet. Is the girl suspicious, too? Out loud he said, 'It's silly you should know more about the household routine than I do. But that's the trouble with being the wage-earner. You're never around.'

'Yes, it is silly,' said Heidi, looking at him steadily.

There was a silence. The sun drifted behind a grey fist of cloud and a chilly wind gusted through the garden. Charles got up heavily. 'I think I must go upstairs and try to do some work.'

'Do you not think you should rest?' Heidi enunciated each word carefully, her voice full of concern. But her exposed legs and shoulders and face said, 'Stay here with me.'

Charles smiled at her in a fatherly way. 'I'm fine,' he said and went inside. So, he thought as he toiled up the stairs, not all the young think I'm ridiculous and untouchable. That's nice. His study took him in like a lost child come home again. He closed the door and leaned against it, looking slowly round the lined walls. He knew the place of each book. His instruments: subtle, pierc-

ing, obedient. His first love and his last. He sat down at his desk
and opened his fountain pen. But when he tried to read the neatly
written page on his blotter, the words swam and he saw faces:
monkey faces shrouded in silk scarves, moustached faces with
ragged mouths, Sam's face but beaked and sneering like a carica-
ture, then Julie's, serene, stony, her teeth gleaming wet, saying
'You make me sick.' When he looked round at the books for reas-
surance they seemed to pulse in and out like a warning light. The
women were right: he should have stayed in bed.

He got up and went to the window. Down below an elderly
woman was being towed along the street by a fat black Labrador.
At every lamp-post the creature stopped, sniffed and lifted its leg
while the woman swung on past like a sling-shot, each time jerk-
ing to a halt and looking back at the dog in surprise. Charles stood
at the open window watching them. His teeth were chattering.
Last night, on that wet empty road, he had nearly died. Not that
the youths had had murder in mind. Nothing so dramatic. They
had merely wanted to humiliate him, have a bit of fun. But ulti-
mately they wanted him dead. Strange that he hadn't understood
this before, since it was so obvious and so close. He was in their
way. He owned the things they wanted to own, enjoyed the
pleasures and comforts they lusted after. He kept the light off
them. All of them. So far as they were concerned, he owed them a
death. He was an obstacle standing between them and their
rightful place at the top of the heap. They didn't hate him, they
were simply impatient. Our turn, they were saying; high time
you were gone.

He wasn't going yet. He sat down again at his desk and surveyed the pages of manuscript, the orderly piles of books and
papers. There was too much to do, although his head felt hot and
the hand holding the pen trembled against the blotter. Of course,
he would see to it that Sam's university career was finished. But
suddenly that seemed to him a flavourless recompense for what
he'd been through. *Revenge is a kind of wild justice.* Those were
the days. He saw a Jacobean stageful of corpses, all of them young,
with Julie herself as the Duchess of Malfi, dead on dead. The
image was flickering and badly lit, like an old movie, but oddly
appeasing. They were waiting for him to die, jostling him towards

the exit. The real wild justice would be to make them jump the queue.

He looked round at the patient shelves of books. No help there. He never read detective stories – their prose offended him – and the days of the Renaissance assassin were long over. Or were they? Again he saw the leather-coated youths with their swathed faces and flick knives. Violence is as violence does, he thought. It merely changes its uniform. He sat daydreaming at his scholarly desk: find them, pay them, turn them loose on Sam, then shop them to the police. For a moment, it seemed as clear and simple as a lyric poem, and as pure.

> O, let me not be mad, not mad, sweet heaven !
> Keep me in temper : I would not be mad !

He focused with an effort on the page in front of him : 'Ben Jonson's decision to publish his collected works was, at that time, unprecedented. Unlike Fulke Greville, he believed . . .' Again the bandaged faces swam before him, and Johnny's mouthful of rotting teeth. They were alien and beyond reprieve; their souls were corrupted. Odd, then, that he should envy them after all these years of lecturing about morality : morality and literature, moral discrimination in Shakespeare, in Jane Austen, in T. S. Eliot. He had never dreamed his own was so fragile. Maybe violence was like a bad marriage; once exposed to it, the civilized habits drop away and the real person comes burrowing out, brutish, bullheaded and undeniable. He wondered what Fulke Greville would have made of that.

He heard the front door open and the sound of the children's voices. Cautiously, he got to his feet. O, let me not be mad, not mad, sweet heaven ! No, indeed. He unfolded a clean handkerchief and mopped his forehead, then went carefully down the stairs to greet his wife.

13

'I had a letter from Tante Ilse today,' said Julie at dinner.

'What did she have to say for herself?'

'Nothing in particular. The usual high-flown nothings. I think she's offended I've never been to see her. But it took six pages to fail to say so.' She had a picture of her aunt's thin, sharp-nosed figure bending over the notepaper, grimly composing her florid sentences. 'She's a scrawny old bird,' she said, 'but she writes as if she was rolling in fat.'

'That's the German language for you,' said Charles. They were friendly again, making an effort to pretend nothing had happened.

'Maybe I should go and see her sometime.'

'Maybe you should.'

After dinner they went into the drawing-room with their coffee and sat listening to a Schubert record. Julie closed her eyes, letting the music go over her. So wistful, so poignant, but with a vague feeling of something terribly wrong. It reminded her of Germany and of being a child. When she opened her eyes she saw Charles watching her lugubriously.

'Why are you staring at me like that?'

'Like what?'

'You know. An old-fashioned look. Disapproving.'

'I was just thinking how young you look.'

'At my age that's no longer a compliment.'

'Isn't it? I'd have thought you'd like it. Want a brandy?'

She shook her head and closed her eyes again: such sad music. When the record ended she said, 'Will you go to the police to-morrow?'

Charles shrugged. 'I don't see the point. They'd want facts, proof, witnesses, that sort of thing. I haven't got any, really.

101

They'd probably think I was imagining it all. You know, a bit dotty.'

'Maybe you're right.' She remembered Sam's sardonic, incredulous, 'That's what they call paranoia.' For a moment she hated her lover, and this confused her. 'What will you do then?' she asked.

'There's nothing much I can do. Sweet though vengeance would be, I'd better leave it to the Lord, as the Bible recommends. Though I doubt if He'll be much more helpful than the police.' He slumped, crumpled, in his chair, an old man, grey faced. It was her fault.

'There ought to be something you can do.'

'I know what I'd like to do all right.'

'What?'

'String them up, personally, with my own bare hands. Preferably in the garden where I could see them.'

'My,' she said mockingly, 'I thought you didn't approve of capital punishment.'

'That was yesterday.'

'That was a whole lifetime.'

'Maybe I've been wrong all my life then,' he said bitterly.

She changed the subject. 'Are you feeling any better?'

'I'm all right. A bit shaky still, but all right.'

'You need a good night's sleep.'

He finished his brandy and stood up: a sack of old clothes; grey face, thin grey hair; her husband. He bent down and took her arm. Christ, she thought.

'You come too,' he said, pulling her up to him.

She did not resist. He held her tightly against him and she could feel his heart bumping, bumping in his chest. There seemed to be no desire in him, only a leaden determination, like fate. Her head lay unresponsive against his white shirt. He was sweating gently and illness made him smell musty, like a disused room. Unseen, she wrinkled her nose.

He turned her round and pushed her by the shoulders towards the staircase, repeating, 'You come too.'

She went like a child to punishment, thinking, Christ have mercy on me. Christ have mercy.

Afterwards she lay in bed watching the shadows on the ceiling. You've done it now, she said to herself. A real whore. It's like my adolescence all over again. Every man a rapist, in uniform or out. Predators all. I've been had three times in twenty-four hours, violently and against my will, but loving it in the end. When was I last so excited? Maybe this is how I've wanted it all along. I'm a rapee. Charles was snoring gently and peacefully at her side. She felt curiously tender towards him. Poor old thing, she thought. My husband the professor. My husband the rapist. My lover the rapist also. Such intellectual men in other ways. I suppose I'm to blame. She began to giggle softly in the darkness. At least it was better than being like all the other mothers she saw in the super-market, piling the economy, family-size packets of detergent and cereal into their trolleys, wiping noses, barking out military orders, their looks fading. So tired, always so tired. No, thank you. She didn't want to be like that. As she fell asleep, she heard an owl hooting forlornly from the garden behind the house.

She dreamed she was walking quickly on her own down a street of red brick Victorian houses. A gang of urchins mocked her in a thick northern accent she couldn't understand, but she took no notice. One of them, a fat, greasy child with a snub nose and hyperthyroid eyes, jumped out in front of her, dropped his shorts, thrust his great bum towards her and farted loudly. She smacked it, outraged, and the child ran howling into the house opposite. When she looked down at her hand fragments of fat were con-gealing on her fingers. She was flicking them away, nauseated, when her aunt appeared at the bay window of the house into which the boy had fled and began to scream abuse in German. 'Don't think you'll get away with this, you whore. My son and I know all about you and your Ruritanian affairs.' 'My what?' 'Ruritanian,' repeated the aunt contemptuously, as though the word were too long for her to understand. Julie looked at her dumbfounded. She wore her white hair in a bun and an emerald green dress which reflected upwards, shading her face with acid. The old woman's eyes were narrowed and her lips drawn back on her teeth like a dog's. Julie realized she had never seen real hatred before. 'What have I done?' she pleaded. 'You'll see,' her aunt hissed. 'I've called the police. You'll see.' She's the neighbour-hood nut, thought Julie in her dream. The police probably know her. They'll be on my side. I haven't done anything. But she woke full of foreboding.

The children were playing in their room across the landing. She went into them gratefully and sat on the bottom bunk, her body aching from the strain of the dream. They were puzzled that she did not hurry them as usual into their clothes, but played on, pretending not to notice. The boy was building a rocket out of Lego while his sister scrawled wildly across a picture book which she lifted, every so often, for her mother's approval. Gradually, the dream slipped away. Her head felt numb and empty. Finally, she roused herself and began to hustle the children into their clothes. As she was pulling a dress over her daughter's head, she suddenly thought, I might lose them, and hugged them both pas-sionately. They looked at her warily, not sure what to make of this outburst. Then they all laughed self-consciously. She finished dressing them and shooed them downstairs. The strain had gone to her stomach; it felt lined with hot, steel wires. If I got ill, she thought, I'd be out of this. Then there'd be no need to choose. Or I could go to Germany and see Tante Ilse. Sooner or later I must face my dreams, anyway. Better than this confusion.

Charles came down to breakfast at his usual time, his nose lifted as usual to the weather, his voice booming as usual, his nightmares gone. They ate in silence, the children even more subdued by his recovery than they had been by his illness, Heidi watching him sideways while she nibbled her diet of dry toast and drank her sugarless, milkless tea.

'You don't look well,' he said to Julie after he had read the front pages of *The Times*. 'You don't look at all well.'

'I don't feel well.'

'Why don't you see a doctor?'

'I'm just tired. I'll be all right.'

There was another silence. Charles rustled his newspaper and sniffed noisily. Julie watched him in annoyance. With his nose lifted like that, he might have been reading the ceiling rather than the newspaper on the table in front of him.

She said, 'Are you going to the police?' Hoping to needle him.

'Maybe later, when the library closes. I've already missed a whole day's work.'

'Does that matter? It's silly to put it off.'

'It's probably equally silly to go. There's nothing they can do.'

'At least you can give them the name of the gang. They probably have a whole file on them already.'

'Look,' said Charles in his heaviest lecture-room voice, 'there's no point in going on about this. I'm a professor at this university. I have a position to keep up. If I took this story to the police, I'd look a complete fool. What's happened's happened. Now leave me alone.'

'It's up to you.' Julie shrugged. Last night he had seemed rampant and dangerous, now he was just a pompous old man, full of rectitude. Her waking life was as unstable as her dreams. An acid was eating away at everything, changing comfortable old faces into tribal masks, wolves into sheep. She felt giddy again, as though there were nothing left to hold onto, and wondered if she were really getting ill.

After she had left her son at school, she walked slowly up the High Street, her shopping bag slung over the handle of her daughter's push chair, absentmindedly answering the child's chatter, one of an army of young mothers on their morning patrol. She paused outside Sainsbury's and peered through the great plate-glass windows down the long rows of gaudy packets and bottles and tins where women like herself, in jeans and without make-up, moved with children perched on their trolleys. And again she felt the strength go from her. The profusion of goods exhausted her now in the same way as starvation had in her adolescence. It had been easier to scheme and cajole for a loaf of bread tasting like sawdust than to cope with this senseless abundance. She walked on past the big stores, turned into a side street of smaller, more expensive shops and went into an old-fashioned grocer's, its windows piled haphazardly with tins of imported delicacies, its interior shadowy with racks of wine, boxes of biscuits and packets of tea with the shop's name on them. The place was empty, the shopkeeper and his assistant white haired, grey coated and obsequious. She gave her order without bothering about prices and asked for it to be delivered. The shopkeeper saw her to the door and bowed as she went out.

Pushing her daughter determinedly in front of her, she walked to the police station. The sergeant in charge was stout and heavy jawed, with iron-grey hair like her father's. He looked at her childish figure and drab clothes coldly and condescendingly. Ho hum, his eyes said, Another of them. I'll listen but don't expect any sympathy from me, my girl. I know you. But when she explained who she was he turned deferential, town paying its expected, traditional dues to gown. Julie told him the story Charles had told her, while the policeman took notes, nodding occasionally and clucking his tongue, though whether from sympathy or satisfaction she couldn't tell.

'Why hasn't the professor come to us himself?' he asked when she had finished. He sounded faintly offended.

'He thinks there isn't enough evidence for you to be able to do anything.'

'He's right in a way. This lorry driver now . . .'

'My husband has his name and address.'

'But he didn't actually see anything happen?'

'No. When he stopped they ran.'

'And the professor,' he pronounced the title with relish, as though it added dignity to his own job, 'wasn't actually hurt?'

'No. But only by luck. There's damage to his car, though.'

'But there's no witness, apart from the professor, to say who did it?'

'For God's sake,' said Julie, 'these are dangerous thugs. They carry flick knives and use them. Isn't that enough?'

'In certain circumstances. But if the professor isn't hurt there's no charge we can bring which we can make stick.'

'I thought it was your duty to protect the public.' She wished she didn't look so absurdly young; perhaps then they might take her seriously. She felt angry that Charles wasn't here doing his own complaining. Damn the lot of them.

'Of course it is, ma'am,' said the sergeant soothingly. 'But it's not easy bringing a charge in a court of law. Juries can be very unpredictable.'

On the wall by his desk was a poster of a dark-haired girl in a gipsy dress. Under her picture was written 'Have you seen this girl?' then, in smaller print, the details of her murder: 'Found in Cross Street on the night of 4 May with multiple stab wounds in . . .' Etc. The face in the smudged photograph was smiling, as though she was pleased with her new dress and liked whoever it was who held the camera. One of us, thought Julie and again the strength seeped out of her, her wrists felt like water.

'Are you all right, ma'am?' the sergeant asked solicitously.

Julie nodded. 'It's been rather upsetting, that's all.'

'I'm sure it has, ma'am. Watkins.' A tall young policeman with a large Adam's apple came across to him. He eyed Julie appreciatively. 'Have we a file on a motor bike gang called "The Outcasts"?'

'I'll see, sir.' The constable went out, past the poster of the dead girl. Julie stared at it, saying nothing, while the sergeant made fatherly noises at her daughter, who refused to look at him. In a couple of minutes the young policeman was back. 'I'm afraid not, sir. There's nothing in the files.' He sounded disappointed not to have found anything to make him seem important to Julie. He watched her out of the corner of his eye.

'I'm very sorry, ma'am,' said the sergeant, 'I don't see that there's anything we can do at the moment. There have been no previous complaints.' He rolled the official phrase importantly off his tongue and leaned back with satisfaction. 'Of course, if the professor wants to come down here and talk it over with me, he could file an official complaint himself. There may be some important details you've missed.' We men, his tone implied, can work these things out better between ourselves. Man to man and no hysterics. Clearly, it would be a feather in his cap to meet the distinguished professor.

Back in the street Julie walked with a shut face, fighting off tears. If only she didn't look so unspeakably young, or at least had mastered the brass, shattering, county accent that made them all skip. Then they might listen to her and know she was serious. She hurried home, handed her daughter over to Heidi and went out again, without bothering to make excuses. She went straight to Sam's rooms, thinking, How old must you be to be a whore? They made love wildly on his still unmade bed, while the morning traffic rumbled outside and Elsie pottered below in her kitchen. To him, at least, she was an adult.

When Charles came home that evening she said nothing about her visit to the police station, but made love to him, too. Down, down, down.

That night she dreamed she went into her father's room and found him with a dark-haired girl in a gipsy dress. He was standing naked, his back to the door, while the girl lay on the carpet before an unlit fire, her long dress up above her waist, her pants torn off. When Julie looked closely she saw stab wounds in the tender, exposed belly, but the girl merely smiled at her wanly, one victim to another. Her father didn't move.

When she awoke she was running a temperature. The doctor came, tapped, prodded, listened, and drew blood from her arm, appalled by her pallor and frailty. He ordered her to stay in bed and keep quiet until he came again. Heidi bustled about triumphantly, her strong, blunt body swollen with importance. Each evening she prepared an intimate dinner for herself and Herr Professor which he ate, each evening, absentmindedly, then went grimly upstairs to his wife's bedside.

14

When Julie announced she was dying Sam wanted to die too. Her face was pale as a handkerchief. Wisps of gold hair had come loose from the knot at the back of her head and curled damply onto her thin shoulders. She no longer looked delicate; she looked skinny. An Auschwitz child. He wanted to gather her up, take her off somewhere in the sun, feed her nourishing food, put her to bed early and make love to her tenderly. Above all, make love to her. He was embarrassed by how much her debility roused him. *Down, wantons, down.* He tried to concentrate on his heartbreak.

'What can I do?'

'Nothing at all.' She spoke quietly, playing the tragedy in a minor key. 'I think I'll go back to Germany.' She paused, brushed the strands of hair from her shoulders, then twisted the knife: 'To a clinic.'

He looked at her helplessly. Her calm overwhelmed him even more than her pale, untouchable air. *Shiksahs.* The Jewish girls he knew could whistle up tempests for no reason at all: a broken necklace or a cold in the nose, and they'd be weeping and invoking heaven. Now this blonde waif was announcing her death as calmly as if it were a cricket score. It was his turn to keen and cry and carry on.

But he knew better. Five years at an expensive boarding school had taught him, if nothing else, the virtue of silence. Keep quiet, whatever happens; never complain. The compulsory games six days a week, and cold baths every morning, the bullying, caning, uneatable food and absolute lack of privacy had been worth it in the end. All through his tropical Jewish childhood he had longed for the cool, minimal response to disaster, the stiff upper lip: 'I'm just going outside. I may be some time.' His father said that, or its equivalent, every time he went, unsuccessfully, to the lavatory.

Now Julie was saying it in the authentic Captain Oates tones and with the authentic meaning. Of course he loved her. Why had he hesitated? The paleness of her face, eyes, hair, even her unnatural thinness were what he had always been after. She cooled the air so that he could breathe.

The sunlight, slanting through the pub windows, turned the cigarette smoke into faintly stirring columns of blue light. The lunchtime crowd had gone. Two college servants in polished blue suits were playing shove ha'penny in one corner, a third leaned against the bar chatting quietly to the landlord. The shadows of people passing on the pavement outside made the smoky columns of light tremble. The sound of traffic was subdued, lulling.

'Can I come with you?' Sam asked. Julie sipped her drink and did not answer. 'Can I?' he repeated, pleading.

'I suppose you might,' she said at last. 'But it won't be easy.'

'Is Charles going?'

'No. I'm going on my own. He'll stay behind with the children and the au pair.'

'Then what's the problem?'

'The place I'm going to is a couple of miles from the nearest village and . . .'

'That doesn't matter.'

'. . . and my aunt will be there.'

'At the village or the clinic?'

'I don't know yet. I've only just written to say I'm coming. Maybe she'll just visit me. It's not far from Heidelberg.'

'Well then?'

'I suppose so.'

Sam took a swig of his beer to hide his triumphant smile. He, not her husband, would be in at the death. She had made her choice. Him. He put down his glass and pressed her thin hand. 'I love you,' he said.

'I know,' she replied, thinking, At least he takes me seriously. He sees how ill I am and is sorry. Whereas Charles was merely irritated. Her week in bed had spoiled his routine. He sat with her dutifully while she shivered and tossed, but all the time he was thinking about his footnotes. His holy footnotes. Although he tried to seem sympathetic, underneath he was ice. For the first time, she understood why Gentiles resent the Jews. As a child, she had listened to the Nazi propaganda as she had listened to fairy stories: the ogres had black, curly hair, hooked noses and liver lips, just as witches were hunchbacked and rode broomsticks. As for Charles's anti-semitism: she had always thought it another of the innumerable snobberies of a working-class boy made good, like his snobbery about wine. Wrong. The Jews are resented because they are sympathetic; they understand that people have feelings and make allowances for them. No wonder the founder of psychoanalysis had been a Jew. 'It's all right,' she said, 'I love you, too. Don't worry.'

They sat for a while in silence, enjoying the smoke-filled sunlight and the indolent minutes before closing time.

'Last orders, please,' said the landlord. When he spoke loudly the folds of flesh hanging over his collar wobbled hysterically. 'Last orders.'

Sam took a swig from his glass. 'I saw Charles, you know. Did he tell you?'

'No. When?' Her voice was suddenly light and strained.

'Two days ago.' He had been about to gloat but he saw her expression. 'Look, I'm sorry. I couldn't help it. I hadn't heard from you for five days. Not even a note. I was frantic. You might have been dead for all I knew.' He realized what he had said, stopped and squeezed her hand. 'I'm sorry. I mean ... I didn't know what to do. So I started lurking round your house. I got there about eight-thirty in the morning. I thought I'd catch you taking the children to school or something. But all I ever saw was that great bosomy au pair of yours. I was watching her, wondering if I could stage a meeting and find out where you were, when Charles came out and saw me dithering on the other side of the street.'

'What happened?'

'I felt as if I'd been caught with my fingers in the till. He strode across the road with his eyes staring and his fists clenched. Just like Groucho Marx: "I'd horsewhip you, if I had a horse." Honestly, I was terrified. But all he did was boom at me. "I think you and I had better have a word," he said. So we marched off down the road in silence. We must have looked a couple of real idiots.

The long and the short of it. I had to skip to keep up.' He giggled, unable to hold it in any longer.

'Go on,' said Julie grimly, 'for God's sake.'

'Well, he didn't say a thing until we got into the park. Then he launched into an extraordinary tirade about . . .' He giggled again, overcome. 'You won't believe me.'

'What?' She spoke impatiently, but under her apprehensiveness a little flame of laughter was flickering up. It was all over. No more lies.

'Morality and literature.'

'You're joking.'

'So help me God. Morality and literature. He quoted Tolstoy's *What is Literature?*, Leavis on *Othello*, Camus' *Myth of Sisyphus*, one of Henry James's prefaces, Lawrence on pornography, T. E. Hulme, Wellek and Warren, Eliot, not to mention, of course, Matthew Arnold. Lots of Matthew Arnold. He'd have quoted himself, too, if he hadn't thought I was an enemy. I think he was giving me the rough draft of his lectures for next term. I felt I should be taking notes.'

'May I have your glasses now, please,' said the landlord, his neck trembling with the effort. Sam and Julie got up and went out into the afternoon glare. She was trembling with suppressed laughter, her lassitude and illness for the moment forgotten.

'You know something,' Sam went on, smelling victory, 'in all that time he didn't look at me once. He just pointed his nose at the heavens and stared down it. Or up it.'

'I know.' Julie could feel the laughter beginning to bubble up like a broken water main. 'I sometimes think he's never once looked at me fair and square. Not in all these years.'

They walked past the newly washed front of a college, biscuit yellow in the sunlight, giggling like schoolchildren in church.

Finally, Sam stopped and said in a sober voice, 'He's mad, you know. Mad as a hatter. All the time he was ranting on he had his fists clenched, wanting to hit me. The knuckles were white. He kept sticking them into his pockets and they kept creeping out again, almost of their own accord.'

'There's nothing mad about that. In the circumstances.'

'All right, all right. So it was natural to want to hit me. Then why didn't he, instead of just talking about books? Fucking books. I ask you. Never once did he come out with it straight. He never asked me a thing. Thank God. Just rambled on and on about literature. That's what's crazy. Don't you see it?'

No answer. She stared at him fascinated. 'OK, so he has a passion for literature and a passion for you. But he can't tell the difference between the two. Nothing's real for him outside books. Not even you. He's not really jealous. Not him, Charles Stone. He's simply become Othello. His whole life is just a series of footnotes to other people's texts.'

He stopped. They stood together at the corner of his street, under the crumbling medieval wall which had once marked the limits of the city and where dandelions now grew and pigeons strutted. She looked at his excited face and thought, So that's why Charles dislikes the Jews. How did he put it? 'Too clever by half.' But sane, also sane. Too sane by half, too?

'I'd better be getting back,' she said. 'I'm supposed to be in bed. They watch me.'

Instantly, Sam's triumphant mood collapsed. 'Not yet.' He was whispering, although the street was empty, for the moment, even of traffic. 'Come back to my room with me. Please. It's only quarter to three. You've plenty of time.' She shook her head. His eyes misted over. 'For Christ's sake. It's been over a week. *Please.*'

So much for her theories about Jewish sensitivity and concern. He was like a child who had been denied his wine gums.

'Please,' he whispered, 'please come with me.'

'All right,' she said and went.

15

It was decided that she would leave for Germany a week after she was well enough to get out of bed. Charles had talked vaguely of a holiday with her aunt, but it was Julie herself who suggested the clinic. The name came to her out of nowhere from her remote childhood : Iserthal. Before she said it she had forgotten the place existed. 'Somewhere in the sun,' said Charles and she nodded. Yes, yes, in the sun. And saw her father walking ahead of her through deep pine woods. A hot day. The trees glassy with heat. Insects buzzing. The smell of resin everywhere and the path uncertain and overgrown. As always, she is hurrying to keep up. The brambles swing back after his dark figure and catch at her bare arms and legs. Occasionally, they come out into a mossy clearing, cool, green, full of shadows, but he never pauses. Then the light changes and they are out of the trees, standing on a curving ridge, a green sweep of field running down and away from them to form a grass cup, studded with flowers and surrounded by forest. At the bottom of the cup, shimmering in the heat, a cluster of low, whitewashed buildings with red tiled roofs. And at their centre, enclosed by a grey stone patio, a turquoise swimming pool, like a jewel in a ring. Its surface shivers in the sunlight. The place seems unpeopled. She takes her father's hand. 'It's beautiful, papa. Can we go for a swim?' He smiles down at her and shakes his head. 'It's private. Strictly private. It's for the rich and the sick. The rich sick.' She looks up at him puzzled. 'A clinic,' he says, 'and full of party members.' 'What's it called?' 'Iserthal,' says her father.

'Iserthal,' she said to Charles.

All those lost years. Under their debris that jewel of greeny-blue water had been waiting patiently for a name to release it.

Their family doctor had never heard of it, of course. But he phoned a colleague in London who made inquiries. The next day they had their answer: the place still existed and was highly recommended, though pricey, very pricey. But it had everything: saunas, masseurs, gymnasium, its own mineral spring, even an operating theatre. Its reputation, however, rested on a special diet worked out by the director. It had been known, they said, to work miracles. 'I have the impression,' boomed Charles, 'that they have testimonials from every hypochondriac since Lazarus.' So he telephoned and made a reservation. At the clinic's request, he confirmed it by telegram. Six hours later he had a telegram back, confirming the confirmation. The next morning Julie was booked on a flight to Munich. Iserthal: all she had done was say the magic word and suddenly wheels turned, messages flew and rock doors of the past swung open for her. She had never dreamed it would be so easy.

Their doctor insisted she leave the children behind. 'You're to have a complete rest. No worries. Nothing. Read if you must, but only trash; nothing to stir you up. Sleep's what you need above all, or a condition as near to it as you can manage during waking hours. Don't even write letters. You have a devoted husband and a perfectly competent au pair. The children will be all right.' He was a big, blunt-nosed man with the pot belly of an ex-athlete and wrists like a coal miner. Despite a lifetime's practice in a university town, he still secretly believed that the intellectual life was unhealthy: 'Too much thinking, not enough fresh air.' He was damned if this pretty young woman was going to be dragged under without his trying to help her. She looked like a ghost. Her husband was a nice enough man, but too old for her. An unhealthy situation. God knows how she had ever got herself into it. 'Go away for a month and forget about everything,' he ordered, 'that's my advice. Take it or leave it.' 'A week,' retorted Charles, 'surely that's enough to get her back on her feet?' 'My dear sir, you don't understand the seriousness . . .' And so on. They finally compromised on a long fortnight, sixteen days. Julie lay in bed letting the battle flow over her, looking from one to the other like a spectator at Wimbledon, saying nothing. But when they had gone the children came in to see her and she wept bitterly. Iserthal: her childhood for theirs. Why was nothing ever simple?

The next day she got out of bed for the first time in a week. All morning she sat in the sunny garden playing quietly with her daughter. After lunch Heidi took the child for a walk in the park before going on to collect the boy from school. Charles, of course, was at the library. A blue and silver day, with pale, running shadows. Julie finished her coffee and went into the hall. The empty house seemed full of echoes, as if the intense lives of the children continued to vibrate in the air even after they had gone. She stood listening to the steady tock of the grandfather clock, waiting for the echoes to die away and her head to empty. Then quickly, so as not to give herself time to change her mind, she went out of the front door and hurried to the pub to meet Sam.

When she got home at teatime the colour was back in her cheeks, her eyes were clear, she moved as if her mind were made up. Iserthal was her vanished childhood, Sam her vanishing youth. So she would take him with her. Not Charles. The life they shared was one that came after the fall, strictly postwar; he had no part in what had gone before and no meaning in it for her. But Sam was all right, too young to interfere. She could trust him.

They had drawn the bedroom curtains on the afternoon sun and he had slid down, as usual, to kiss her belly and thighs. But she had pulled his head up to hers. 'Come into me now,' she had said, 'straight away. I want you inside me.' And they had lain like that for a long time, unmoving, for the first time at peace. I *can* trust him, she thought. That's that. And the illness and exhaustion left her; her body no longer hurt.

But at the back of her mind she was frightened. Perhaps she was only going deeper into the dream she had begun ignorantly to act out weeks before. But now the dream had a name: Iserthal.

16

Charles was delighted to find his life suddenly become easy again. A few telephone calls, a few hundred pounds and, hey presto, Julie smiled, talked to him about his work, spent hours with the children, drew up lists for Heidi and even made intimate jokes with him about her now dispersed pack. It was like old times. He was astonished that it should cost so little. Four hundred pounds was a bit steep for two weeks at a glorified health farm. But as a ransom for his marriage it was cheap, dirt cheap. Admittedly, she said she was still too weak to make love, but she told him so gently, stroking his thin hair and kissing his forehead as though she were sorry. He said he understood and held off. There would be time enough when she came back. A lifetime, in fact. It took so little.

Yet when she lay languidly in his arms before sleep he thought he could still smell on her the faint, musky smell of arousal. *Oh thou weed, that art so lovely, fair and smell'st so sweet That the sense aches at thee*. He couldn't get the words out of his mind. But he told himself that he was the cause of it and that it was merely illness that stopped her. Sam had disappeared from the library; perhaps he had been frightened off at last. And he fell asleep contented.

The night before she left they went out to dinner. The restaurant was at the back of an old stone pub on the river, just below a weir. 'The food's indifferent,' said Charles authoritatively, 'but no more so than anywhere else in these parts. At least it's a pretty place.' Meaning the river, the sunset, the trout flickering and trembling in the turbulent water below the weir. Dark, powerful shapes, some of them two feet long. They were strictly protected, but they brought in the crowds who sat on the terrace over the pool, sipping their drinks, mesmerized by the ominous, slippery presences in the spotlit water.

Half the cars in the crowded park had foreign number plates. Charles drove slowly between them, looking for a place big enough for the Jaguar. In the far corner of the park a jumble of motor bikes leaned on their stands, chrome glinting, garish tanks bulging. His stomach turned over once, abruptly. He drove back down the next row and found a slot near the entrance, as far from danger as possible. He felt his hands sweating on the steering wheel and was angry.

As always when the weather was fine, the place was packed. They found room at the end of the terrace, in the shadows away from the bar door. He left Julie sitting on the parapet, staring into the churning water, while he went in to confirm their reservation and get drinks. Inside it was all horse brasses, oak beams and Merrie Englande, ho-ho. Ghastly place, he thought. Can't think why we came. But in the dining-room the glasses and cutlery winked at him in the candlelight and the Spanish waiters scuttled about enthusiastically. 'Good evening, Professor. Of course, Professor. The table is ready, Professor. Twenty minutes? Of course, Professor. Thank you, Professor.'

How they love the title, thought Charles. It gives them a sense of grandeur. He went into the saloon bar and elbowed his way through the packed tourists. What big bottoms the Americans have, he was thinking complacently, and the Germans. And the Japs with their flat, secret faces. Weird. When he reached the bar he boomed 'I say,' in his loudest, most upper-class voice, but the sweating barmen took no notice. All around him were foreign faces and foreign voices. But in the corner, at the far end of the bar, a group of youths in leather gear were laughing together raucously. He looked at them sideways on, afraid to stare. Then he realized that he wouldn't recognize their faces. All he could remember were masks of white silk and a mouthful of rotting teeth under a black moustache. He wondered if he was equally vague to them.

'I say,' he boomed again, but with less conviction. A barman noticed him at last and took his order. One of the youths glanced at him contemptuously, without recognition, then buried his face again in his pint glass. Lank hair, acne, sallow features. He realized they were teenagers, none of them older than his impressionable, deferential students. How could they be the instruments of his terror? Butchers' boys, garage mechanics, apprentices at the local brickworks. It was inconceivable. Then one of them turned and leaned his back against the bar. Emblazoned across his leather shoulders was 'The Outcasts'. Charles's stomach turned over again. He looked away. When he brought out change to pay for the drinks his hands were shaking feverishly.

He elbowed his way out of the bar, the drinks slopping in their glasses. Julie was sitting as he had left her, staring into the spotlit water. He sat down heavily on the parapet beside her. His breath whistled in his throat and his face streamed with sweat. 'Sorry to have been so long. The place is packed.'

She looked at him alarmed. 'My God, what's the matter? You look as if you'd seen a ghost.'

'Not a ghost. But I've seen that motor cycle gang.'

'Where?'

'In the bar, swilling pints. It seems they're having a night out.'

'Are you sure it's them?'

'I don't know any of their faces, except one. And I didn't recognize him. But one of them had the gang name on his jacket.'

'Did they recognize you?'

'I don't think so.' He was silent a moment, then said in a puzzled voice, 'You know something? They're kids. There's not one of them over twenty. It makes me feel ashamed.'

'There's nothing to be ashamed of. It doesn't matter how old they are, they're a gang of sadistic little thugs. Why don't you phone the police?'

'Don't be ridiculous. There's no law against a few louts having a drink at a pub.'

'It's not a question of what they're doing now. It's a question of what they did.'

Charles peered at her disdainfully down his nose. 'You're not going to start that again, are you? How would I explain it all to the police over the phone? If I launched into that complicated rigmarole, they'd think I'm crazy.'

Julie stared at the water in silence. Finally she said, 'They know about it already. I went to see them a couple of weeks ago, before I got ill.'

Charles lowered his nose at her menacingly. 'You what?' He should have been angry but all he felt was shame redoubled on shame. 'What did they say?'

'You were right. They said there's nothing they can do without positive proof. The sergeant sounded as if he'd been given a hard time by juries. But he wanted to see you. He seemed to think there might be something you and he could work out between you, some sort of charge.'

'That's what he told you. He just wanted to see a middle-aged man who could let himself be made an idiot of, first by a lot of pimply adolescents, then by his interfering wife. You had no right, Julie. You had no right.'

She stood up. Tomorrow she'd be gone. Tomorrow there'd be an end to his self-importance. 'There's no point in having a row about it,' she said indifferently. 'I was only trying to help. If you don't want help, that's your affair. Let's go and eat.'

'Yes, it's my affair,' muttered Charles.

A stone passage led directly from the pub door to the dining-room. Halfway down it was a serving-hatch opening on to the bar. Julie stopped and looked through. 'Is that them at the end, in the corner?' Charles nodded, his face averted. She stared at them. Her husband was right: contemptible children. Then one of the gang looked up and saw her. He winked heavily and nudged the youth next to him. They all turned and began whistling and waving. With their greasy black hair and greasy black jackets they looked like a line of agitated jackdaws on a gate. One of the barmen crossed irritably to them, then turned to see what they were looking at and grinned conspiratorially: a blonde is a blonde.

'For God's sake,' Charles hissed, his face still averted, 'what are you trying to do?' They went on down the passage.

'This way, please, Professor.' The head waiter pounced, rolling the title sanctimoniously round his tongue. He was a red-faced little man with a genial face and beady eyes. Charles smiled at him gratefully. They were back in the predictable, obsequious world of social distinctions. Safe, he thought, safe.

They made the best of their dinner, despite the food. Charles ordered a disproportionately good wine, then expensive brandies. There was no point in quarrelling with so little time left. Over the second brandy Julie said, 'I'm sorry I interfered. I only wanted to help. I couldn't bear it that nothing was being done.'

'I know,' said Charles. 'And I'm sorry I was touchy. You see, I feel such a bloody fool. Absolutely impotent.'

She smiled. 'That's not the right word, all things considered.' He smiled back and they held hands for a moment across the white tablecloth, like young marrieds.

When they came out the bars were closed, the tourists gone. They went and stood on the terrace, looking down into the water. The dark bullet-shapes still flickered restlessly beneath its marbled surface. 'I wonder if they ever sleep,' said Julie. 'It makes me weary to look at them.' At that moment someone inside the pub switched off the spotlights. The pool became black, with vague, shifting smudges of foam. In the darkness the thunder of the weir seemed louder. A swollen yellow moon hung low over the willows on the river bank. Charles took Julie's hand. 'The food may be lousy,' he said, 'but it's a beautiful place.'

The car park was empty. They climbed into the Jaguar and rolled down the windows to let in the summer night. Charles drove slowly, a little muzzy with drink and not wanting to show it. It was only a mile to the roundabout at the edge of town; after that the road was lit. He had nothing to worry about.

He was halfway round the roundabout when he saw them: helmeted, booted, sitting astride their bikes in a layby on the road north, passing round quart bottles of beer. He stabbed nervously at the accelerator and the tyres squealed. Instantly, the gang rasped into life. He heard the blare of their engines starting up and saw in his mirror a confused glare of headlights. Then once again the inside of the Jaguar was white with light. He wondered if the trout felt naked like this in their spotlit pool. Julie gripped his thigh. This time, at least, he wasn't alone.

And this time, being familiar like a road he had travelled before, everything was speeded up: the same white blaze splitting into separate daggers of light, the same battering din of engines, the same shrouded face at the window under the same yellow and red helmet. It nodded across at him almost jovially and from behind the mask a voice shouted, 'Hi, dad. Remember us? Who's the bird? A bit young for you, ain't she?'

Then the speaker accelerated away and, one after the other, the rest of the riders rasped past, bunched for a moment in front of the car, waving their quart bottles and making the V-sign. then shot away down the sodium-lit road, a cluster of red lights disappearing into the brightness of the town. The whole nightmare had lasted less than two minutes.

Charles drew in to the curb. 'Jesus Christ.' His teeth were chattering. 'Jesus Christ.'

Julie stroked his wet hair. 'It's all right. It's over. They've gone.'

'The bastards,' said Charles. 'The bloody bastards. What have I done to them? Why me?'

'Now will you come to the police?'

'Don't you see?' His voice rose. He was near to tears. 'There's nothing to complain of. They've done nothing· illegal. I almost wish they had.'

Julie said nothing. There was nothing to say. They drove on slowly, turning off the main road, taking side turning after side turning, as though they themselves were criminals on the run. There was no one about.

'Why me?' Charles repeated.

Julie stroked his plump thigh as he drove. 'God knows. I suppose they're just having fun. What they call fun. You happened to be around. They picked you out of a hat. Or rather, a crash helmet.' She began to laugh but stopped abruptly when she saw his haggard face. 'It could have been anyone.'

When they got home she poured him a large drink, helped him off with his clothes and then gently, patiently made him make love to her. He was still faintly trembling when he fell asleep.

Julie, too, was trembling, but not with fear. A current flickered along the tracery of her nerves like St Elmo's fire round the rigging of a ship. She felt lit up on the inside with a vague, ghostly excitement. It was like her father, like the time they came for her father. The bed swayed under her and for a moment all the small noises of the summer night ceased. She had been there before, in the oyster half-light, not even the birds awake, listening to the shuffling pause before authority hammered at the door. She recognized the insignia: the boots and black jackets, the absurd badges of the elect, the same violence and the same fear. It was like being naked. Blessed are the really powerful, for they can do anything. She had been young then and they had left her desolate, with a life amputated at the hip. Now it was different. She felt curiously peaceful, somehow reassured. There was a life elsewhere, after all, undomesticated and unanswerable. It was good to be back.

Poor Charles. He didn't doubt for a moment that she belonged there, along with Sam, along with everybody under twenty-five. And because he was so certain, she had believed him. His fantasies became hers. For the first time she realized that it was Charles who had made the affair seem dangerous and exciting, not Sam. What had really attracted her was the thought that he might appear at any moment, like the Gestapo, out of nowhere and catch her at Sam's front door or on his shabby staircase or upstairs in the act. So she had gone back again and again, shivering with excitement, daring him to appear, with his booming voice and his belly and his unspeakable self-assurance. He must have imagined she was experiencing God knew what delights. But the truth was it was just an affair; a surreptitious fling before middle age caught her; a delaying action. Was it always the same, she wondered, listening to his troubled breathing. Is infidelity only glamorous to the person betrayed? Poor Charles.

Poor Sam, too. He was as innocent and as tame as her husband. Because the university bored him he thought he was a rebel. So he would go down to London, let his hair grow, wear jeans and denim shirts, go to bed indischiminately with a crowd of grubby, speechless girls, smoke a little dope, write a little free verse and imagine he was an outsider. But he'd finish, sure enough, in advertising or publishing or television, well paid, well married, well housed, and only occasionally adulterous, like the rest of his kind. Tame, tame, tame.

Even the motor bike gang would go the same way in the end: the wife, the kids, the pub, the union. They'd trade their bikes in for Ford vans and console themselves by souping up the engines. Perhaps one or two of them wouldn't join and would finish in prison or a psychiatric ward. But it was unlikely. In time they'd volunteer for safety like all the ex-Gestapo bullies who ran banks or baked bread and now were snoring peacefully in this lovely, still night.

Lying in bed, Julie felt that she alone knew how the world was run. Under the solid buildings, the houses of commerce, shops, factories, garages, offices, the libraries, hospitals and neat domestic cages, was a river of pitch. Those on the surface thought of it as the municipal sewer, engineered for their benefit to dispose of all the waste and keep the world sweet-smelling. But she knew better. It was a real river flowing from a real spring, and somewhere, every so often, its current deepened and quickened until the containing walls cracked and the complacent world above lurched in. As she lay watching the street lights sway in the leaves outside her bedroom window, she could feel the current trembling through her again. 'Just like old times,' she said half out loud. Charles muttered her name and grabbed her hand under the bedclothes. She nestled against his sweating chest but he went on muttering confusedly in a thick, anxious voice. Lucidly and without much feeling, she understood for the first time that when they had taken her father away she had gone with them. That's how it is, she thought and closed her eyes.

17

When Sam thought of anything – Julie, books, music, films – he thought also of money. Sadly for the most part, as something he would never really have, but compulsively. The intensity of his yearning surprised him, but not its poignancy. He knew the way things were going with him. The university was the only mooring he had ever had or ever wanted. Now he had cut loose and was beginning to drift, moving out from the shore on some dim current he could scarcely feel, so faint, so easy that he could almost mistake it for a natural tide which would bring him inevitably back to where he started. Yet he was gone. The shore was at his back and receding, the familiar figures and landmarks diminished with distance. All that was left was the grey, implacable heave of the sea. Going, going, gone.

Nevertheless, he thought about money. Things in shop windows pursued him voicelessly as he hurried past, pretending not to notice : cameras, hi-fi equipment, soft and subtle clothes in unexpected colours. He yearned for them like a thwarted lover, resentfully. And then there was Germany : how could he raise the fare and the money to keep him there?

He lay on his back in the river, staring up at the arching trees, calculating. I must sell my books, he decided. Make a clean sweep. He rolled over and began to swim slowly back upstream towards the bathing place. The chill, amber water braced his body, making it shrink into its proper limits. When he reached the steps he held on to them with one hand and lay for a while face down in the water. He felt complete, defined, in charge of himself. Then he climbed out, shook himself like a dog and walked over to his towel.

'Beautiful,' he said to the keeper as he rubbed briskly. For the moment he had no worries. The blood ran fresh in his veins as though he had been reborn.

'Ay,' said the keeper, 'it is that. This morning it was all covered with mist. Then the sun came out and the whole place began to steam.' The keeper was more than ten years older than Sam but looked younger. His broad face and chest were tanned, he had innocent brown eyes. 'It sort of does something to you,' he said.

'You're lucky. They pay you to be here.' The old weariness returned. Here we go again. Always money.

'Not enough,' said the keeper. 'But it's a nice job. God knows what I'd do if I had a wife and kids. Give it up, I suppose, and go into a factory. I wouldn't like that.'

'God knows what any of us would do.'

'It's a bugger,' said the keeper.

A muscular young man stepped onto the springboard, paused, gathered himself together, then ran carefully forwards as though in slow motion, hit the end of the board, soared up, arched and cut into the water.

'Not bad.' The keeper nodded approvingly. The young man swam professionally away upstream, his feet faintly churning the water behind him.

'Haven't you ever wanted to get married?' asked Sam.

'No,' said the keeper slowly, 'I never saw the point of it.'

'But haven't you ever been in love?' There was something about the man's unlined face and innocent stare that made Sam think he knew the secret that eluded all the wrinkled, subtle wiseacres among whom he usually moved.

'Love?' The keeper's voice was puzzled. 'I've never reckoned it much. I couldn't see what all the fuss was about. I mean, you take a girl out for the evening, wine her, dine her, slip her a few bob, then – wallop!'

'Wallop?' echoed Sam.

'Wallop,' said the keeper decisively.

Sam looked at him with awe. 'What about the girls?' he asked.

'What about them?'

'Don't they object?'

'Oh no,' said the keeper, 'that's all they seem to want.'

'Really?' Sam brooded. 'Maybe the pill has changed things.'

'Maybe,' the keeper replied. 'Or maybe they don't reckon me much either.'

'Why shouldn't they?'

'Search me. I've never been much of a one for understanding women. Maybe they know it. It's funny what they know and we don't.'

'Yes, it's funny.'

'You know something?' said the keeper, 'maybe it's just because I love this place so much. I mean you can't love everything, can you? I never thought of it before. But I really do. When I get here in the morning at six and there's no one around, just the trees and the mist and the river, it gives me a real kick. Even after all these years. I wouldn't give it up, you know. No. I've never met anyone I'd give it up for.'

'You're lucky,' said Sam, 'you're really lucky.'

'I don't know about that,' said the keeper. A kettle whistled imperiously from his hut. He went in to make tea.

The park, as Sam walked home, was like a roofless cathedral, columns of light between the soaring trees. Wallop! he thought. Was that how the French girl had been, with a little more sophistication? I give you pleasure, you give me. No questions asked. How do you reconcile that with the landscaped park, the placid, medieval buildings and the books? A pigeon glided contentedly down a shaft of light, as though down a banister, and settled by another pigeon which fluttered slightly at its approach. The two birds paraded together on the grass with intricate steps. When Sam came close they moved heavily into the air and flew away. Do pigeons fall in love? he wondered. Doves marry and are faithful to death. Which is more than human beings manage. Are single doves as restless as we are, so much at the mercy of their brief, fussy copulations? For a few weeks each year, perhaps. Better if we, too, had a mating season. Then there might be some peace.

Near the entrance of the park was a fenced-off area enclosing a sandpit, a climbing frame and a rough circle of interlocking logs. He paused to watch a line of children balancing along the tree trunks. The leader was calling out orders to her smaller followers: 'Stop. Jump twice. Now run down the long one like this.'

Julie's son and daughter sat on the grass watching the other children. Their faces were shut and pale; they seemed to have aged. Heidi sat by them on a bench: ponderous, unhappy body and spectacular hair.

Sam opened the gate in the fence and walked across. He said, 'Hullo. I'm a friend of the Stones.'

'Oh, yes,' said Heidi, 'you came to dinner. I saw you then.' She blushed extravagantly.

Sam turned to the children. 'Hullo. I'm Sam. What are your names?' The children looked up at him blankly and did not answer.

'They are missing their mother,' Heidi explained. 'She left yesterday for a holiday.'

Sam registered surprise. 'Did she?'

'Yes,' said Heidi, 'she's gone to Germany.'

'Not like her to leave the children.'

'She is not well. The doctor says she must rest.'

'I'm sorry. Awfully sorry. Has she gone for long?'

'Only for two weeks, but the children are very upset.'

'I'm missing my mummy,' announced the boy, taking his cue. He began to cry self-consciously and his sister immediately joined in. Heidi gathered them both up and held them to her awkwardly. They made a plaintive, whimpering counterpoint to the excited shouts of the children parading among the logs. 'There, there,' she said and smiled apologetically over their heads at Sam.

He said, 'I'm sorry. I didn't mean to upset them.'

'They make too much fuss,' said Heidi impatiently. The children cried even louder, the little girl joining in the refrain: 'I missing mummy.'

'I think I'd better go,' Sam said. He knew he should try to jolly the children out of their tears, but their grief turned him cold. He was out of his depth.

There was an ice-cream van at the entrance to the park. He bought two cones, hurried back to the enclosure and thrust them towards the children. 'Look,' he said. They stopped crying and held out their hands, unspeaking.

'Say thank you,' said Heidi. The children glanced at Sam unforgivingly, then concentrated on their ice-creams.

'It's all right, for heaven's sake,' Sam said. 'I'm sorry I upset them.'

'It's not your fault,' said the au pair girl.

Sam walked quickly home. It was.

'There was a gentleman to see you,' Elsie called from her kitchen as Sam closed the front door.

'Who?'

'He didn't leave his name. An elderly gentleman with a loud voice. He went up to your room and then came down a few minutes later. I suppose he's left a note.' She was sitting as usual at her table, nursing her morning glass of Guinness. The sink was piled with greasy plates. 'I hope he didn't look into the bedroom,' she ducked her head bashfully and giggled, 'I haven't got round to it yet.'

'Isn't today the day for clean sheets?' Sam asked. 'Do you want me to strip the bed?'

She sat up straight and looked at him indignantly. 'That's my job. Don't you worry, I'll get round to it. I'll get round to it.' She took a decisive pull at her Guinness. 'I'll just get the washing-up done.'

Upstairs, there was no note on Sam's green baize table cloth and nothing had been disturbed. He crossed the passage and surveyed his unmade bed and the ring-marks round the basin. Wallop. He thought of Julie's silvery body lying there, slippery as a fish, waiting for him, and felt his blood thicken. Then he remembered the children in the park, their pale faces and exclusive grief. It was time to go.

He went back across the landing and began to pull his books from the shelves: fat blue editions of Oxford poets with monumental gold lettering, slim volumes by modern crooks and hopefuls, expensive American collections of criticism and literary history. Off to the knacker's yard with them. He had thought he could use them to build a life of a kind: *dignified, clothed by erudition and time*. Who said that? Not that it mattered any more. A pity, in a way, it hadn't worked out. He wondered how much he'd get. So many books for so many days of freedom, rudderless and with no known destination. For the moment, he wasn't sure he wanted it.

It was odd to imagine Charles standing in this room, peering contemptuously down his nose at Sam's paltry library and brooding about adultery. What was he after? Sam wondered. Proof perhaps. Letters. More likely another blundering confrontation on morality and literature. God forbid. He felt embarrassed for the old boy, almost sorry. It was Julie's fault. If it hadn't been for her, he'd still be a bright young man, buzzing ambitiously up the university ladder under his professor's benign and expert eye. Well out of that, he told himself. Yet he was sorry to have missed Charles. There was something he wanted from him. Recognition? Forgiveness? God knew. He felt suddenly close to the old man. Intimate. Through Julie they were tangled inextricably together like bodies in an orgy. Sam wished he had left a note.

He turned back to the shelves and went on pulling down his books. Anything with a hard cover was sellable. The rest he would leave. He filled a rucksack, then a suitcase, then another. Without books the room no longer seemed his own. Just a collection of battered Edwardian furniture awaiting another transient. Sam's pictures on the wall would be replaced by other pictures covering the same pale patches; his notebooks, files and stacks of paper by others, probably tidier. Was that all he amounted to: so much paper? He shouldered the rucksack and picked up the suitcases. Bowed over by their weight, arms and fingers aching, he walked slowly to the bookshop to sell his past. They paid him twenty-five pounds.

He went back home and packed what remained of his belongings. His room had been dusted and his bed made, but he didn't stay. When he told Elsie he was leaving and wouldn't be back she said 'Oh' and began to cry, bobbing her head to and fro like a child trying to avoid punishment. He gave her ten pounds to help her through the summer and watched the tears soak down her mottled cheeks. That leaves fifteen, he calculated, plus twenty odd in the bank. Enough, at least, for the ticket. Maybe his parents would help.

'Don't spend it all on Guinness,' he said.

Elsie ducked her head, giggled, then cried louder.

18

That morning Charles had woken early, his head full of confused, foetid images and sly voices. The sunlight poured onto his bed. He lay with his eyes closed, while a thrush performed in the tree outside. *Liquid siftings.* Slowly his head cleared and he began to enjoy the luxury of solitude. He wondered if Julie was already awake in her clinic bed, listening to the hushed, expensive sounds of private nursing beyond her room. More likely she was still sleeping off the journey. Her face at the airport had been pale, strained by the effort of saying good-bye to the children. Thin and chill, even before she disappeared through Passport Control she seemed to be losing all substance. Already he had difficulty in remembering her, as though she were a presence at a seance, incorporeal, vanishing into the shadows of the room the moment the lights went on and the spell was broken. All that remained were the vibrations of her infidelity. He remembered the pain she had caused him, and the uncertainty, but he couldn't remember her face. Would she take another lover in Germany? Probably. He realized, with surprise, that he didn't care. The thought of her being handled here, by a man he knew, was intolerable, like fire on the skin. But someone else's mouth on her body, someone else working her up blindly, hundreds of miles away, didn't matter. In every sense, it was beyond him. He would never know and, even if he did, there was nothing he could do about it. Let her go. If he gave her a long enough string, she would either come back in the end or strangle herself. And that was that. The thrush went on singing, high, pure and eerie. He would see no more of the motor bike gang. Somehow he was convinced that they and Julie were linked, at least in the imagination. If she went, they went too. He was at peace.

At seven-thirty Heidi brought him in a cup of tea and the newspaper. He smiled at her and said, 'What a beautiful day.'

She beamed with pleasure, taking it personally: 'Yes, it is a beautiful day.' She lingered hopefully at the door.

Insufferable, thought Charles. The whole lot of them. Insufferable and impertinent. He opened his newspaper irritably.

At breakfast the children were pale faced and subdued. Immediately he sat down his daughter climbed on to his lap and wouldn't budge. She and her brother had cried all the way back from the airport, refusing Heidi's lumpish solace – exaggerated for Charles's benefit – and his own booming attempts at jollity. Now the little girl moved in on him imperiously and would eat only if he fed her. The boy paid no attention to anyone. He had desolate rings round his eyes and his face was putty coloured, as if he had been crying in his sleep. Charles would have liked to console him but didn't know how. He was relieved when Heidi took them off to school.

In the library he had a private alcove off the main reading room where the books he was working on were permanently piled: variorum editions, concordances, bound volumes of the publications of learned societies and old leather folios of heavy, greyish paper and faded print, smelling of time. He closed the door, pulled up his chair and stretched his arms and legs pleasurably, relishing the silence and the privacy. The switch in his head clicked automatically:

> Love ruined me and I am rebegot
> Of absence, darkness, death, things which are not.

How wrong can you be? he thought. Absence makes the heart grow fonder. Or shall it be stronger? Or simply colder? A blessing anyway.

He opened his briefcase and pulled out a pink double file: notes on one side, manuscript on the other, everything neat and ordered. The pink offended him, unseemly as a nursery pudding, but when he began to read over his new essay it no longer seemed to matter. He read carefully, checking and rechecking, and as the sun shifted across his desk his calm increased. Not bad. Yes. Not bad at all. He leaned back, closing his eyes against the sunlight, and realized that he didn't care. When he tried to think of his smug colleagues grudgingly measuring out their respect and tempering their malice, all he could think of was Mr Rotherham, with his shabby suit and fiery face. He was holding a typed letter Charles had handed him. The paper was rich and yellowish, like cream, and embossed with the crest of an Oxford college. It was addressed to Charles and announced, with pleasure, that he had been awarded an Open Scholarship. Mr Rotherham nodded and did not smile. 'I thought you'd do it,' he said. 'That's the first hurdle over. But don't forget, it's only the first.' Charles's elation vanished; he felt terribly depressed. 'Yes, sir,' he mumbled, thinking, Bastard. Give me my due. Now he realized that the old man had been right. There was no end to it. The hurdles stretched out to the limits of his life. The moment he jumped one he was gathering himself for the next. And the last landed him in his grave.

It hadn't felt like that at first. More like falling in love. Day after day in his college's medieval library, swathed in overcoat and mittens during the long winters, nose red, fingers chillblained, his arse aching from the hard bench and his eyes from the inadequate lighting, he had become besotted. The rows of old books, with their fading print and footnotes cantilevered from the side of each double column, their dying odour and the loud, drawn-out crackle the pages made as they turned, excited him like an exotic mistress. After them, there was no way back. So Mr Rotherham died of cancer, with chalk under his fingernails, while Professor Charles Stone went marching on. Glory, glory, alleluia! In some obscure way he didn't properly understand, he felt he had let the old boy down. What did it all amount to in the end? Sensuality of the mind.

Now it was his turn.

> Die for adultery! No:
> The wren goes to't, and the small gilded fly
> Does lecher in my sight.
> Let copulation thrive.

On the blank page in front of him he saw Julie's head flung back and Sam nuzzling and licking her throat. The image was detailed, brutal and convincing, like a dream. Its ferocity shocked him. It seemed to him to belong to the younger, more vulnerable man he had never, in his scholarly obsession, had time to be; not to the portly, distinguished figure he now was. Like an adolescent, he thought. Like the sexual fantasies of an adolescent. He crossed his worsted-suited legs, feeling a vague stirring in his groin. Not heat, but emptiness. Desolation. It was the mystery that excited the adolescent, the violent, Oedipal mystery. And it was the mystery that stirred him now in age, chill and hollow. He didn't know. Maybe there was nothing to know. Maybe he had simply turned his wife into literature, as he turned everything else. A Desdemona caught in his belated sexual imaginings. He looked at the ranks of books in front of him and they returned his stare complacently, giving nothing away.

He pushed back his chair irritably and stood up. At this rate he'd dribble away his precious two weeks of freedom in prurient daydreaming. 'Do something,' he said out loud, 'for once in your life.' He opened the door to the reading room and surveyed the studious bowed heads with a proprietorial air, then walked firmly to the reference shelves and looked up Sam's address in the university register.

It was only when he rang the doorbell that he realized that he had no idea what he would say. Listening to the cracked jangling of the bell at the end of the passage, he felt his stomach swarm and contract with nerves. Like being interviewed for my first job, he thought, and that made him feel foolish. Elsie opened the door, twinkling and ducking her head in embarrassment. When she told him Sam was out he sighed loudly from the depths of his being, as though he were exhaling his past.

'You don't mind if I go up and leave a note?' he boomed.

'O-o-o-oh, no-o-o-o,' she lengthened the words out, overawed by his grey, important presence. She held the door open for him and, as he went past her down the passage, bobbed him the ghost of a curtsey. He sniffed disapprovingly at the nimbus of drink that surrounded her.

Sam's room was as he had expected: shabby and disorganized, the books on the shelves predictable. Charles closed the door and crossed to the window: no sign of the boy in the street below. No sign either of Julie's large, childish handwriting among the piles of paper on the table. No sign of her anywhere. The room smelled of bacon and tobacco. There were breadcrumbs on the baize table-cloth, dust on the mantelpiece and bookshelves. The place filled him with distaste. When he pulled out some books to see if there was anything hidden behind them, he felt his fingers were irredeemably soiled. Even the faintly savoury air was a contamination.

He went back to the window: nothing but two queues of cars fuming in the sunlight. Then he crossed the landing, opened the bedroom door and stood for a moment surveying the intimate disorder of someone else's private life. The house was silent. He closed the door quietly and leaned against it, feeling his heart beating, beating. Again he began to search, rifling through the shirts and socks and sweaters in the chest of drawers, with its chipped veneer, pulling aside a curtain to inspect Sam's one suit, his academic gown and old corduroy jacket. Nothing and again nothing. He turned and stared at the unmade bed. It was high and old fashioned, with a brass head and foot which rattled when he pushed them. The blankets were khaki ex-army issue, the sheets needed changing.

Quickly, so as not to give himself time to change his mind, he pulled back the covers. There were wide, greyish stains on the rumpled sheets. Blindly, he bent down and sniffed the faint, undeniable smell of sex. Her sex. He was certain. The wide stains spoke to him of a wide pleasure, unthinking and without limits. Tears began to stream down his face, although a sane voice whispered, 'It could be anyone. They all smell alike. You know nothing of the boy's sex life.' He went to the basin and splashed his face with cold water, looked at the dirty towel and then wiped his eyes with his own crisp handkerchief. He pulled the bedcovers back as they had been, returned to the basin and washed his hands, then went out quietly. He was still crying. But it was shame that grieved him, not adultery. Charles Stone, distinguished scholar and critic, world authority on the Renaissance and Professor of English at a great university, sniffing the sheets of an uppity research student like a child at his parents' bedside. He was more perverted than his betrayers. *All the perfumes of Arabia* ... the voice began automatically. He stretched his mouth wide open to stop it, sniffed violently, hiccupped and fled down the stairs out into the engulfing din of the traffic.

A warm, dusty wind had got up, sweeping round the corners of the old buildings. He faced into it and strode out in the direction of the library, an imposing figure, though a little on the heavy side, in an expensive suit. The wind which rustled his thin hair also, apparently, made his eyes water. This added to the impression he made on wandering tourists of age and achievement and seriousness. A camera clicked, freezing him against the carved gateway of his own famous college. Inside he was howling like a child.

19

Sam began to feel better as soon as his car rattled into the yellow-lit fringes of London. The mile after mile of dingy semi-detacheds interspersed with hopeful little factories of breeze block and plaster induced in him a kind of peace. All passion spent. This was where he belonged. The closer he drove to the centre, the wider his calm became. It was a warm summer night and the streets were still full of people, clustered with their drinks outside pubs or strolling aimlessly under the dusty trees. Sixteen million of them swarming across seven hundred square miles. There's peace, there's privacy. An ocean of busy lives to sink into without trace. No Julie, no Charles, no dinners at high table, no footnotes, no university politics and backbiting. Buy, said the billboards, buy, buy, buy. The summer night smelled of money, the effort of it, the triumphs, the erosions. A Jensen swished contemptuously past him as he chuntered along the edge of Regent's Park and he gazed after it with admiration. He was back where he belonged, among the nerves and the scrabbling, the flashy rewards and sombre houses.

When he let himself in the front door the air in the hall was trembling with music. Mahler, he thought. The old man's feeling sorry for himself. He set down his suitcases and rucksack and called 'Hullo,' but his voice was swallowed by the thundering orchestra. He tried again : 'Hullo.' His mother came out from the back of the house : a small, plump, vigorous woman, her face scrawled with make-up haphazardly, as though her eyes weren't quite right. Yet they took in Sam, his shabby clothes and shabby baggage, missing nothing. Her first words were, 'I thought you'd forgotten me.'

Sam pecked her rouged cheek. 'I'm sorry I didn't phone,' he said, 'I've been terribly busy.'

'At my age,' there was a throb in her voice, 'you don't expect to be remembered.'

Sam said, 'For God's sake,' then stopped. Why argue? After all, he was glad to be back. 'How are you keeping?'

'Fine. Weary but fine.' She gave him her distracted, gimlet look again and announced, 'You've lost weight. You don't look after yourself.'

'I'm all right. God forbid I should look like my cousin Harold.'

'Your cousin Harold earns five thousand a year and is married to a nice respectable girl. And he's the same age as you.'

'He looks like a tub of lard with five o'clock shadow.' Sam followed his mother into the kitchen where she began dismantling a chicken with her fingers and piling the pieces on a plate. 'I'm not hungry,' he said weakly.

'Eat. I worry about you,' said his mother; then without pausing or changing speed she added, 'She's expecting a baby in November.'

'Who is?'

'Josie, of course. Harold's wife.'

'That'll give her two to look after.'

'It's her first.'

'What about Harold?'

Mrs Green giggled, then said in a false shocked voice, 'You have no respect. Your cousin Harold doesn't give his poor mother sleepless nights.'

Sam gnawed a chicken bone, standing at the kitchen table. 'There's nothing in this world,' he swallowed, 'that could keep Queenie awake. As you well know. Not even Uncle Joe.'

'Samuel.' His mother registered mock approval. 'Sit when you eat. You'll give yourself ulcers.'

It was as if he had never been away. They had played this game since he was a child: she gave him his cues and he compensated her for her forty years of meddling in-laws by insulting them. It bred between them a conspiratorial affection which passed for family love.

On the way back to the dining-room, she suddenly stopped and faced him. 'Tell me, Samuel, I've never liked to ask, but what are you doing up there?' She made a vague northwards gesture with her head in the direction she thought the university ought to be.

'I'm doing a doctorate.'

His mother's face lit up suddenly like Guy Fawkes Night. 'Darling,' she said, 'You mean you're going to be a doctor?'

'Of philosophy.' He watched her face fall. 'I'm doing research.'

'Oh.' She turned out the kitchen light.

'Don't worry,' he said consolingly, 'I'm packing it all in.'

'Oh,' his mother repeated, as if she hadn't heard.

In the dining-room the vibrating air smelled of food. There were crumbs in the meshes of the lace tablecloth. Sam's father slept in front of the thunderous radiogram, his face inches from the loudspeaker. Mrs Green rattled cutlery onto the table with deliberate, unnecessary clatter. Her husband stirred slightly and opened his eyes. 'I wasn't asleep,' he muttered.

'Hi, pa.'

The old man's eyes focused with an effort. He smiled. 'Nice to see you, stranger.'

'Likewise.'

Although Mr Green's neck rolled over his stiff white collar, his stomach protruded comfortably and what remained of his hair was white, he had the hopeful, vulnerable face of a very young man. He looked like a boy who has stuffed a cushion under his shirt and dressed himself up in his father's sedate suit only to find himself stuck with his absurd disguise. He seemed surprised by his weight and his wrinkles, as though age had taken him unaware.

'How's business?'

'Lousy,' said Mr Green, 'It always is. Even when it's good it's still lousy.'

'Maybe you and I should change places.'

'Don't joke about these things. You don't know how lucky you are. Stick with what you've got and be thankful.'

'I haven't got much at the moment.'

'You've got your freedom.' His father leaned back again in his armchair, closed his eyes to the music and moved his hand faintly, beating time.

'New record?' Sam asked.

His father shook his head. 'Old favourite.'

'Eat up,' said his mother to bring herself back into the conversation. Gnawing his chicken bone out in the kitchen, Sam had realized that he was starving; he hadn't eaten since breakfast. Now, with his mother leaning watchfully and imperiously over him, his appetite went as suddenly as it had come. 'I'm not very hungry.'

She gave him a tragic look through her lopsided make-up. 'You only say that to upset me.'

'I don't. Honestly. I'm just not hungry.'

'Just to please your old mother,' she wheedled, then added with heavy cunning, 'Otherwise I'll give it to the dog.'

Sam glanced at the terrier asleep in front of the empty grate, its rhinoceros skin sparsely covered by wiry hair. His old rival. 'All right,' he said sullenly, 'I'll try.'

His mother leaned back smiling. 'I've only got stewed fruit to follow. You should have warned me you were coming. I'd have had a proper dinner for you.'

'This is lovely. I don't want anything else.'

'Just a little stewed fruit to follow.'

'No, nothing else.' She couldn't give stewed fruit to the dog.

While the gramophone boomed passionately on, the Greens went into their usual silent act: Sam ate, his mother watched, his father lay back with his eyes closed, vaguely beating time to the music to show he wasn't asleep. Finally, Sam laid his knife and fork together and pushed back his chair.

'You haven't finished,' said his mother reproachfully.

'That's all I can manage.'

'You don't like my cooking?'

'I love it, but that's all I can manage.'

'What's the matter? Are you ill?'

'I'm fine. I'm just full, that's all.'

'You eat like a bird.'

'A vulture.'

'It's not funny. You'll get ill.'

'Mother. For God's sake.'

She rose tragically and picked up his plate. 'Chum.' she called, 'Come and eat.' The terrier heaved its tubular body reluctantly upright and waddled out after her. 'At least you won't let me down,' she said to it as she closed the door.

Mr Green smiled at Sam and shrugged. 'A marvellous woman,' he said, 'but difficult. She thinks in food. Feels in it, too, I suppose. It restricts the conversation a bit.'

'I never knew you cared.'

'I don't any more. I have my music.'

They sat without speaking while the symphony blazed and died. When it was over Sam's father pulled himself to his feet as though his body were too heavy for him, bent over the gramophone and blew at the needle, then lovingly replaced the record in its sleeve. He turned to Sam: 'Want anything else?'

'It's up to you.'

The old man sat down again. 'How's the university?' he asked.

'I've had enough. I'm leaving. In fact, I've left. Burned my boats.'

His father looked at him in alarm. 'You don't want to come into the business, do you?'

'God forbid.'

The old man eased himself back again in his armchair and sighed with relief. 'I was just wondering. You'd hate it. I always have and you, with your education ...' He brooded a little. 'Have you told your mother?'

'Yes, but she didn't listen.'

'She never does. It's just as well. She'd only worry and then I'd have no peace.' He brooded again, dejected at the thought of his music being interrupted night after night by pointless discussions of his son's future.

'I don't think she'll mind much when she gets used to the idea,' said Sam. 'She's always distrusted the university. She just wants me to make money.'

'She wants you to be happy,' replied his father, pretending to be loyal.

'For her it's the same thing.'

'She may be right.'

'Sometimes I think so too.'

They lapsed again into silence. Finally, his father asked, 'What will you do now?'

'I don't know really. For the moment, I just want to get to Germany.'

'Why Germany, of all places? That's no country for a Jew.'

'That's ghetto talk, pa. The war finished a long time ago.'

'You haven't answered my question.' When Sam didn't reply his father asked, 'Is it a girl?' Sam nodded. 'Be careful,' said his father. 'A *shiksah?*'

'What else?'

'Be very careful. Who is she?'

'A girl I know from the university.'

'A student?'

'Not exactly.'

Mr Green looked at his son fondly: 'I suppose she's married.'

Sam looked back at him with awe: 'How on earth did you work that out?'

'I'm seventy years old,' his father replied. 'You're not the only one in the family with brains. Or experience. Don't tell your mother.'

'I wasn't intending to.'

'Just be careful. You're young, you're free. You won't stay young, but at least you can try to stay free. Don't tie yourself up.'

'Free to do what?'

'To travel. To go. To get out. The world is big and beautiful, Sam. Think of the places there are to see: South America, the Pacific, China . . . One of these days I . . .'

'Come off it. You haven't even crossed the Channel since your honeymoon.'

'But that's just it, you see. I couldn't go on my own, could I? I'd have to take your mother. And she'd want to do it all so expensively and go to all those awful Jewish places in the South of France. You know, Juan Les Pins, St Tropez, Sainte Maxime. That's not what I want. It's cheaper to quarrel at home.'

They both laughed, but anxiously.

'Well,' said Sam, 'I'm free as a bird for the time being. The trouble is to know what to do with my freedom.'

'Use it,' said his father.

Mrs Green came back in looking martyred. 'At least the dog enjoyed it.' She sat down. 'Thank heavens you've turned off that awful noise.'

'It wasn't awful,' said her husband, 'It was Mahler.'

Mrs Green surveyed her son critically and said, 'What's wrong with you?'

'Only the usual things: I'm undernourished, I don't sleep properly and I don't earn enough.'

'Don't make fun of me. I'm your mother. I have a right to worry. And a right to know.' Without any warning, she seemed on the edge of tears.

'Of course you have,' Sam said soothingly. It always ended in the same way: with him doing the parental thing to his parents. 'There's nothing the matter. I'm just tired, that's all. It's been a long day. A long term, for that matter.'

'You need a holiday,' said his mother, suddenly motherly.

'I know. I want to take one. I thought of going to Germany. To walk in the mountains, maybe climb a little.'

'Well, why don't you?' When Sam didn't reply she looked at him resignedly and said, 'I suppose you're broke.'

'More or less.'

'So that's why you're honouring us with your presence.'

'Mother!' Sam tried to sound exasperated, but failed.

'I know.' Mrs Green was using her tragic voice again. 'Don't think I don't.'

Sam turned to his father: 'How are the slogans?'

Mr Green brightened and sat up. 'I've got some new ones. They're different. I think you'll like them. Come on, I'll show you.'

He laboured to his feet and went wearily upstairs, Sam trailing behind him. The same dried and dusty bullrushes stood in the Chinese vase at the head of the stairs, the same bottles of hair lotion and aftershave were lined above the basin in his father's dressing-room. Nothing had changed and nothing had happened in the house since Sam had left years before. Two lives preserved in amber, unmoving. It would be like this forever. Inexplicably, he wanted to cry like a little boy crying for no other reason than that he wants to be comforted. His empty room was still waiting for him in the darkness, all his old knick-knacks intact. Well, it was only for a couple of days.

Mr Green pulled out a bunch of keys and unlocked the doors of his wardrobe. Then he selected another key and opened a drawer. Sam was enveloped in the fresh, familiar smell of unsmoked tobacco. His father's smell. The drawer was deep in boxes of cigarettes, tins of tobacco, pipes and boxes of cigars. Its odours permeated the drawer above which held his father's shirts. The old man moved in a faint, clean, aromatic air. He pulled out a biscuit tin and opened it tenderly. 'Here it is : the story of my life. I'm a wasted talent.' The tin was full of white postcards. He sorted through them and handed a couple to Sam. 'These were the first two. Remember?' He knew Sam did, but this was part of their ritual. Dutifully, Sam looked at the carefully stencilled cards :

IF YOU CRAVE A CIGARETTE
CRAVEN A

*

BUD
AS YOU GROW OLDER
YOU'LL GROW
BUDWEISER

*

'I like them,' said Sam. 'I always have.'

'So do I. But they didn't. They never even acknowledged them. Not a word. '

'That's not right.'

'Too true. But there you are. Anyway, it pissed me off. At least they could have said why they didn't like the things.' He went on sorting through the cards. 'It kept on happening, again and again. Finally, I tried this one on the booze firm' :

DON'T JUST ASK FOR GIN
SAY
BOLS
TO THE BARMAID

*

'They must have loved that,' Sam said.

'I don't know about them,' said Mr Green, 'But it certainly cheered me up. It was after that I thought of "Prim For Personal Hygiene". Then there was my detergent, Fug. Remember?' He handed Sam another card.

IF TIDE WON'T CLEAN IT
AND DAZ DOESN'T DO IT
FUG IT

*

'It's a pity,' said the old man in a meditative voice. 'From what I hear, most of the people in advertising look down on the job. They think they should be writers or something, and they're just prostituting their wonderful talents. But me, I was really keen. I'd have loved it, just as I've always hated the bloody rag trade. But I never got a chance. I suppose it's a closed shop, like everything else. You've got to know the right people, or have been to university like you.' He stared at the open box and brooded.

'What about the latest ones?' Sam asked.

His father shuffled through the cards. 'I've given up brand names,' he said. 'How do you like this? I thought an American radio might use it.'

DON'T FORGET FOLKS,
YOGA
SPELT BACKWARDS
IS
A GOY

Sam snickered. 'You could always try Radio Tel Aviv,' he said.

'Just a passing thought,' said his father. 'Ah, here are the new ones.' He passed the cards to Sam.

IS THERE A LIFE
AFTER
BREAKFAST?

*

YOU'RE NEVER ALONE
WITH
A FAMILY

*

Sam looked at his father tenderly. 'I think they're marvellous,' he said at last. 'And profound.'

'I knew you'd understand,' the old man said, gratefully. 'Everyone else thinks they're jokes. Which is all right by me. But you know, those two have taken me seventy years to write. Seventy years. Three score bloody years and ten, and that's all I've got to show for it.'

'It's more than most people have.'

'Maybe you're right. They do keep me going.'

Mrs Green appeared at the dressing-room door. 'What are you two up to?'

'Pa was just showing me his latest slogans.'

'Oh, those things. I can't see the joke. Never could. It's a pity you can't think of something that would make a little money.'

'You don't lack for anything,' said Mr Green.

'How do you know what I lack? You've never bothered to ask.'

Sam said, 'Oh Christ.' Then: 'I'll go down and get my cases.' And left them to it.

Later, as he lay reading in his old room, under the same old counterpane, with the same old pictures on the wall, his father came in and sat down on the end of the bed. 'I suppose you need money,' he said.

'I've got a bit, but I don't know how much this German trip will cost.'

'How long are you going for?'

'I don't know for sure. It depends. It may all fall through. If it does, I thought of going climbing for a bit. I've had a note from a friend who'll be in the Dolomites and wants me to join him. I'd hitch-hike from Germany. Once you're up at the huts, you can live for bugger all.' The letter was in his wallet, a reminder of the sane world where people were Sam's age, made jokes, drank beer, held down any old job that would give them time off to get away to the mountains, went to bed with their stringy, quiet birds and didn't worry: 'Drop me a line at the Poste Restante, Cortina, and I'll leave a message for you there, saying which hut I'll be at – Jim.' It sounded so simple, so desirable. He didn't know why he'd ever allowed himself to get sucked in to the middle-aged whirlpool of guilt. What had Julie and her husband and her children to do with him?

'I'm awfully short at the moment,' said his father apologetically. 'No, that's a lie. I'm always short. But I could probably let you have a tenner.'

'That's wonderful,' said Sam. He paused, then added, 'Look, I'll be getting a job directly I get back. If you could lend me another fifteen, I'd be all right. And I'd pay you back immediately I started earning. Promise. But I don't want to get you in a jam.'

'What difference does it make at my age? I know how it is. Woman trouble. Believe me, they're always trouble. Only later, you don't care so much. Just be careful, that's all. Don't get yourself caught.'

'I'll try.'

The old man got up and smoothed down the collar of his plum coloured dressing-gown. He looked at his son fondly with his hopeful, pale blue eyes. 'It'll be all right,' he said.

'I'm really grateful.'

'Glad I can help for once.'

'Henry.' Mrs Green's querulous voice drifted across the landing. Sam's father shrugged and gestured resignedly with his hands. He said, 'You mustn't mind us, you know. We're used to each other. As marriages go, it's a good one.' He went out.

Sam read on. A clock ticked peacefully, the street outside was silent. The shade over the bedside lamp was like a pair of frilly knickers. It glowed orange, warming the room. It had been like this as long as he could remember, and would stay so. Is that what it was all about: two lonely people sharing a house. Is there a life after breakfast? The clock on the mantelpiece said one o'clock. The beginning of the bad time, he thought. I a.m. equals I am. His father would like that; he must pass it on. He tried to think of Julie – Was she dying? Did he love her? – but she no longer seemed real among these familiar things. Is there a life after breakfast? There had to be, if he didn't want to end up like his father, aged seventy and still waiting. That's why he needed Julie; she belonged to another world, blonde, different, detached.

He got out of bed and opened the door stealthily. In the glow of light from his room he could see the old terrier lying stifflegged in front of his parents' bedroom door. It growled at him, showing yellow teeth, but did not move. He crept down the stairs without turning on the lights, felt his way across the hall and went into the kitchen, closing the door behind him. Then he switched on the light and opened the fridge. The ruins of the chicken lay on a greasy plate among fragments of stuffing. He pulled off a piece of breast and swallowed it ravenously. Then another and another. He scooped at the stuffing with his fingers, then bit with relish into a cold roast potato.

There was a noise at the door. He turned like a thief, chicken in one hand, potato in the other. His mother stood at the door, the dog beside her. She smiled at Sam tenderly and with pride.

'I *knew* you were hungry, darling, Do you think you can fool your old mother?'

He stared at her guiltily, his mouth full. Is there a breakfast after life?

20

The room was full of shadows. Shadows in the angles where the walls met the ceiling, gross shadows from the chairs and cupboards, shadows moving with the curtains, swelling the piles of toys. The bottom bunk was a cave of shadows, although above the upper bunk the dim night light held them back precariously with its yellow glow. Charles sat in shadow gratefully, his face shrouded, his bulk disguised, while the children finished their evening milk. He had read them their stories, Heidi had said good night and gone, the nightly rituals were almost complete. In a moment he would take their empty cups, kiss them, close the door and go downstairs to face the long evening. He lingered for a while, unwilling to break the shadowy peace.

'Sing us a song, daddy,' said the boy. And his sister echoed, 'Song, song.'

'It's getting late.'

'Please.'

'Song, song.'

'All right. Just one.' Charles leaned back in the comforting gloom.

The water is high, I cannot get o'er,
Nor have I wings with which to fly ...

His voice was growling and unmusical, but he sang softly so that the stillness of the room seemed gradually to extend into the melody.

Give me a boat that will carry two,
And both shall row, my love and I ...

The children settled rustling under the bedcovers. Leaning forwards, Charles caught his daughter's warm, bathtime smell, faintly soapy. He sang on.

Down in the valley the other day . . .

To be clean and sleepy, smelling of soap. Along the back of his thighs, he could feel again the cool, slightly scratchy texture of his mother's apron and heard her voice in the shadows. Half a century ago. All gone.

A-gathering flowers both red and blue,
A-gathering flowers both white and gay . . .

Poppies, cornflowers, forget-me-nots, daisies. He had never been much of a one for flowers. He hadn't had time. Maybe he should have made time, as his father had done.

I little thought what love can do . . .

A breeze stirred the curtains, letting in a slither of evening light. The shadows flickered and thinned. Might as well finish. He sang on more strongly, labouring to keep tune.

A ship there is and she sails the sea,
She's loaded deep as deep can be,
But not as deep as the love I'm in.
I know not if I sink or swim.

Oh, love is simple and love is free,
And love's a jewel while it is new.
But when it is old it groweth cold
And fades away like morning dew.

What a choice, he thought. Darling, I'm singing our song. But not even that was true. There had never been anything simple and free between him and Julie. Nor between any consenting adults. Folk songs were for adolescents. Yet he felt a pang of regret, hearing the old melody echoing in his head. After all, it was beautiful; so were the words. Was, were. It was his own childhood he was grieving for through the song, and for his mother who had once sung to him, too, and was now dead. Her mother must have sung to her, and her mother's mother to her mother. And so on, back through the anonymous generations. He got up with a show of briskness, though his bones felt weary.

'When will mummy be back?' his son asked as Charles kissed him.

'Not long now, darling. Go to sleep. She'll be back soon.'

'I wish she'd hurry.'

'She will, she will.' The child's eyes were wide and dark, as full of shadows as the room. 'I'm here. Now go to sleep.' Charles kissed him again, then bent and kissed his daughter who put her arms round his neck and hung for a moment possessively. He picked up their empty mugs. 'Night, night.'

On the landing he paused to make sure they had settled, then went downstairs and poured himself a large whisky. He drank it down immediately and poured another. It tasted clean and faintly abrasive, purging his gullet. But the world stayed where it was, tilted askew between the shadows in the nursery upstairs and the shadows into which his parents had long since gone. He saw himself that morning, as portly and silver haired as his father, sniffing the adulterous sheets like a child. *Adulterous sheets*: good old Shakespeare. Was it his own wife he had smelt? He took another long swallow of whisky and went back upstairs to his bedroom. But the laundry basket was empty, cleared out by Heidi in the burst of efficiency which had followed Julie's departure. Trying to get rid of all traces of the opposition, he thought. And once again he saw himself, as if from some high corner of the room, holding the plaited lid and peering down into dark, empty basket, looking for evidence. Evidence: the smell of arousal and urine on his wife's underclothes to match the smell of his student's stiff, stained sheets. What of his own arousal at the thought of her and Sam together? There was nothing to choose between her excitement and his. They were mutually dependent. She had released in him all the foetid imaginings he had never had time for in his industrious adolescence. The thought of her in bed with someone else was secretly more titillating than the fact of her in bed with him. He had become her accomplice, watching from the outside, as he watched himself now. So it didn't matter that his shame was private, since he himself was always there to witness it. A wife can't testify against her husband. But in the court in which he was arraigned he was the defendant, prosecutor, judge and witness all rolled into one. *Felo de se*. Was that what he had been leading up to all this time? What childishness !

He put the lid back on the basket and stood listening. Outside in the street, a starter motor churned and churned monotonously: aaarrr, aaarrr, aaarrr. Finally, after what seemed minutes, the motor coughed into life, the driver blipped the engine viciously and the car moved off down the street. The birds resumed their settling noises in the dusk. Charles was sweating. He took a bottle of Julie's cologne from her dressing-table, shook some on to his hand and dabbed his forehead. Her clean, public smell enveloped him and with it the sudden image of her with her legs locked round the buttocks of some faceless, hairy lover under a churning sheet. Fascinating. *Oh, insupportable.*

He went back downstairs, swallowed the rest of his drink and refilled the glass. When he put the bottle down he found it was on the tray a fraction before he expected. I must be tipsy, he thought, but his mind was clear.

Heidi came in from the kitchen with her long hair and doggy, devoted eyes. 'When would you like to eat?'

'I'm not hungry yet.' He spoke carefully, afraid that the whisky might show itself. 'Why don't you eat up and go to the pictures? You deserve an evening out after all your hard work.' He gave her an unsteady but paternal smile. She blushed as usual.

'You are very kind. Are you sure?' When he nodded benignly she said, 'I phone my friend, please. And I leave your dinner in the oven. It is stew. It will not spoil.' She went back into the kitchen. He heard the telephone ping as she lifted the extension, then the muffled, glottal sound of German. He sat holding his glass of whisky. Prisoner at the bar, indeed. He took another long drink and stared mindlessly at the night gathering outside.

A quarter of an hour later, Heidi knocked again. 'The dinner is in the oven, please. It is very nice. I go now. I will be back soon after eleven.'

'Don't worry. I'm babysitting. There's no reason to hurry back.'

'Thank you,' said the girl, blushing again.

When he heard the front door close behind her Charles sighed deeply from some remote fastness of his gloom. He felt the muscles of his shoulders relax and realized that he had been tensing himself all evening against her intrusion. He took another pull at his whisky and refilled his glass.

The French windows into the garden were open. He walked across to them quite steadily, surprised that the drink was having so little effect. When he leaned against the doorway it met his shoulder a little earlier than he expected, otherwise everything was as usual. He stood inhaling the cool air and the subdued night scent of the flowers. The garden was full of small, secret noises, faint rustlings and stirrings, as though there were hidden creatures on the move. By day it was a mere extension of the house, a dull oblong of grass, two apple trees and a border of unwilling flowers. But at night it seemed to breathe with a vague life of its own, reaching out into the room behind him. He glanced back to where the half empty whisky bottle stood in a pool of light under a reading lamp at the end of the sofa. The lampshade cast deep green shadows on the shelves of books and the restrained pictures, so that for a moment he had the illusion of a forest clearing, creepers, vines, leafy fingers stretching tentatively forwards towards the light. A puff of breeze came and went in the garden, disturbing the apple trees. Their leaves seethed together briefly, like surf on the open sea.

Years since I heard that sound, he thought. How many? Twelve? Fifteen? Christ, another lifetime. I was free then. The only time, really. He saw the stretched belly of sail and heard the creak of spars, the water hissing from the bows and the waves quietly answering each other into the distance. Moving in a great bowl of bluish silver, with a full moon, like a half-crown, nailed above the mast and Tom asleep below. Charles himself, released for once from the library and no longer confused by the strangeness and precision of the ship's routine, absorbed into the huge, unquiet silence of the sea. Perfect for a moment, perfectly happy. Of course, it had ended badly. He had put them miles off course and at dawn the wind rose and swung round into their teeth. They finished creeping down the Blackwater under bare masts with the auxiliary motor churning and stinking, and Charles vomiting stalely over the side. He had never been invited again and two years later Tom dropped dead of a heart attack. His death left

Charles feeling cheated. He had been denied the chance to re-deem himself of his friend's contempt. He hadn't even had time to say he was sorry.

He never had, he realized, and took another drink of whisky. Never. When death came he always managed to be elsewhere: at university when his father died, in Germany when his mother's time came. 'Come at once,' said the telegrams and although he went at once he always arrived too late. At the time he had been relieved. Much more convenient, when all's said and done. Spar-ed all that fuss. It was only later he understood that, because he had not been there, everything was left hanging in the air, like an urgent conversation he hadn't finished. Yet in the end all there was to say was 'Sorry'. Sorry you're going. Sorry I didn't do better by you.

I can't go on apologizing to the dead forever, he thought. I must be the drink. Drink and the loamy night smell of the garden. Weird how it opens you up. Like those evenings with his father at the allotment, sitting on an upended orange box, legs dangling, watching the trains clang and snort on the embankment above while the old man placidly dug and hoed, or crouched over the thick-smelling earth, scraping and patting. 'Look at this, then.' Runner beans, lettuces, ribbed giant marrows, clusters of greenish tomatoes. All done by magic, Charles used to think, from packets of seed bought at Woolworth's. His father's fingers were stubby and deft, with earth beneath the nails. When it got dark he'd brush the loam from his knees, wash his hands under the com-munal tap and relight his pipe. Then they'd walk back under the streetlamps to the pub, where the old man supped his pint and Charles drank lemonade through a straw. But it didn't last long. Before he was ten his homework kept him in and, as that increased, he became contemptuous of his father's mindless satisfactions and his ignorance. The broad, comforting accent became some-thing to swallow back. No trace of it now in his own plummy Oxford vowels. They were strangers long before Charles moved on to the university. The inevitable telegram summoned him to the funeral of someone he hardly knew.

He took another drink and peered into the garden, half expect-ing to see his father's broad, absorbed back crouching out there in the darkness. An owl hooted from the next garden, ghostly, boding no good. He had let the old man down, undermining his dignity with his own brilliant career. What would he think now of his son, the professor, distinguished sniffer of sheets and underclothes?

His face felt hot. Drink, shame, or excitement? Jealousy is its own reward, he thought. Shakespeare knew that. He knew everything. Trust old William. Automatically, the quotes clicked in his head like answers from a computer: *Pish! Noses, ears and lips. Is't possible? ... Naked in bed, Iago, and not mean harm .. Then laid his leg over my thigh, and sighed, and kissed ... Oh thou weed ... Too hot, too hot! To mingle friendship far is mingling bloods. I have a tremor cordis on me: my heart dances, but not for joy, not joy ... paddling palms and pinching fingers ... Is whispering nothing? Is leaning cheek to cheek? Is meeting noses? Kissing with inside lips? ... The sense aches at thee ... The sense aches at thee.*

What mockery! There was nothing in this world that could happen to him which he couldn't turn, with patience, into a learned article or fighting footnote. Maybe Julie was right, after all, to give up on him. Why should she, too, live her life at second hand? The owl hooted again and the computer in Charles's head clicked with it:

Wits who, like owls, see only in the dark,
Forever reading, never to be read,
A lumberhouse of books in every head.

There was no end to it, no end at all. He emptied his glass and walked unsteadily back into the room. No doubt about it, there was a certain poetic justice in her betraying him. Whom hadn't he betrayed in his own quiet way? Father, mother, poor old Mr Rotherham in his shiny suit, the nameless colleagues of his earlier days in the provinces, even self-sufficient, organized Tom. They had all gone down like skittles before his ambition and his contempt. The thought burst in his head like a triumphant explosion of fireworks, illuminating for a second a whole area of upturned, half forgotten faces: Fuck the lot of them. What do I care? He felt releaved, light-headed. Then the moment passed and he was exhausted. I need a good night's sleep, he thought. Ten hours without dreams.

He picked up the whisky bottle by its neck and carried it upstairs to the bathroom. He fumbled in the medicine cabinet among the tins of Elastoplast and ointment, the bottles of aspirin and shampoo, and finally pulled out a plastic phial: 'The Tablets. One to be taken at night as required'. It was half full. He slopped whisky into his glass and swallowed two of the innocent white pills. Then he went into the bedroom and locked the door behind him. He set down the bottle, glass and phial by his bed and walked towards Julie's dressing-table. The room lurched sideways and he had to steady himself on the edge of the bed. He opened a drawer and took out a white nightgown. He stood for a moment, looking at the shadow of his hand under the surf of nylon frills, then carried it back to the bottle, refilled his glass and sat down on the bed. The room tilted sporadically like Tom's boat in a heavy sea. 'Fuck the lot of them,' he said out loud. He emptied the phial into his hand and began gulping the pills down with whisky. 'Sleep, that's what I need. Real sleep.' Finally, he lay back on the bed and gently, very gently, ran his wife's nightgown over his cheek, mouth, eyes in a final, second-hand caress. Like it always was he thought, as the darkness flooded into his head.

Across the landing, the children slept on undisturbed.

21

Every time Sam looked out of the train window he saw hawks. Or were they kestrels? Or falcons? He couldn't tell for sure. Predators, anyway. He never dreamed there could be so many. Alone or in pairs, they hung trembling above the pine forests or turned in slow, watchful circles where the fields broke free briefly from the ocean of trees. The train climbed steadily under a hot sun, stopping at every station. Little buildings of red brick set down like toys by the railway lines; behind them clusters of neat, newish houses; then the engulfing forest. At each stop Sam leaned out of the window to watch the passengers leaving the train and the one or two who got on: heavy figures, for the most part, short haired and solemn with health. Sleepless and unshaven, he watched with awe as people filed into one side of the stations and cars left the other. Like a meat factory: cattle go in, sausages come out. But apart from the cars, nothing moved on the ordered streets. The world seemed to have become unpeopled, leaving only machines and the hawks wheeling on their invisible axes.

Once the train came out onto an embankment running along the side of a hill. Below lay a great wooded amphitheatre, then soft folds of arable land, honey-gold, waiting to be harvested. Beyond them, a line of ragged peaks shone vaguely, like a promise. Sam glanced up at the rack above his head. Beside his suitcase of holiday clothes lay a bulging orange rucksack, crammed with climbing equipment and topped by a rolled sleeping bag and a rope. His insurance policy. If Julie decided to have done with him, he'd have somewhere to go, someone to welcome him. In a way, he wouldn't be sorry. Although this was her country, she no longer loomed as large as she had in the closed world of the university where he scuttled monotonously between the library and his rooms and the pub. There his one relief had been the chill, muddy water of the river. Now his horizon was edged with mountains, vague, beautiful and unknown.

The train climbed higher and the forest closed in again. At the next stop a well-dressed middle-aged woman got in and sat down opposite Sam. Her grey hair was neatly coiled in a bun, her linen suit dull and expensive. She sat very upright, reading a paperback novel. On its cover a girl in a swirling dress, with large eyes and hair spread over her shoulders, looked passionately out at Sam; behind her the turrets of a castle rose above pine trees against a stormy sky. The intense expression on her face made Sam want to laugh. The woman read steadily and fast, without looking up, occasionally lifting her forefinger to scratch absentmindedly at the corner of one eye. Sam watched her idly, envying her absorption, then turned back to the window and began counting hawks. When he reached twenty he glanced back at the woman. She had put her book down in her lap and was rummaging in her handbag. Finally, she brought out a small, red enamel box and carefully, terribly carefully, tapped a dozen tiny pills onto the palm of her hand. Then with a sudden, furtive jerk, she slapped her hand to her mouth and swallowed the lot. Carefully again, she brushed the traces of powder from her hand and straightened the cuffs of her cream silk blouse. Then she looked up and saw Sam watching her. She blushed like a young girl. He turned quickly back to the window and when he glanced at her surreptitiously a few minutes later she was reading as steadily as before. But her face was running with sweat. I don't know a thing, he thought. It's all strange, wherever I look. It was as though he had waited twenty two years to be properly born.

The woman got out at the next station, her face cool again, her clothes immaculate. The train rattled laboriously on, climbing, climbing. Sam dozed and woke uneasily in his corner seat by the lowered window, feeling the hot summer air on his face, sniffing the gummy smell of the pines, listening to the chatter of the wheels: Loves me, loves me not, loves me, loves me not. Moving peacefully between an old life and a new. Gradually, his eyelids drooped and the sound of the wheels modulated to a thin, electric buzzing. He was lying in bed in the afternoon sun, looking down at Julie's sleek head moving above his groin. He could feel, in a kind of slow-motion excess of sensitivity, her blonde hair on his thighs. Slowly, he stretched out his hands and took hold of her shoulders. He felt the bones moving under her delicate skin. Charles's voice boomed in his ear:

Noli me tangere, *for Caesar's I am,*
And wild for to hold, though I seem tame.

He looked up and saw Julie's two children standing by the bed, staring at him with solemn, shut faces. Someone hissed and jerked the bed angrily from behind. A different voice cried, 'Iserthal', as if announcing the end of the world.

Sam jolted awake. The train jerked again more gently and settled, brakes hissing. Outside, the gutteral voice called again, 'Iserthal'. He got up in a panic, still partly in the hold of his dream, pulled his things off the luggage rack, heaved the sack unwillingly onto his shoulders and hurried down the corridor, his suitcase bumping against the compartment doors. As he stepped down from the train, his eyes were dazzled by the sun. He rubbed them and blinked, finally coming awake. Further down the platform, Julie stood in the glaring light, a small tense figure. She waved nervously.

He had forgotten how skinny she was, how unprepossessing. A child's figure in elderly clothes, isolated in the unforgiving light. As he walked towards her, lugging his suitcase, he noticed that her hair was lank and unwashed, her face thinner than he remembered and somehow dowdy, like her dress. He had always thought she never wore make-up; now it occurred to him that she probably spent hours each day achieving that virginal, unmade-up look. But for their great reunion she hadn't bothered. Instead, she seemed to have gone out of her way to make herself look unattractive. Perverse bitch. She was showing her contempt, as if to say, You may have travelled hundreds of miles, but see how little I care. Once again he felt he was drowning in an alien world. The sun was too hot and the voices bluffly greeting each other were as incomprehensible as the familiar figure standing in front of him.

When he bent to kiss her she proffered her cheek, then quickly drew back and said, 'My aunt's here. I don't think she speaks much English, but you'd better be careful.'

'Jesus Christ, a chaperone. In this day and age. What have you told her?'

'That you're a friend of the family on your way through Germany, and are just stopping to see how I am, and get a break in the country.'

'Thanks very much. Do I get to stay the night or am I to leave on the afternoon train?'

'Don't be tiresome. It's difficult enough as it is.'

The aunt was waiting in the little ticket hall. Small and thin like her niece, dressed in black, her hair iron-grey and severely crinkled, a woman without pleasure. Her face was hollow and bitten-up, as though she were gnawing at herself from the inside. She offered Sam a bony hand and eyed him disapprovingly.

'*Guten Tag*,' he managed, smiling.

She smiled back grimly and said something in German, then added, 'I can very little English speak.'

'*Und ich kann kien Deutsch sprechen*,' Sam replied, trying to look rueful and charming.

The aunt smiled more warmly and rattled something in German. Her voice was colourless and faint and seemed to come from a long way off.

'She says you have a good accent,' said Julie.

'I bet she says that to all the boys.'

Julie smiled at him for the first time and said, 'I've found you a room. It's in the local hotel. The pub really. It's nothing much, but at least it's clean and cheap.'

They walked together up a street of straggling modern houses, freshly painted and crowned with television aerials. Whenever Sam glanced at Julie, he could see her aunt, like some black and forbidding *doppelgänger*, moving beside her.

Behind the new houses, the village huddled together as though for protection from the forest which loomed above it at the end of the steep main street. The hotel was low and whitewashed, its doorway a couple of steps below the level of the street. There was no vestibule, simply a big room with scrubbed floors and scrubbed tables where the mountainous landlord was waiting for them. His triple chins ran all the way round his neck, so that his head seemed to be mounted on tyres. His eyes were almost lost between fat cheeks and the band of bony fat below his narrow forehead where his eyebrows should have been. When he looked at Sam appraisingly Sam saw only a glint of suspicious blue between rolls of pinkish lard. 'A monster,' he whispered, but Julie took no notice.

She ordered coffee and the three of them sat in a corner of the big, low room, drinking in silence. I'm damned if I'll play your game, Sam thought, whatever it is. Finally, Julie got up and muttered something explanatory to her aunt. 'I told her I'd go up to your room with you and the landlord to act as interpreter.'

Like the bar, the stairs, corridors and walls were wooden, scrubbed and smelling of resin. The landlord lumbered ahead, his boots echoing; Sam brought up the rear, bowed under his sack and suitcase. Like the three bears, he thought. Why should they make me feel so childish? The bedroom, too, was wooden, small and bare: a narrow bed, a basin, a pine cupboard and chair. There was a red rug on the floor and red cushions on the seat built into the window embrasure, with its view of the deserted street and the hot dark forest beyond.

The landlord bellowed something in his false, jovial voice. Sam nodded uncomprehendingly and muttered '*Gut, sehr gut*', feeling ridiculous and somehow mocked. Then the man went out, leaving the door open. They stood unmoving while he clumped heavily downstairs. When the door into the bar closed Sam walked quickly over to Julie and took her in his arms. The expression on her uplifted face was quizzical and withheld. Again Sam had the feeling he was being mocked. But when he kissed her she softened against him, as if her jaw and teeth, spine and pelvis were melting under the pressure of his body. She slid her leg between his thighs, her tongue softly explored the inside of his mouth, and for a moment she was gone. Yet when she pulled away the mocking, quizzical gleam was still there. I might be anyone, thought Sam. She is simply taking her pleasure. And again she seemed alien and incomprehensible. He felt terribly depressed. I've lost her, he thought. He brushed his mouth across her cheek, inhaling the subtle, unperfumed smell of her skin. A voice in his head said, as clearly as in his dream, 'She has another lover.' So this is what

161

poor Charles feels when he holds her. Christ, what a farce. He tried to kiss her again, but she stepped away.

'Not now. I must get back to my aunt. She's *vairy* proper.' The accent had come back in her voice. She seemed impatient and far off. Now she was out of England, he realized how much of her life had always been elsewhere. He really had lost her. He felt a brief pang which was half regret, half relief.

When she had gone downstairs he unpacked slowly, then stripped off his clothes and washed himself in cold water, standing one-legged while he soaked each foot, feeling the beautiful chill seep upwards from his toes to his eyes. He peered at himself in the little mirror above the basin. The water had brought a briskness back into his face, but it was still shadowed with stubble. 'Let 'em wait,' he muttered and unpacked his razor.

As he opened the door to the bar, Julie got up impatiently. 'You've taken your time.'

'I needed a wash and a shave.' He looked round the empty room. 'Where's auntie?'

'She's gone back to her room. She's staying down the street, near the station. She comes out to see me at the clinic in the afternoons.'

They went out into the glaring sun. The road climbed steeply through the village, swinging left where the houses ended. Julie clambered over a fence and walked straight on up through a pasture where insects shimmered in the heat. Sam followed her resentfully. He was sweating already, his legs ached, he needed sleep. He could think of nothing more desirable than to lie down in the grass among the white clover flowers and buttercups and drift away into nothingness, inhaling the heavy smell of summer. But she did not pause. She walked quickly up the tilted field, her back stiff with irritation. Sam plodded after her.

When she reached the edge of the forest she waited for him to catch up. 'The road also goes to the clinic,' she said, 'or near it. There is a turning. But it is much quicker this way.'

'What's the hurry?'

But she set off again without answering. As he followed her down the vague, narrow path, he remembered the dream voice booming, 'Noli me tangere, for Caesar's I am,' and was suddenly angry like a rebuked child – angry and ashamed and impotent. He watched with venom her thin, receding back and the blonde hair flapping on her shoulders. *Shiksahs!* Maybe his father had been right after all.

The forest was thick and dark and tangled. It seemed old and a little ominous, like a place that has been long avoided. He remembered something she had said about the Romans never penetrating it. Above their heads a bird squawked angrily and beat up through the resisting branches. Then there was silence again, except for the muffled sound of their feet on the path and the rustle and swish of the undergrowth catching at them as they went. The calf muscles in Sam's legs began to ache fiercely, but there was no clearing among the trees to rest in. The sun filtered down at intervals, where the upper branches thinned, streaking the trunks with yellow. The still air smelt of resin.

They came into a clearing at last – pine needles, moss, a greenish, underwater light – but Julie didn't pause. She had plunged into the bushes on the other side before Sam, who was ten yards behind, had time to call to her. He tried to remember why he had come: to lumber with aching legs after a stranger who seemed to resent him? He told himself that he had come because she wanted him to, because he was in love, because she said she was dying. Dying. He began to giggle foolishly. She moved like a long-distance runner, relentlessly, while he stumbled and sweated behind. As always in moments of confusion, he began to calculate. Two pounds a day for the room. How much were the meals? Probably another two pounds at least. That made £28 for the week. He couldn't afford it if he was to go on to the Dolomites. Which he was. Maybe if he bought food at the local shop – if there was a local shop – and ate in his room, he could manage on a pound a day . . .

Julie had crossed another clearing while he was calculating. Ahead of them the trees thinned and the light sifted palely back. He wiped the sweat from his face with the back of his hand and stumbled on. Finally, they came out of the forest and stopped. Julie stood looking down into the wide green cup beneath them at a sprawl of red roofs and white walls, with an oval of turquoise water glinting at its centre.

'There it is,' she said.

Sam flopped down on the grass. 'It looks expensive.'

'It is.' She sounded almost boastful, like a child with a new toy.

'I didn't know that kind of thing appealed to you.'

'Oh, it's nice to live well from time to time.'

'Provided somebody else is paying.'

'You're too bothered about money.' She sat down beside him, but at a distance. They both stared as though hypnotized at the jewel of water below them.

'That's easy to say when you have it.'

'You will, believe me. I know. You're going to be a great success, Sam.'

'I don't know how you work that out. As of this last fortnight, I have no prospects at all.'

'Don't sound so sorry for yourself. It's not my fault. You left the university because you wanted to. High time too, if you ask me. Anyway, I'm right. You don't have to worry. I can smell success on you.'

'You make it sound like something to be ashamed of. Like bad breath.' He lit a cigarette and lay back in the grass watching the smoke drift away, blue on blue. Bitch, he thought. Bitch. Bitch. Bitch. For a while neither of them spoke. Finally, he said, 'I take it you wish now I hadn't come.' He could hear how pompous he sounded. Just like Charles. And that made him more angry.

'No,' she said slowly. 'No, I'm glad really. Just don't push me, Sam, don't push me.'

He turned his head towards her. She was looking down at him and her face, for the first time, had softened. He reached out and took her hand. 'I'm sorry,' he said, 'I didn't get any sleep on the train.' That pale gold hair. His anger melted away.

'It's all right. My aunt makes me edgy. Always talking about the past. As if she wanted to apologize for the murder of my father. It gets on my nerves.'

'I'd have thought it would break your heart.'

She moved her hand, with his still in it, and rubbed his cheek. 'I'm sorry. I don't know what got into me.'

Sam half moved towards her, but she stood up. 'Let's go on down.'

The interior of the clinic was white, hushed and full of light. Every passage seemed to end in plate-glass doors opening on to the pool or the fields. White-coated attendants moved on rubber soles over the slate-grey rubber floors, pushing chrome trolleys on rubber wheels. Discretion, the wheels whispered, discretion, discretion. Julie opened one of the doors. 'This is mine.' White walls, white bed, but on the pale wooden table by the window a bowl of flowers as red and violent as a wound.

'It looks like a nunnery,' said Sam, 'an antiseptic nunnery.'

She closed the door again without going in and said, 'It's good to live an uncluttered life.'

Sam didn't answer. Numb, he thought. Like scar tissue. White and numb and impervious.

They went on down the passage, through the plate-glass doors to the pool. The bodies exposed on deckchairs were old and well kept, the wrinkled flesh oiled and tanned, the silver hair severely ordered. An elderly couple swam side by side down the pool, solemnly, as if on parade. Their chins made faint blue waves. Sam and Julie stood blinking in the glare. He could feel his shirt sticking to his back and glanced round self-consciously. Then he saw Julie's dowdy, plum-coloured dress and realized that he looked no more out of place than she did.

'Christ, I'd love a swim.'

'*Streng verboten*. For patients only.'

'They look too old to enjoy it.'

'What do you expect? Muscle Beach? It's a clinic.'

On the opposite side of the pool a tall young man got up from his chair, sauntered to the edge of the water and arched gracefully in. He swam indolently and without fuss, as though it were one of his things. When he reached the edge he slithered up out of the water in one continuous, sinewy movement, like a snake. His hair was as blond as Julie's, his eyes colder and as blue. He walked up to them smiling: 'Hullo.'

Julie smiled back. 'Sam Green, Kurt Wolheim,' she said. The

two men shook hands. The German's pale and elegant body made Sam feel gross, as if he had been cast of cheap material and in the wrong mould.

'Welcome to Iserthal,' said Kurt, 'Julie told me you were coming.' He spoke English easily, with an American accent, and smiled like someone who understood the uses of his charm. But his eyes watched Sam ironically and from a distance. When he sat down he settled his body with small animal movements, like a cat.

Sam flopped into a deckchair beside him. His shirt was soaked, his legs ached, his head buzzed with fatigue. He closed his eyes for a moment, then opened them again. In the glare he saw that Julie had taken a chair on the far side of Kurt, making him the centre of attention, as if that were his natural right. Sam smiled with a show of amiability. 'You don't look like a patient.'

There was a tiny moment of silence before Kurt replied, 'I'm not. I keep an eye on the pool in case anyone gets into trouble. I help out.'

'Who are they all?'

'They are our past. They are what happened to the last days of Hitler.' He made a vague, languid gesture which took in the wrinkled bodies round the pool and the two sedate swimmers. 'You would be surprised. Of course, they look better with their clothes on.'

'What do they do all day?'

'They eat wheat germ and oranges and salads. They drink mineral water. They sunbathe, swim and do exercises. They are massaged. Believe me, they lead a full and controlled life.'

Sam looked at him suspiciously. He was smiling his charming smile, but his eyes were as remote as ever.

'Watched over by you?' Sam asked.

'No, no. Watched over by the good Dr Klaus. I am merely an attendant lord, as your poet says. Not even that. Just an attendant.'

'You like Eliot?'

'Natürlich. A great poet. I studied him at Princeton.'

'What was that like?'

'Charming. Full of the sons of gentlemen. I learned about Eliot and poker. All sorts of things.'

'This is an odd place to end up.'

'Oh, I am simply, how do you say, filling in time. Resting. A little break before I set out on life.' He looked at Sam ironically, his eyelids half closed. 'You see, my father is a friend of Herr Doktor's, an old friend.'

'Your father's a doctor, too?'

'Not at all. He runs an art gallery. He is what you would call a smart figure. These days the rich prefer paintings to money or shares. So much safer.'

'Is the doctor a collector?'

'Not seriously. They were friends during the war.' He leaned forward smiling and said in a confidential voice, 'You see, my father was a colonel in the Waffen SS. Very diligent, very highly thought of. That was where he knew Dr Klaus. He also was highly thought of. But today you are not supposed to mention these things. I find that silly.'

'Really?' Sam tried to sound cool and incredulous, but his voice was unsteady. 'I'd have thought you'd find it embarrassing.'

'Why should I be embarrassed? I wasn't born. It's no concern of mine.'

Sam peered through the glare at Kurt's smiling face and sardonic eyes. He's trying to make a fool of me, he thought. He knows I'm a Jew and is doing this for Julie's benefit. 'Then why boast about it?' he said.

'I do not boast. I state the facts. Truth has a special purity of its own.' His voice, with its careful American accent, was soft and reasonable, yet also faintly mocking. What's he after? Sam wondered. He might as well be challenging me to race the length of the pool. Julie lay perfectly still, her eyes closed, her face to the sun, taking no interest. Sam felt a surge of anger against her, too. Her and her uncluttered life. He squinted again at the relaxed and indolent young man beside him. When he spoke he could hear his voice rising childishly in indignation. 'What's pure about that kind of truth? Murderers are murderers. They don't have to have my approval.'

'Believe me,' said Kurt in his easy, reasonable way, 'they don't need your approval.' He gestured again at the figures round the pool. 'Do they look as if they do? They get along very nicely,

167

thank you, with it or without it. And I'll tell you something funny: it is we who shock them. The young. They are shocked by our little experiments with drugs and our promiscuity. Ridiculous, isn't it? After all, they made it all possible for us. They showed us that no one is answerable to anyone else.'

'For God's sake!' It was Sam's turn to sound contemptuous.

'It's true. They're living proof that anything goes.' Kurt's languor lifted slightly and his voice quickened. He watched Sam coldly as if wondering where to strike. 'All that liberal indignation about the mass-murderers, the monsters, the perverts alive and well and living in South America. And the rubbish about escape routes and the Odessa line. All crap. The Odessa line took them straight to their own back doors. Most of them are alive and well all right, but living where they always lived, and running the dear old country. Very efficiently, too.'

The sun beat down. Even by the pool it was as airless as a closed room. Sam thought of the bottle of duty-free whisky in the wooden cupboard of his wooden hotel room. He imagined it glinting amber in the sun, and its sharp, clean taste. 'Well?' he said.

'Well, who are they to call us immoral?'

'Surely,' Sam tried to sound ironical, despite the heat and fatigue, 'a real immoralist doesn't need excuses.'

'Too true. But it is interesting, no? Our fathers were patriots, men of principle in their way. And what happened? They gave us our freedom. Because of them and their principles, there is now a generation free of moral restraints. That's paradoxical, *ja*?'

The light clashing off the pool intensified his icy blue stare. He's mad, thought Sam, mad as a hatter. He said, 'It seems to me they did the opposite: made all those humane, liberal values you despise seem much more important.'

'You're a sentimentalist,' said Kurt.

Sam shrugged and sat up. 'You're keeping very quiet,' he said to Julie.

She opened her eyes and looked at him without interest. 'I wasn't listening,' she said. She stood up and stretched. 'Perhaps you should go. I have massage. Then I'm supposed to rest before lunch.'

When Sam got to his feet he was swaying a little, dizzy with the heat. Above the forest was a dark edge of cloud, knotted thickly like tarred rope. 'There's a storm coming,' he said.

Kurt sat up and extended a languid hand. 'I will see you again soon, I hope. It was most interesting.'

'Surely,' said Sam.

Julie walked with him to the gate where the path up to the forest began. 'When can I come back?' he asked.

'It's difficult. My aunt comes in the late afternoon. Perhaps she'll return to Heidelberg soon.'

'Please God,' Sam muttered fervently.

'The doctor doesn't approve of patients going out in the evening. Early bed is part of the cure.' She looked at Sam's hangdog, resentful expression and relented. 'I'll see what I can arrange. Come tomorrow morning, about eleven.' She kissed him quickly on the cheek and walked away.

Sam stared after her until the glass doors flashed good-bye. Then he began to slog slowly, sweating, up the hill towards the pine trees. Him, he thought. Him, him, him.

22

The gristle was thick and translucent, yellowy-orange, rubbery to the teeth. The top of his throat closed against it, as though all his intestines, coil upon silvery coil, were pressing in revulsion against the root of his tongue. 'Eat it,' said his mother, 'eat it.' She seemed enormous. The gristle lay where he had left it at the side of his plate, a white crust of congealed fat stretching away from it. Again his mother said harshly, 'Eat it.' She stretched out an arm like the leg of a bullock, speared the gristle with her fork and thrust it against his lips. The weight at the back of his throat exploded in his mouth and he began to vomit. He felt his whole life was heaving up at him from the pit of his stomach.

Charles hung over the edge of the bed, staring at the yellow, lumpy pool that spread over the carpet. The muscles of his face had gone soft so that his nose, lips and cheeks seemed to be hanging slackly down towards it. The sour smell which came up at him made him retch again. Through swaddling clouds of nausea the old, idiot voice whispered, *He cracks his gorge, his sides, with violent hefts.* He flopped back against the pillow appalled, knowing he should get up, find a rag and wipe this monstrosity from the floor. But his body wouldn't answer. He could feel the weight of his flesh and his shuddering intestines on his bones. Dead weight. Not dead enough.

His ears buzzed. A switch clicked in his head and he felt he was lurching sickeningly downwards, like a plane in an airpocket. He closed his eyes against the vertiginous emptiness. His mother smiled at him: 'There, there, darling. It's all over.' When he opened his eyes again the ceiling was back in place. Something tickled his left cheek. With immense effort he turned his head and found that his nose, mouth and one weeping eye were buried in the delicate folds of his wife's nightdress. Gratefully, he inhaled the faint, cool scent of her eau de cologne. It's all over. Is it all over? Gradually, very gradually, the room darkened. He muttered out loud, *'I have drunk and seen the spider,'* then drifted back into sleep, breathing his wife's smell.

23

By the time Sam reached the edge of the forest the clouds had
built up into great bronze and black towers, their tops fuming in
the sun. They progressed massively, but oddly fast, across the sky,
rifting occasionally for a shaft of brassy sunlight. Somewhere
high up the wind blew strongly and thermals sucked the clouds
upwards like burning castles. But down below nothing moved.
The air was stagnant and enervating, stretched tight by the
raaaasp-raaaasp of the cicadas. He could see a hawk balancing on
a pillar of light between two swollen banks of cloud. Waiting,
waiting. Sam pulled open his sticky shirt and blew down his
chest: 'Phew'. The forest was silent except for the steady shrilling
of the cicadas.

He looked back at the clinic. The eye of water at its centre
seemed greenish now in the thickening air. He thought of the
doctor working away with his health foods, mineral water and
massage to preserve the last shrivelled specimens of the Master
Race. Nice work if you can get it. They were survivors to a man.
Julie, too. He wondered how he had ever convinced himself that
she was dying. All that anguish, all that drama. It seemed absurd
now: another world, another person. For all he knew, she had
died already and been resurrected with fruit juice in her veins,
wheat germ in her tissues and salad in her breasts, blue-eyed,
blonde and pure, *echt Deutsch*, with her blond and blue-eyed
lover. There was no way he could compete with that long-limbed,
icy young man, with his casual, crazy talk about freedom. Anything goes, he'd said. But only, thought Sam, over my dead body.
Or the bodies of Jews like me. He stopped short, thinking, That's
ghetto-talk, and standing alone at the lip of the forest he blushed
for shame. Just like his father. The man's dotty. Why should I be
drawn in? Dotty and depraved, beyond appeal. A cold-eyed

bastard. Yet secretly he envied Kurt because he knew Julie found him attractive.

Far off the thunder coughed apologetically and the air darkened. He turned in among the trees and began to follow the faint path. He was empty-headed with fatigue and walked unsteadily, occasionally wavering into the bushes which scratched his arms and picked at the fabric of his jeans. The thunder coughed again, louder and closer. A sweltering wind began to stir through the trees, making the pine needles rustle together maliciously. The Romans never got here, the Romans never got here. The thunder rolled closer. Neither did the Jews.

The rain came on over the tree tops, hissing like surf. Sam lifted his sweating face gratefully as it began to splash down through the branches. Suddenly, to his left, a finger of lightning sizzled into the trees and thunder crashed directly overhead. The rain bucketed down furiously. He stood there, head back, arms out, shirt open, soaking up the blessed coolness. Another flash of bluish white and the thunder crashed again. Jesus. He shoved on through the bushes, head down to the tiny stream which was the path, while the trees heaved angrily in the dark air. The thunder spoke again, but further off, and the rain steadied. He trudged on.

The hotel bar was crowded with men. Not a woman to be seen. The steam of drying clothes mixing with the smell of food and drink made the air heavy. All the lights were on. When Sam pushed open the door everyone turned and stared at him inquisitively, as though he were a curiosity they had been told about but never seen, and there was a moment's silence. His shoes squelched loudly as he crossed the room, his hair was plastered to his scalp, his clothes were soaked. But he was weary beyond embarrassment. The mountainous landlord behind the bar said something he didn't understand in a hearty, encouraging voice, his little eyes jumping with pleasure. Some of the drinkers laughed and Sam smiled with them but did not stop. When he got up to his bedroom he locked the door behind him. The room was dark and filled with the sound of rain. He closed the window, stripped off his dripping clothes and towelled himself down. Carefully, he wrung out his shirt and jeans, socks and underpants, and hung them along the foot of the bed. He banged his shoes together and stood them neatly under the basin. Then he walked naked to the wardrobe and took out the bottle of whisky. He stared at it for a moment, holding it in both hands, then took a long, glugging swallow. He paused, listening to the rain, feeling the warmth spread down his throat, along his veins, until even his fingertips tingled. Then he drank again. When he climbed into bed at last he slept as though assassinated.

24

Julie lay in bed with Kurt watching the rain, veil after veil drifting across the window beyond the vivid roses. They lay side by side in their sweat, quietly, fingers entwined. The air was cool and soothing. She had come home. All the lost years. Her father squalidly dead in a camp, her cousin, shifty to the end, dead on the Eastern Front, her aunt shrivelled in rectitude. She alone had survived. She looked down at her smooth, pale body. I've been spared, she thought. How odd. But her heart felt tired.

She turned slightly towards Kurt and moved closer. His body, too, was smooth and elegant. Impervious. The hair on his chest and legs was pale gold, burnished round his genitals. She slid her hand lazily across his stomach, as flat and taut as her own. He stirred in his sleep, muttered inaudibly, rolled over towards her and slipped his hand between her thighs, but did not wake.

She looked back at the rain beyond the window. Why not? she thought. He's beautiful. My mirror-image. Why should I be denied it? I've been docile long enough. She shivered, remembering Charles's flaccid, greyish flesh. Strange how easily Sam had cancelled all that for her. And now she had come home. Who'd have believed it? She eased onto her back again and opened her legs, took Kurt's hand in hers and pressed it against her clitoris, then lay still again. Again Kurt stirred and did not wake. Poor Sam, she thought. So earnest, so in love, but so strident. Yet he had set her free. None of her smooth-talking young admirers had managed that. The wittier they were, the more they irritated her and the more she valued her stolid husband with his prejudices and his unending pronouncements on morality and literature. After all, they had a marriage of a kind, they had children. Why should she sacrifice that to the vanity of young academics on the make? At least Sam had been passionate and vulnerable. He had thought more of her than of his career. He had made her feel obscurely powerful.

She realized, with a little tremor of amusement, that she was thinking of him in the past tense. Poor Sam. Her Odessa line. Why had nobody ever told her that sex was for use, that through pleasure she extended her boundaries? She moved Kurt's hand against her wetness. He half woke and began to stroke her lazily, lazily. She lay still to attend to the far off tremblings in the pit of her body, while the rain shushed down outside. There had been too much sweetness and light. It was time to find out about the darkness. Her hand moved with Kurt's, probing, touching herself. Otherwise, neither of them stirred. Discreet steps passed down the passage outside her door. A trolley squeaked briefly. He was the perfect instrument, no more moral or immoral than a stone. Simply himself, contained within himself, content with his own limits. Like a stone. You must go down, down. What does a stone know of the ordinary decency they all talk about? Down. Their twined fingers moved more busily. The father had committed 'crimes against humanity' and the son had inherited blankness. Slowly the excitement mounted in her, but her face, upturned to the ceiling, was slack. She could feel, like a hallucination, her own skull pressing against her skin from the inside. Their fingers moved together more urgently and her body began to quiver as if in the grip of some primitive electrical machine. Her pelvis heaved up and down, her buttocks laboured while Kurt, now leaning coolly over her, propped on one elbow, watched her closely but dispassionately, as he might have watched a conjuror explaining his tricks. And as she reached her climax, her head cleared of all its confusions and she emerged into a world as stark and white as the walls of her hospital room. That's it, she thought. That's it. Yes. Kill him. Kill me. Through him she was embracing her father's murderers. It was what she had always wanted. There was no pity left. None at all. She began to sob, weeping for her father as she had never grieved before, burying her streaming face against Kurt's elegantly muscled chest, while the rain hissed on outside.

25

Far off he heard the faint thud of a hammer. Its tempo was different from the steady throb at the back of his head. What were they working at? Then a voice, less faint, when the hammering stopped: 'Professor Stone, Professor Stone.' What did they want with him? Go away. But the hammering began again more loudly than before and this time the voice called with it: 'Professor, professor. Please, Herr Professor.'

Someone had passed an iron bar through his head from one ear to the other. It twisted and rang when he tried to sit up. He lay carefully back down again. But the voice calling his name clanged brutally on. Why were they persecuting him? He opened his mouth to tell them to stop, but his throat was raw and tender and the words came out a formless croak. He swallowed twice, painfully, and managed: ''S all right'. The voice, mollified, said something incomprehensible, then went away.

Charles sat up again gingerly. The sunlight, streaming through the window, hurt his eyes. The room was full of the bitter stench of vomit. Christ, what a mess. His heart, doggedly beating in his chest, was offensive to him.

A puff of summer breeze billowed the muslin curtains and let them fall. Tentatively, he lowered his feet to the carpet and stood up, steadying himself on the bed with one hand. He felt as fragile as an old vase; a voice could shatter him. But he wasn't dead. Well, then. One step, then another, then another. He crossed from the bed to the dressing-table to the linen cupboard and took out a towel. Then he turned again and faced the sunny, reeking room. His head throbbed evilly. Again he set out on the long journey to the bedside, gently, gently, treading on glass. He lowered himself onto the edge of the bed and rubbed his sweating face with the towel, then he went down heavily on his knees and began to wipe up the stinking mess on the floor. On his knees by his bed as in childhood. Our Father, Who art in the library. Rubbing patiently, as though erasing his past, his mind emptied.

When he had finished he rested again on the edge of the bed, thinking, If I lie back down, I'll never get up. His mouth tasted foul, his body was stale and itchy. Wearily, he got to his feet and unlocked the bedroom door. His morning tea-tray and neatly folded newspaper were outside. He dropped the stinking towel beside them and went into the bathroom. Heidi, lurking below, came up at once and knocked discreetly on the door.

'Herr Professor, are you all right?'

Charles swallowed a glass of water to lubricate his ravaged throat. 'Of course I'm all right. But I was sick in the night. I'm afraid there's a mess.' His usually booming voice sounded like brown paper tearing.

'That is all right. Do not worry. I clean up everything.'

'Thank you.' He looked at the presence facing him in the mirror: ashen face, sack of a body in a shirt stained with vomit. Portrait of a Professor the Morning After. While the bath slowly filled, he brushed his teeth, again and then again, trying to eradicate the taste of defeat.

When he went back into the bedroom the bed was made, the dressing-table tidied and there was a large damp patch on the carpet, smelling of disinfectant. The whisky bottle was gone, but the little phial still stood on his bedside table. There were two tablets left. The windows were wide open on another delectable day and the summer air moved gently in and out.

In clean clothes, talcumed, deodorized and cologned, Charles went down to the kitchen, where Heidi hovered anxiously, large-eyed and full of concern.

He smiled at her encouragingly, sat and opened his newspaper as though everything was normal. She brought him his coffee and a rack of toast.

'You are feeling better?'

'Yes, yes, I'm fine.' But his head still throbbed and he was glad to be sitting down again. He sipped the coffee. Heidi settled her large form at the table with him, leaning forward and cradling her breasts in her arms. 'It worried me very much when you did not wake. And then when I had taken the children to school and you were sleeping still.'

'I was awfully sick in the night. But it's nothing. I'm afraid I drank too much whisky. I'm sorry about the mess.' He tried to sound charming, but his heart wasn't in it. Why should he bother, now or ever, with her or anyone?

'It is nothing. I clean it all up. But please,' she blushed and her doggy eyes deepened, 'I have done something. I hope you are not cross with me.'

'What?' Charles felt he was speaking across a great distance. If only she would go away and leave him in peace.

'When I see how sick you have been I telephone the doctor.'

'For God's sake!' His cup hit the saucer too hard, slopping coffee on the table. There was no end to it. He said angrily, 'There's nothing the matter. I drank too much on an empty stomach, that's all.'

The girl's eyes moistened, her blush intensified. 'Please do not be angry with me. I am worried for you. I'm sorry.'

'It's not your business to worry.' He wished his voice were adequate to his frustration, not dry and crackling.

Her eyes brimmed with tears and her mouth began to tremble. 'Please,' she said, 'please.'

What was the use? He reached out and patted her shoulder. 'It's all right. I'm sorry I was cross. You weren't to know. You're very kind really.'

Her burly frame was shaken by a single sob. The tears brimmed over and streamed down her cheeks. She fumbled for a piece of Kleenex, wiped her eyes and looked at him adoringly. 'Thank you,' she said. He felt like crying with her, from weariness and relief, and in gratitude for her adoring, comforting presence.

The doorbell rang and Heidi went out, leaving Charles hunched at the table sipping his coffee. He heard voices in the hall, muffled by the closed kitchen door, but did not listen. When Heidi returned she was blushing again and apologetic. 'It is the doctor. He is in the drawing-room.' Charles swallowed more coffee, then rose wearily to meet the next enemy.

With his powerful belly and florid face, the doctor seemed like a visitor from another world – healthy, sane, unperturbed and, by

Charles, long abandoned. He pumped Charles's hand, eyeing him critically. 'What's all this, then? I hear you've been sick.'

'It's a fuss about nothing. I drank too much whisky on an empty stomach. God knows what possessed the girl to call you. I suppose she got a bit hysterical when I overslept. I can only apologize for wasting your time.' That's not bad, he thought. Keep it up.

'No need to apologize, old boy. Glad to see you. And God knows, you look a bit seedy. Sound it, too. Let's have a look at your throat.' He got out his little torch. 'Say Ah.'

'Ah,' said Charles obediently.

'Just a drop too much whisky, you say?' The doctor's voice was quizzical.

'Well, I took a couple of sleeping pills as well. I've had terrible trouble sleeping these last few nights.'

'You mean since the little woman went away? Just a couple you say?'

'Well, no. Perhaps three or four. Maybe more. You see, I was a bit tight. And desperate for sleep.'

'Is that all you were desperate for?'

'Of course,' said Charles. 'What else?'

'Hmm,' said the doctor. 'Do you mind taking off your jacket and shirt?'

Charles did as he was told and found, to his annoyance, that he was sweating with the effort. The doctor moved his chill stethoscope over his chest and back. 'Hmm,' he said again, musing, critical. Finally he unplugged the instrument from his ears and said in a portentous voice, 'You're lucky they weren't barbiturates.'

'Weren't they?'

'Not if they were the ones I prescribed. And I suppose they were. They're a new kind of pill, specially designed to prevent stupid accidents like this. They don't kill you. They make you vomit.'

'I see.' Once again Charles was overwhelmed by a childish desire to weep.

'You're lucky all the same. You could easily have swallowed your vomit and blocked your lungs. Then where'd you be? Dead or dying. That's where.'

180

'I'm sorry,' said Charles unsteadily. 'I didn't realize.'

'Now look, old boy,' the doctor's bluff, beery face was sympathetic, 'I'm not asking you if this was a mistake, though I hope it was. I just want to make you realize how lucky you've been.'

Charles mustered his shattered dignity. 'I assure you it was a mistake. I only wanted a good night's sleep.'

'Glad to hear it, old boy. Very glad.' He sounded relieved to have been spared an unpleasant responsibility. Charles buttoned his shirt, eyeing the watchchain which drooped across the doctor's massive stomach. There was a moment's silence.

'Well, then.' The doctor rubbed his hands briskly together and pulled out his prescription pad. 'I'll give you something for your throat. You must take it very easy for a day or two. I don't think you'll have any more trouble sleeping.'

Charles smiled back at him. 'I don't suppose I will.' The confrontation had been avoided. But he wished he didn't feel so tearful.

Alcohol and sleeping pills, thought the doctor, as he climbed into his car. A rotten combination. Almost as lethal as young wives and old husbands.

26

The first thing Sam heard was the rain muttering outside his closed window. It was like waking inside a packing case: wood all around and the smell of wood in his nose. He had slept for eighteen hours, but his body ached as if he had been bounced heavily off the walls all the long night. Damaged in transit. When he opened the window on the rain the air was cold. So much for summer. He might as well have stayed in England.

Downstairs there was the rank odour of drink and tobacco, although the floor and tables had been scrubbed, the glasses shone in their rows and the ashtrays were empty. The landlord's wife brought him coffee, dark bread and salty butter. She was as massive as her husband and as padded with fat, but comfortable. When he fumbled out his few words of German she talked back cheerfully, almost as if she were sorry for him. She understands, he thought gratefully and had a sudden yearning to gossip about nothing in particular with this placid woman with motherly breasts and mottled forearms. But his German wasn't up to it. And there was no comfort to be had from Julie. He wondered what wrong he had done that he should be left in the lurch so abruptly. Sipping his coffee he thought complacently, this is what it is to be heartbroken. He watched the landlady behind the bar, taking down the bottles one by one, dusting them, then putting them back as tenderly as if they were the toys of a lost child. Had she ever been heartbroken? In another age perhaps, before she settled for her monstrous husband with his creased neck, malicious eyes and *lederhosen*. Heartbreak was the prerogative of youth. The old had other things on their minds. Was Charles heartbroken? He doubted it.

In London now his father would be sitting, like him, over his morning coffee, the paper in front of him, the scent of tobacco and lavender in the air. Lavender soap, lavender shaving cream, lavender brilliantine and aftershave. He should have bought shares in Yardley. On the lapels of his carefully brushed suit there would already be flakes of ash from his first cigarette as he smoked, sipped and brooded about the injustices of his life: his lack of money, his lack of interest in the need to raise money, the shop with its dwindling clientele, the machinations of his unspeakable relatives, his indulgent, nagging wife. (And his mistress, was she also indulgent and nagging? Probably.) And the longer he brooded, the heavier his inertia became. How could there be a life after breakfast? If it weren't, that is, for Mrs Green, bustling, fractious, impatient to clear the table. You're never alone with a family. Sam could feel the vibrations of the old man's gloom coming to him across half of Europe and it occurred to him that he, too, had now added to it. For years he had been the beloved only son for whom there was always nothing but the best. My son the undergraduate. My son the research student. My son the would-be professor. Now he had become my son the new nail in his parents' coffin. He wished he could say sorry. He wished ... He realized, with surprise, that he was homesick.

He finished his coffee and went back upstairs. The rain still beat down outside. He unstrapped his rucksack, pulled out a pair of boots and a waterproof kagoule, and put them on. The kagoule reached down to his knees. With the hood up he looked like a plaster gnome. No matter. He went out into the streaming street. The clouds were low over the forest, weeping without remission, as though the end had come. He slogged uphill towards the trees across the steep field where yesterday he had wanted to sleep among the buttercups. Buttercups, for Christ's sake. The earth was chill and drenched. So much for his grand passion. Even the weather was against him.

Julie must have been watching for him, for she was waiting at the glass doors when he arrived. 'You're soaked.' Her voice was friendly but distant, vaguely amused. He pulled off his waterproof and wiped his sopping boots on the doormat. She seemed less spectral than yesterday. There was colour in her cheeks and her hair was washed. Sam gestured towards the drowned landscape.

'Look at it,' he said. 'Now we're really fucked.'

'I don't know. Are we?' She didn't sound interested.

He changed the subject: 'You look as if the cure's beginning to do you good.'

But she wouldn't rise to that either. 'Is it?' she said in the same distant voice. 'Well, it's high time. It costs enough.'

He followed her into the reading room where half a dozen survivors sat dozing behind their newspapers. The armchairs were black leather and very modern. Thick rubbery plants punctuated the whiteness of the walls and pillars. It looked like the waiting room of a private airport or a space-age industrial concern. The silence was oppressive. There should have been a subdued, far off hum of engines or computers.

'Do we have to stay here with these ghouls?' Automatically, he found he was whispering in the churchly hush. Julie nodded. 'Can't we go to your room, for God's sake?'

'It's not allowed.'

'Oh boy, it's like being back at school. I thought this was a luxury clinic.'

'The doctor's a great one for rules. They're supposed to be part of the cure. Complete rest and quiet.'

'I bet he is, with his background.'

She didn't reply. Her averted face was stiff with impatience. They sat listening to the discreet sounds of aged leisure: the rustle of newspapers, the occasional surprised snore and hollow cough, the faint bubbling of the coffee percolators. Finally, Sam hissed, 'This isn't possible. What are we going to do?'

'You're in too much of a hurry,' she said coolly. 'That's your trouble. You want everything your way and at once. Like a spoilt child.'

'But look at it,' he pleaded. 'The place, the weather, the fucking rules. Everything's against us.'

'Don't whine. It gets on my nerves.'

But he couldn't stop himself: 'I've travelled halfway across Europe on money I don't have in order to be alone with you. And all we do is sit cooped up with a lot of dying Nazis and watch the rain bucket down.'

'You mean you want what you've paid for?' Her voice was low, icy and full of venom. She didn't look at him. 'Would you like me to drop my knickers here and now? Or should we go out to the lavatory and I'll give you a quick blow-job? Then you can be on your way. Off to your beloved mountains.'

He looked at her delicate profile in amazement. Amazement and awe. His blonde Madonna, as fragile and exquisite as a glass statuette. But she talks like a Greek Street whore. And she knew his secrets, had sized him up. Unanswerable.

'That's not true.' His face was red with shame. 'I love you. You know it. Why else should I have come here? And you wanted me to come. You said so.'

She looked at him at last, her eyes a little softer. 'Poor Sam. You really do sound just like a child. I warned you it would be difficult.'

'You didn't say how difficult.'

'I didn't know. You must be patient. I'm here because I've been ill. I might as well do what they tell me.'

'And what *does* the doctor tell you?'

'Oh, Doctor Klaus. I don't really see him. Nobody does. He examined me when I arrived, did a lot of tests, took samples and all that stuff. Then he prescribed a diet and a routine, and that's that. I suppose he works it all out by some special theory.'

'It sounds like an easy way to make a living.'

'There you go again. What does it matter, so long as it works?'

'Mind if I join you?' Kurt was standing over them, smiling his charming smile. He was wearing white trousers and a pale blue shirt, crisply laundered. He looked as if he had just strolled in off a yacht. Sam's toes curled in embarrassment in their great, wet boots. His old jeans were filthy and his hair bristled wildly.

Julie smiled up at him. 'Of course not.' She seemed relieved. 'We were talking about Doctor Klaus.'

Kurt arranged himself elegantly in an armchair opposite them. 'Oh yes, the good doctor without a past.'

'I was saying he was onto a good thing,' said Sam.

'He always has been,' Kurt replied, 'in one way or another. There are some people who can't lose, whatever they do. He's one of them.'

'It seems a pity.'

'That depends on how you look at it. It's like we were saying yesterday: if you believe there's such a thing as justice in this world, then it would be nice to see the doctor get his, no?'

'But you know better?'

'Oh no. I make no claims. I know only what I see. No more, no less. And I see the doctor does very well.'

'You two aren't going to start up again, are you?' Julie said in a bored voice.

'There's nothing to start. I think Sam and I agree. We just put it differently.'

'Really?' said Sam sarcastically. 'Well, well.'

'Oh dear,' said Julie and turned away from them both to watch the rain against the windows.

'But yes. Didn't we have the same kind of comfortable childhood? Well fed, well clothed, denied nothing unless it was good for us to be denied. I'm right, yes? We were both brought up to think the world was arranged for our benefit and all we had to do in return was behave properly. Be polite, say "please" and "thank you" and "sorry". Be responsible for those under us and deferential towards our superiors. And generous when it was appropriate, but not too generous. All that crap. Wash our hands before meals and our teeth after them. Love our parents, work hard, get on. Above all, get on. This is true, *ja?*'

'So what? There are worse ways of being brought up.' Sam looked at the young man's chill, handsome face and suddenly saw his father asleep in front of the thundering gramophone and his mother stuffing her old terrier with delicacies and love. There was no harm in them. 'Anyway, it's all over and done with,' he said. 'Why get so worked up about it?'

'Things happen.'

'Yes, yes,' Sam made an impatient gesture, 'your father. You told me.'

'That was later, much later. I had seen how things were years before, when I was just a little boy.'

'Don't tell me. Let me guess.' Sam felt that the other man was somehow trying to humiliate him with his seductive, knowing talk, and this was his last chance. 'You found your father's wartime diaries,' he said contemptuously. 'Or was it his old uniform in mothballs in a trunk? Anyway, you had a vision of evil and have never looked back. I wish I'd been so sophisticated. But there it is. We can't all be lucky, can we?' He looked belligerently from Kurt to Julie, but she took no notice of him.

Kurt smiled. 'No, no,' he replied soothingly, 'I tell you it was nothing to do with my father, nothing so spectacular. Just an old aunt, an aunt I was supposed to kiss.' Suddenly, his eyes narrowed and his voice became thin and venomous. 'She was repulsive. She had stale breath, a moustache and eyes like a lizard. But I used to kiss her anyway, because I was told it was the proper thing to do. Yet I know she no more liked me than I liked her. We had a compact, you see, a compact of hypocrisy. Everyone must seem to love everyone else. Then one day I realized that it was all lies, every single detail. I was five or six at the time. I felt I'd solved the mystery of the universe. All lies. But I kept it to myself, of course. Then, when I was in my teens, I found out about my father. And you know something? All I felt was relief. I'd been right all along. After that, I was free.'

'Then why carry on so, if you're free?' said Sam. It occurred to him that if he could once put him down and keep him down, Julie might come back to him. But he wasn't hopeful.

'I'm sorry,' said Kurt, and for a moment he seemed it. Then the shining obsessed look came back into his eyes. 'People are swine, you know. All of them. But they're worse when they've got a bit of money and pretend to be proper. Pigs in party clothes. The very rich aren't so bad, some of them. They don't have to pretend if they don't want to. They're above it, provided they're not too stupid. And the very poor. They don't have to pretend either because they've got no reason to pretend.'

'And you've joined them, I suppose? You're one of the truthful?'

Kurt leaned back in the leather armchair, his eyes veiled again. 'I try.'

'And you think I'm either dumb or hypocritical not to join too?'

'You're not dumb. You'll join in time.'

'I'm flattered. But what are the initiation rites?'

'There aren't any. It's an imperceptible process. Like nature.'

'Like nature,' Sam repeated ironically. 'And what about you, Julie? Have you joined?'

Kurt answered for her: 'Julie joined years ago. My father's friends initiated her.'

She sat perfectly still, as though unhearing, looking at the rain washing down the plate-glass windows. Her face was pure and indifferent. Sam knew for sure now that he had lost her.

Kurt's voice came again, but so quietly that it seemed part of the rain suddenly intensifying in a fresh gust of wind. 'In everyone is this core of darkness,' he said. 'If you can reach down into it, you are free.'

Sam noticed that his boots were steaming faintly in the heat of the room. Why should he be made a fool of? 'You aren't as free as you claim to be,' he said. 'If you were, you wouldn't be so obsessed with your father.'

Kurt smiled indolently. 'Maybe you're right. But I try.'

'I suppose you do,' said Sam. The rain and wind bullying the windows, the geriatric hush in the room, and the girl at his side whom he'd lost: everything was unreal and foreign, as alien as the language spoken by the landlord and the louts in his bar, or as the dense forest on the hill. He should never have come.

Kurt was leaning back in the deep armchair, his arms negligently outstretched. The sleeves of his shirt were partially rolled up. There were little blue marks on his forearms, like bee stings, like baby love bites.

So that's why he's here. Sam felt a great surge of triumph and release. He thought of the long-legged, enviable body slithering out of the pool. Just another walking wounded, after all. Who'd have believed it? As wrecked as the thin old hulks washed by the rain into the corners of this opulent room. It had all happened so long ago, yet the disasters went on and on. There ought to be a smell of blood in the air. Sam sniffed energetically and with relish: only the reek of his drying boots and the fainter scent of coffee from the neat row of percolators on the table by the door. He turned cheerfully to Julie: 'Where's auntie?'

She turned her face slowly and looked at him with curiosity, as if she had forgotten he existed. He wondered if Kurt had been giving her drugs, too. But the pale skin on her arms was unmarked.

'She comes in the afternoon.' A sleepwalker's voice.

'That rather puts the kybosh on the day, doesn't it?'

'Maybe she'll go home soon.' There was a tremor of interest in her voice, like a corpse reviving. 'We've had two hours every day for a week now. There's nothing left to say. And her silences aren't interesting. Not that we ever had anything much to say. But we don't mention that.'

'What do you talk about?' He was determined not to let her drift away again. Keep her talking. Maybe he should walk her up and down, slap her face and feed her coffee, like someone who has taken an overdose.

'The good old days, of course. When my father and her son were still alive. The good old days before that Nazi bastard of hers pointed the bones at us.'

'Poignant stuff.'

'Poignant enough.' There was a moment's silence. Then she added in a low, angry voice, full awake now, 'I wish she'd go away. I wish she'd go away and leave me alone.' She looked Sam full in the face. Her cheeks were hot with feeling. She meant him too, but Kurt's languid presence kept her quiet. He knew he should get up and leave, but couldn't bring himself to end it all so abruptly. Now he was sure he'd lost her, he loved her hopelessly again. Just like the old days. A whole month ago. She had seemed unattainable at the beginning and she was unattainable again now. She had always been unattainable. Those afternoons in his room were no more real than some story he'd read and half forgotten. Blonde calls to blonde. His father knew a thing or two, after all. He had never stood a chance. He was her experiment with infidelity. The experiment had worked and she had gone on to other things.

He got up and went over to the coffee table. While he was pouring, an attendant came in and said something to Kurt, bending low over him as though sharing a secret. Kurt shrugged and got up. He gave Sam an ironic half-wave across the room, shrugged again in mock helplessness and followed the attendant out.

Sam carried the cups of coffee back to Julie and they drank in silence. Finally he said, 'He's a patient, isn't he? That was all crap about working here?' Julie nodded. 'What about his father?' Sam went on. 'And the Gestapo, and all that stuff? Is that crap too?'

'Probably. I don't know,' Julie said wearily. 'And I don't think I want to know one way or another.'

'But you know he's a junky?'

She nodded again and said, 'How do you know?'

'I saw his arms. Doesn't it bother you?'

'Why should it?'

Sam swallowed. 'You seem keen on him.'

'I simply like him. He's someone to talk to. I'm not *keen* on him. Whatever you mean by that.'

'But you don't care if he takes heroin?'

'Don't be so melodramatic. I'm not Florence Nightingale. It's not my business.'

'It is, if you like him.'

'I don't like him that much.'

'Don't you? I see.' There was silence again. Sam looked at her beadily. 'They say dope ruins your sex life.'

'I wouldn't know.' She paused, then added venomously, 'You're beginning to sound just like Charles.'

'Maybe that's what you do to all your men.'

'You don't own me, you know.'

'Boy, do I know.'

They were silent again, as if each had realized at the same moment that they were quarrelling like an old married couple. The continual mutter of the rain expanded in the hushed room.

Julie stood up suddenly, her face tight with dislike. 'Come on,' she said abruptly.

'Where're we going?'

'My room.'

'I thought that was against the rules.'

'Let's break the rules for once, shall we?'

He followed her out truculently, trying to make his boots clump noisily on the obsequious, muffling rubber tiles. But the old heads, sunk behind newspapers or dozing open-mouthed to the ceiling, took no notice. No matter what he did in this place, no one took him seriously.

27

He followed her down the hushed corridor, thinking, Now you've done it, watching her thin, smooth shoulders. Beyond them the plate-glass door, and beyond that the wild, grieving weather. He pictured his father waiting in his shop among the racks of dresses for the rain to drive in customers, watching the river of cars, the buses with their steamed-up windows, dreaming about the Amazon, Tahiti, Bali, and his only son off with a *shiksah* somewhere in Bavaria. The father dreams dreams and the son lives out the gloomy reality. If only the old boy could see him now.

Julie opened the door to her room and waited while Sam walked in past her, then turned the key behind them. The noise of the rain was louder, more imperious. In the greyish light the flowers on her table seemed to be stretching their throats to the window in longing. He waited in the middle of the room, uncertain what to do, knowing what was coming, while she leaned against the locked door, her hands clasped behind her, her hair hanging forward over her face, looking down. The rain drummed on. Sam shivered, waiting. Finally, she looked up and flicked her hair impatiently out of her eyes. She said, 'It's over, you know.' Her voice was matter-of-fact, without emotion.

'I know.' He stood in his wet boots, arms dangling. Like a naughty schoolboy, she thought, who's been denied a treat. If I were nice, I'd let him make love to me once more. Then he might even think he'd won. He'd have had his last triumph over Charles. He'd have paid for his journey. But I'm not nice. Neither is he.

'For heaven's sake, sit down,' she said. 'You look ridiculous standing there like a scarecrow in those great big boots.'

He said, 'I'm sorry,' and sat down heavily on the bed. On the bed. So he was still hopeful, despite everything. She felt a flicker of something like admiration for his doggedness. She sat down facing him in the chair by the table. He stared at her stupidly, taking nothing in, then looked away beyond her, beyond the flowers, to the ceaseless, nagging rain. The back of his throat felt tight, the corners of his eyes prickled. When he spoke his voice sounded strained and unnatural in his effort to keep it controlled.

'What went wrong?'

'Nothing, really.'

'Is it something I did?'

She laughed quite kindly. 'Don't be so self-pitying, Sam. No, it's nothing you did or didn't do.'

'Then what?'

'It's the place, Sam, just the place.'

'I don't understand,' he said dully.

'Seeing you here has made me realize that this isn't what I want.' She spoke patiently, as though explaining something to a dim child.

'What do you want then?'

She didn't answer immediately and the sound of the rain took over again. When she finally spoke she seemed to be changing the subject. 'The first time I saw the clinic I was with my father. I was only a little girl. So high.' She raised her hand vaguely, palm down, and the vanished child stood for a moment between them. Her voice was low. 'It was a rotten time. There was never enough of anything. Food, things like that. And when I saw this place I thought, That's what life should be like: clean, cared for, expensive, and with a jewel at its heart, a private, blue swimming pool. I thought, When I'm older I'll come back here with him. I'll bring him here and look after him.' Sam watched her, the tightness growing unmanageably in his throat. She no longer seemed aware of him, talking to herself, explaining the obvious. 'But he's dead, so that's that. I'd forgotten the place existed until two or three weeks ago. Now I've come here on my own I see that that was all I ever really wanted: to be here with him and look after him. The rest was just things that happened to me, some good – like my children – some not so good. They aren't important.' Her voice tailed off again. A gust of wind billowed the muslin curtains at the window, filtering a spray of damp onto the table and faintly stirring the flowers. 'So I'll stay married to Charles, I suppose. It doesn't really matter one way or the other any more. If I'm married, at least I have my baybees. If it weren't for them, maybe I'd go off with you, Sam. I don't know. But you see, you don't matter much either. Not any more.'

'You didn't think so back in England.'

'But that was back in England. This place is different. It's made me see things differently. Maybe that's part of the cure.'

She smiled, but it was no use. Sam sat there lumpishly, tears oozing down his punctured face.

'There, there.' She wanted to stroke his shaggy head like a child's, or a pet dog's, but that would only start it up again. He'd want to make love to her. Better to keep her distance and have done. 'There, there,' she repeated soothingly.

He sniffed, gulped, sniffed, fumbled in his pocket for a handkerchief and blew his nose loudly. 'I'm sorry,' he managed. He fumbled again and brought out a cigarette, but the first lungful of smoke made him choke and the tears didn't stop. Again, he blew his nose like a sea lion. She had never realized how ridiculous someone else's grief could be.

'Look,' she said, 'I've got something that'll cheer you up.' She went over to the wardrobe and brought out a box of Tampax, while Sam watched her dully through weeping eyes. When she upended the box onto the table a plastic phial and some little cardboard tubes fell out with the wrapped cylinders. She took the vanity mirror from her handbag and wiped it on her dress, then opened the phial and carefully tapped two small mounds of white powder onto the mirror. She slid a cardboard tube into one nostril and sniffed up a mound of powder. Her nostrils were delicate and finely shaped. How beautiful she is, thought Sam. Pure, pure, with the pale gold hair falling forward.

'Isn't that coke?' he asked. She nodded faintly, then put the tube into her other nostril and sniffed again. She leaned back smiling.

'That's better. That's so much better. Now you have some. It'll make you feel good.'

He shook his head, his face dry at last, his heart grey in his chest, looking at her. 'Is that Kurt's initiation rite?' he said.

'It could be one of them. It depends on the person, I suppose.' Her voice was light and easy.

'Meaning it's not yours?'

'Yes. Meaning it's not mine. Don't you want it to be yours, Sam?'

He shook his head again, suddenly dog tired. 'I don't need it. I've got you. You're mine.'

'To each his own,' she said, smiling.

'Kurt's your lover, isn't he?'

'I tell you it doesn't matter who I sleep with. Or whom, as Charles would say. None of that matters.' She looked at him with bright eyes, her pupils tiny points of darkness in the clear blue. 'You don't understand much, do you?' When he didn't reply she said pleadingly, '*Please*, Sam, don't be so glum. It's not the end of the world.'

He got up slowly and went to the door. 'I'd better be going,' he said and turned the key.

She watched him from a tower of elation. Everything was vivid, anything was possible. He seemed small and dismal and far off. She felt very sorry for him. '*Please*, Sam.'

He turned at the open door. 'Bye, bye,' he said.

She heard him clump off down the passage, made a move after him, then remembered the phial on her table. She locked the door again, hurriedly repacked the box of Tampax and hid it carefully away in the wardrobe. Then she ran to the end of the corridor and pressed her face against the cold glass door. She could see him, small and hunched against the rain, labouring up towards the forest. Her breath blurred the glass as the rain beat down a quarter of an inch from her face. She went back to her room, put on heavy shoes and a coat, and hurried out after him, walking on air despite the rain and the mud and the chill wind.

At the edge of the forest she saw a hawk humped with bedraggled feathers in a tree. She stopped and stared up at it. Its eyelids flicked open and it stared back, pupil-less eye to pupil-less eye, gold to blue. What had Sam said? Eyes as big as a fist proportionately. She smiled up at it, thinking, I'm as free as you are, friend. I have a husband, children, lovers and a dead father. But

I'm still free. The bird stirred uneasily from one leg to the other, preparing to take off. She hurried on.

A heavy mist of rain swayed between the trees, shushing patiently and monotonously on the forest floor like a creature breathing. At least this was still the same and would stay so, despite the trippers with their Leicas and picnics, and the lovers with one idea in their heads. The same, always the same, right back to the weird little men in skins and paint, paying homage to the oak trees and quivering with superstitious terror. Dense, unforgiving, unchanging. When she was a child it had lain sombrely on the boundary of her world and scared her. Now she felt easy in it, at peace with its darkness. This is what it meant to have come home. She walked quickly, humming to herself, 'Isn't this a lovely day to be caught in the rain.'

The thick, rich air in the hotel bar made her nose tingle with pleasure. It was as if she could smell each ingredient separately : beer, Zwetschgenwasser, sauerkraut, onions, the smoky kasseler and roasting meats, the steam off the soups mingling with the drying clothes and boots. She breathed deeply, inhaling the peasant world of her childhood, redolent and comforting. Then the resiny staircase.

When she opened the door of Sam's room a draught of cold air stopped her at the threshold. He was sitting in front of the open window, a blanket round his shoulders, a little pool of water at his feet. The room was black with the rain and full of its noise.

'For heaven's sake.' Her voice was friendly but exasperated. He seemed to her to be becoming more and more like a child, to be treated childishly.

'I'm cold.' He huddled on the window seat, clutching the blanket tightly round him. He looked like an old woman, crouching under the open square of rain. 'I'm cold,' he repeated.

She closed the door, took off her coat and walked over to him. 'God, you're stupid,' she said good-humouredly. 'Why don't you close the window?'

'What's the use? You can't keep this out.' He jerked his head woodenly at the rain.

Like a marionette, she thought. Hardly human any more. She

looked out at the darkened street. The rain seemed to soak up all movement and light. It was as if the whole landscape had been emptied out, leaving only the dim, swaying veils of water. She closed the window.

'You like it,' she said. 'That's the trouble with you. You enjoy feeling miserable. If you really had your way, you'd go outside and wallow in it, then lie down with pneumonia and weep yourself to death. Bloody fool.'

He shrugged. 'The hell to you, Mrs Stone.'

She smiled down at him from the impregnable height of her elation. 'The hell to you, too.' She bent and kissed him on the mouth. He pulled her down to the window seat with him and clung to her desperately. 'Why did you come?' he whispered.

A great spurt of mirth began to bubble up inside her at the sight of his passionate, sorrowful face. She kissed him back to stop herself laughing. He smelled of sweat under his damp, bushy jersey. 'To say good-bye properly,' she said. She kissed his neck, his ear, his forehead, but the laughter would not be suppressed. Through clenched teeth, it fizzed in her mouth like soda water. Her thin body quivered: knees, hair, delicate rib-cage and shoulders.

He pushed her away furiously. 'What's the matter with you? What's so fucking funny?'

'I'm sorry,' she gasped, 'it's all so stupid.' And she buried her face again in his neck.

He held her stiffly at arm's length. He looked outraged. 'I'm glad you think so.'

She shook her head and pushed against him again, lying in his arms, shaking helplessly. 'Oh, come on, Sam, come on.' And gradually the laughter took him, too. Slowly, drily at first, despite his offended dignity, then whirling up like a duststorm, taking everything with it: the facts and footnotes and learned articles, the bland faces of the young academics he'd envied and the older ones he'd toadied to, Charles's blind, porpoise snout, his worrying, indulgent parents, the food, the cars, the cost of things, his lost career and careerless future, Elsie and her Guinness, the pig-eyed landlord downstairs, the French girl, the seminars, the Collected Works of William Shakespeare, the tears, the tangled sheets, Julie's torn panties, her addict lover and his drugs, the clinic with its mineral water and oranges and geriatric hush. Everything was sucked upwards in a great, roaring spout of laughter. They held on to one another, laughing and crying like reprieved prisoners.

'Look at us.'

'Our grand passion.'

'A new Frieda and Lawrence.'

'A Jewish Lawrence,' he spluttered, 'don't forget that. It's very important.'

'Oh, Sam, Sam darling.' Tears streamed down her cheeks. The muscles of her face ached.

'Our grand passion,' he repeated. 'And what do we get? Old Nazis, young junkies and this unspeakable, fucking rain.' They clung together helplessly while the laughter stormed on. Then gradually, very gradually, it receded.

'But I love you,' he said more calmly, 'I really do.'

'Me too,' she said, 'in a way. But what's the use?' Another ripple of laughter went through her like a last, distant roll of thunder. She stood up briskly. 'Come on,' she said and began to take off her clothes.

They undressed separately in a businesslike way, then stood naked looking at each other in the wooden, rain-darkened room. Julie got onto the bed and Sam stood for a moment looking down at her: the blonde head, parted lips, slender breasts and thighs. She seemed as pale and unsubstantial as a visitant. What had she to do with him? He shivered, suddenly cold and mirthless.

'A goose walking over my grave,' he said.

She looked up at him with her centreless, blue eyes. 'You said that once before, ages ago. Don't worry, darling. It's not the end of the world.'

He smiled and shrugged, spreading his hands in a helpless gesture he'd learned from his father. 'I'd better make the most of this, just in case it is.'

When he climbed onto the bed beside her and took her in his arms she turned to him hungrily, as though this were their first time instead of their last. They made love like cannibals, biting, licking, burrowing, lost. When they had exhausted themselves he cried a little, because he'd lost her, he said. She stroked his armoured forehead and kissed his eyes soothingly, feeling lighthearted, until finally he turned away and slept. She lay for a while listening to his breathing and to the rain and to her own heart beating pleasurably in its cage. Her world was still invaded by a clear light. She was herself, husbandless, loverless, fatherless. Me, said her heart. Me, me, me.

He didn't stir when she got up and dressed. She glanced back at him from the door. His back was thickly muscled, he had heavy arms : a survivor. He'd get over it. She felt only a great relief. 'Thank God that's over,' she whispered. Quietly she closed the door, quietly went down the creaking stairs, through the now empty bar, out into the drumming rain. Then she walked quickly up the hill towards the forest, hurrying to get back to the clinic before her aunt arrived. She felt alert, relaxed, hungry. He'd get over it. She wished she hadn't missed her lunch.

28

For no obvious reason, the town looked beautiful. Nothing that Charles could put his finger on. The florid Victorian buildings at the centre, with their carved stone and red brick, were being crowded out by featureless, dingy boxes of glass and plastic. The standardized shop fronts – Marks & Spencer, Woolworth, Sainsbury, Burton, Tesco, John Collier – displayed their standardized wares to the ghostly Sunday streets. Then a wasteland of semi-detacheds, corner pubs, grocers' shops and shut garages, stretching out towards the country. No grace, thought Charles, no grace at all. But prosperous, comfortable, placid. He was glad to be back.

It had rained earlier and the streets looked pale and washed, still faintly steaming in the sun. A jet trail ran high up in the sky, cotton white on blue, its tail ragged where the wind pulled at it. Who would have thought Derby could be beautiful, or that beauty wasn't always a matter of style and proportion? A place that was at peace with itself could have it. Or a person.

> Nor spring, nor summer beauty hath such grace,
> As I have seen in one autumnal face.

Tell that to Julie. He saw her preternaturally smooth face as clearly as if she were standing in front of him. Her eyes regarded him calmly, like those of a Duccio Madonna. What had she to do with his home town?

'Daddy,' his son tugged his arm, 'where are we going now?'

He had always thought the children looked like him. Now he saw her image duplicated in them. Like her, they seemed absurdly out of place in this gritty town, with their blond hair, swinging clothes and upper-class accents. I have come a long way, he thought, not necessarily in the right direction.

'This is what's called a pilgrimage,' he boomed, realizing with distaste that, no matter what he felt, his voice always sounded as if he was speaking from a podium. The children stared at him uncomprehending. 'That's when you make a special journey to a holy place.'

'What's holy about this town?' his son asked.

'I was born here, of course.' He laughed and the children smiled anxiously in response.

'Let's go and find the house, shall we?'

They climbed back into the car and drove off down the deserted high street, turned left, then right down a row of terraced houses, then left again. He could have driven it with his eyes closed. Right at the 'Keys and Compass', then ... The street had gone, the neighbourhood gone. Where there had once been long terraces of red and purple brick, two up, two down, the lavatories at the end of each tiny garden backing onto the lavatories and gardens of identical terraces like teeth in a clenched jaw, there was now a sea of different, larger boxes, sand-coloured brick and gunmetal roofs, arranged in squares and crescents. Red earth where there would eventually be grass, bordered the new roads.

Charles stopped the car and sat for a moment staring bleakly through the windscreen. 'My God, they don't leave much.'

'Who don't?' asked his son.

'The planners, the developers, the people who put up new houses. They've bulldozed the old place flat.'

'Oh,' said his son, politely but without interest. And his sister echoed, 'Oh.'

'I remember, I remember,' Charles began and the boy chimed in with him, 'The house where I was born.'

'It's just as well I do,' said Charles, 'because nobody else will.'

'It's not much of a pilgrimage,' said his son.

'At least you've learned a new word.' Charles leaned on the steering wheel, brooding. 'Come on,' he said at last, 'my father – your grandpa, but he died before you were born – used to have an allotment, a place where he grew vegetables. Let's go and see if it's still there.'

He drove on tentatively through the new streets in the direction he thought the railway line should be. It wasn't easy. Promising turnings curved back on themselves or became dead ends. He reversed, began again, turned, began again. Men in shirt sleeves polishing their cars paused to watch him curiously. He might have been a visitor from another planet, or the police. Finally, the road dipped and went under the railway line. He recognized the bridge and the sharp right turn that followed it. Maybe, he thought as the car rolled into shadow. But when he came round the corner into the windy sunlight the allotments, too, were gone. In their place was a neat municipal playing field : a football pitch enclosed by a cinder running track, a little pavilion of yellow brick, then a children's playground with swings, climbing frame, a slide and a paddling pool. A single, melancholy chord twanged in his heavy body. 'Oh well,' he said. It was like the Russian version of history : knock it all flat and begin again, as though the past had never been. 'It wasn't like this at all,' he explained apologetically. 'It was shabbier but nicer.'

The children were not impressed. 'Can we have a go on the swings?' asked his son, and his daughter chimed in, 'Please, please.'

Why not? thought Charles. It's probably all they'll remember of the day. So he sat on a bench in the mild and pleasant air, watching his children play. Better not visit the cemetery, he decided, in case they've bulldozed that, too. It was always better not to know. Like with Julie and Sam. Like Julie in Germany. You can keep going if you're not sure. It's certainty that kills. His parents were dead and buried. He'd seen their tombstones. Let them rest.

They drove back to the centre, to the big Gothic hotel with arched halls and red patterned carpets. At least that hadn't changed. They ate lunch in a tall dining-room among the flushed, opulent faces of those who'd stuck it out and won. Charles wondered how many of them he had known and feared in the asphalt schoolyard all those years ago. But he recognized no one. The tablecloth was stiff as wood, the cutlery shone.

Sipping his coffee, he watched his children as they dug into their dessert, napkins tucked under their chins like breastplates of bone. Both were rosy from the food and their half hour in the playground, both had risen to the occasion, awed by the solemn room and deferential waiters, and were eating beautifully and without mess. They had got over their mother's departure.

The girl spilt ice-cream on the tablecloth and her brother scooped it up for her, then smiled conspiratorially at his father and tried to wink. But he wasn't up to it yet. One side of his face stiffened as though paralysed and both eyes closed. Charles winked back. 'That's right,' he said, 'eat up nicely.' His daughter glowed at him across the table, enjoying her moment, the only woman around. Somehow she made him uneasy. Her eyes were bright, yet there was a kind of flatness around them, as though she had seen too much already. He felt his heart contract with foreboding and thought, What's wrong with me? Then she attacked her ice-cream again vigorously. The moment had passed.

He brought out his diary and began flipping idly through the pages trying to remember. In the notes at the back, among references to learned journals in his own microscopic hand, with its Greek *d*s and *e*s, he found Arthur Clegg's address, written in large, painful capitals, taking up a whole page. The head porter gave him directions, held open the Jaguar's door for him and was dourly grateful for a disproportionate tip.

They drove back to the housing estate under which Charles's childhood lay buried. One of the car cleaners, polishing lazily to work down his lunch, pointed out the turning. The gleaming Austin outside showed how Clegg had spent his morning. Charles parked beside it and shepherded the children through the front garden. There were rosebushes, dahlias and a little patch of neat, thin grass. The path had been recently swept.

The woman who opened the door had dark hair, dark eyes and soft skin. Not quite English, not quite young either, but still pretty in a heavy, vaguely hairy way. Her body was full and easy, and she had big hips, as though ripened by much comfortable lovemaking.

'I'm sorry to disturb you,' Charles tried not to boom, 'but I was wondering if Mr Clegg's at home.'

She looked at him suspiciously. 'Arthur's out back, doing a bit of gardening. Come on in. I'll get him.' Under the midlands accent was a trace of something more exotic: a faint roll of *r*s, a fainter, sing-song rhythm.

They followed her into the living-room. Mrs Clegg had a taste for vivid greens, yellows and orange. It was like a greengrocer's shop redone in plastic leather and synthetic velvet: cushions like outsize cabbages and marrows, giant pumpkins and oranges round every light bulb, bunches of straw vegetables on the walls. At the middle of it Mrs Clegg herself, plump, scented and succulent, like a custard apple, an improbable, houseproud touch of the tropics.

They had sex last night, Charles thought and realized, with surprise, that he was envious. There was a time when he never noticed such things. Preferred not to. Misery is a great educator.

'Make yourself comfy,' she said, 'I'll call Arthur.' She turned to go, then paused and said to the children, 'My name's Clara. I wonder what yours is? Anyway, come on out with me. My kids are in the garden. We've got a swing and a sandbox.' They followed her out without hesitation.

He heard voices outside, heavy steps, the sound of a tap running in the kitchen. Then Clegg came in, wiping his hands on his old flannel trousers. His bright red shirt was open, the hair on his chest grizzled like the hair on his head. With his big belly and shoulders, he looked like an ageing bear, shambling and friendly.

'How about that then,' he sounded pleased. 'It's the professor.'

'I wasn't sure you'd remember me.'

'Oh aye. I remember you all right. That were quite an evening.'

'It was indeed.'

'Did you go to the police? I never heard nowt more.'

'What's the point? I didn't have anything to tell them. Not even the numbers of the bikes.'

'That's true and all. They'd have made you feel a fool.'

'My wife didn't see it that way.'

'They never do.'

They smiled knowingly at each other. Charles could hear the children calling excitedly in the garden. For the first time in weeks, he felt at ease.

'Sit yourself down.' Clegg went across to the window and called, 'Clara, put the kettle on, love.' Then he turned to Charles. 'You'll have a cup of tea, won't you?'

'Love one.' Charles settled himself on the green leatherette sofa. He was more tired than he should have been. The pills had made even the simplest routine of living exhausting.

'I'm sorry to burst in on you like this, on a Sunday,' he said.

Clegg waved his apology away. 'Just doing a bit of gardening. Glad to stop. What brings you up this way?'

'Just taking the children out for the day. I thought I'd show them where I was born. At least, that was my ecxuse. Really, I wanted to have a look at the place. I haven't been back for years.'

'Changed a bit, hasn't it?'

'Indeed it has.'

'Well, it's better than it were, believe me. Better than the old back-to-backs.'

'I was born in one of them.'

'Were you now?' said Clegg cautiously. 'So were I.'

'Somewhere round here, in fact. Or rather, under here.'

'Comfier now, isn't it?' He watched Charles defensively, ready to take offence.

'Much, much. You've got a very nice place.' He remembered his parents' dingy, overstuffed house and thought, Well, that's true, anyway.

Clegg brightened. 'That's the missus' doing. She chose it all.'

'She's not English, is she?'

'Italian. She came over to work in a caff for her cousin. Up in Newcastle. You'd be surprised at the number of Eyeties there are in Newcastle. And in Glasgow.'

'I didn't know that.'

'Hundreds of them. All jabbering away and making fortunes. Clever lot of sods. Work like beavers. You've got to admire them.'

'Oh, I do,' said Charles hastily. 'Not like the lazy English.'

'That's right. Not like the English. You've got to hand it to them.'

There was a silence, then Charles said, 'My wife's not English either.' As if this were a bond between them. 'She's German. I met her when I was teaching there.'

'Well, you know what I mean, then.' Clegg looked at him, then looked at the floor. Finally, he said, 'It must be this town.' He paused and studied the floor again. 'Somehow I never fancied marrying a local girl.'

'Perhaps that's because one knows them too well already.'

Clegg ran his tongue over his lips and grinned: 'You're reet enough there.'

Oh, thought Charles, I know you. Off with your girls every day after school. Out in the woods or the back row of the cinema. Kissing, groping, exploring the impossible secrets. Having it off. Yes, that's right. Having it off. While I ground dutifully away at my homework and fingered myself alone in bed. Well, we're all the same in the end, more or less. Or did Clegg know more when it mattered? Enough, anyway, not to have made a fool of himself when he chose a wife. Practice makes perfect, they say. He said, 'I suppose everyone wants a bit of strangeness. You don't want to marry someone you know inside out already.'

'Fat chance of that, professor. Women are always strange, wherever they come from.'

'But some are stranger than others.'

'There's no one will argue about that.'

They both laughed, relaxed, members of the club. Husbands Anonymous. Misery makes strange bedfellows, thought Charles, I'm talking to this man as if I'd known him for years. Which is more than I do with my colleagues. That's something I owe the leather-boys, at least. He heard Mrs Clegg moving about in the kitchen and the sounds of the children's voices from the garden. The room with its hideous plastic furniture, its plaster ducks and bunches of straw vegetables on the walls, and its greenish, submarine light, seemed perfectly at rest. Click. *At the still point of the turning world.* Click. *Anihilating all that's made To a green thought in a green shade.* Click. Silence. He leaned back and closed his eyes for a moment, enjoying the stillness.

'Bit tired, are you?' Clegg said at last. His voice was sympathetic, not inquisitive.

'I'm sorry.' Charles sat forward again. 'I haven't been well.'

'No need to apologize.'

Mrs Clegg came in, carrying a tea tray.

'I were telling the professor about those wop relations of yours.'

She pursed her lips and began pouring tea, as if she hadn't heard. Used to it. Impervious.

'Don't you miss Italy?' Charles asked.

Mrs Clegg shrugged her plump shoulders dismissively. 'It's too poor. I like my comfort.' She spread her hand vaguely to take in the room, the knick-knacks, the grey-faced television.

'I can see that. It's a very nice place you've got.' He heard his own voice. He wasn't being patronizing. He wasn't booming. Miracles never cease.

They drank tea and talked about nothing in particular : Italy – beautiful motorways, pity it was so poor – children, old slums and new estates. I could have been like this, Charles was thinking, if it hadn't been for a trick of memory and the rat constantly gnawing away : achieve, achieve. Much good it's done me. He thought of his books, his paintings, his wines, the years he had spent pronouncing on culture, marshalling facts, correcting errors, putting dead, oblivious authors in their place. He should never have left.

'What a good cup of tea,' he said.

'Aye, she makes a grand cuppa,' said Clegg, then added, 'for an Eyetie.' He grinned truculently at his wife and she grinned back, then rolled her eyes to the ceiling in mock resignation. How strange, thought Charles, they don't take offence. How strange.

'What's happened to the school?' he asked.

'You'd not recognize it. It were torn down, of course, along of everything else. Now it's all glass and recreation rooms. TV sets in every class. Like a sodding holiday camp. Our kids go but they don't learn nowt. Just paint muddy pictures with their fingers. And they call that education. Beats me.'

'Mr Rotherham must be turning in his grave.'

'Poor old bugger. What a life. The same thing year after year, and nobody listening. Then the kids go off to work in the factories, or lay bricks, or drive lorries like me, and by the time they're twenty they're earning double what he ever did. Poor old sod. He must have liked you, though.'

'It was mutual. He changed my life. That's all you ever need, one good teacher to get you going.'

'It would have taken more than one teacher to get me to a university. It would have taken a bloody bomb. Or a brain transplant.'

'Maybe you didn't miss so much, after all. We're all the same in the end, aren't we?' Middle-aged, sagging, trying to make the best of what's left, hoping for nothing. 'You don't look as if you've done too badly.'

'D'you hear me complaining?'

'Well, that's a change, I must say,' his wife said, unsmiling.

There was a sudden clamour of voices from the garden. Charles got up. 'I think war's broken out.'

Mrs Clegg waved him back to his chair. 'You sit. I'll see to it.' She went out quickly and they heard her soothing voice with its tangled accent: 'Now, now, what's all the fuss about?' Then the door into the garden closed.

Charles settled himself back on the sofa. 'I saw those thugs again, you know. Just once.'

'Did you now? Did they see you?'

'Oh yes. They were at a pub just outside town. I was there with my wife. They must have lain in wait for us because when we were driving home they came belting past, just like the first time. But they just waved and shouted and disappeared. I was scared stiff.'

'Stands to reason.'

'But again I didn't even have the sense to get their numbers.'

'It doesn't matter, does it? There's nowt to be done. The pity is, they got away so quick the first time.'

'Speak for yourself.'

Clegg sat forward in his chair, clasping his large hands together tightly. 'I'd have liked to teach them something. Something they'd remember before it's too late. That's all they understand, a fist and a fucking tyre lever.'

'You really believe that?' Charles asked, wondering, Do I? Do I?

'What else is there to believe? Mebbe they're not all like that. And mebbe the ones that are will change when they've got a wife and kids like the rest of us. Mebbe. But meanwhile they don't give a fuck for us or for anything, and don't you forget it. Don't give an inch, that's my motto, or they'll have your balls off.'

'Not an inch?'

'Not one. That's my motto.'

'It's a hard rule.'

'It's the only one that works.'

Charles looked at him gloomily. The blunt, slightly bruised

face, the blue eyes lit with conviction. Him too, he thought. Christ, what a stinking business. Reading books or driving a lorry. It's all one. Clock in, do your stint, keep at it. And at the end of it a pay packet or a grudging article. What's the difference? Just keep at it, because that's all there is. The one true end, the only satisfaction. Just slogging away. Another day done for. Then another. Till there aren't any left. *Let us love one another and work.* Who said that? He hesitated a moment, ransacking the files in his head. Freud. Letter to Martha Bernays. 1884. Had it all taped, didn't he? *Let us love one another and work.* Like poor old Mr Rotherham. What else is there? He wished he knew. Or wished he were like Clegg and didn't want to know: one hand over his balls, the other holding a tyre lever. But with an affectionate wife.

He got up and walked to the window. The children were playing peacefully again. Two blonde heads, two dark. Mrs Clegg sat in a deck-chair watching them sleepily. A veil of thin, high cloud had spread across the sky, filtering the sun.

'You'd think there'd be better advice to offer them,' he said, 'something a bit more cheerful.'

'You tell me what it is. You've got all the book learning.'

'I'm beginning to think that books don't help much. I wish they did.'

'There's not much that does help, when you come down to it,' said Clegg, though he didn't sound worried.

'There should be. After all these years, there should be.'

'That's as may be,' said Clegg.

A wind got up, shaking the line of washing at the end of the garden. Charles's son sat in the swing, the other boy pushing him. To and fro, to and fro.

'It would be nice to be young again,' said Charles.

'Aye, it would be nice to have a million quid. But it won't happen.'

'No, it won't happen.' And Julie won't leave me, he thought. And I won't divorce her. She'll come back smelling of other men, thinking of other places, other beds, and take up where she left off: dutiful mother, the professor's wife. Maybe she'd go off again after a while. Or maybe he'd send her off when he saw the trapped look in her eyes and sensed another storm brewing. After all, what are four or five hundred pounds compared with this peace, this freedom, this indifference? Cheap at the price. But she'll always come back, shopsoiled and unrepentant, with her exquisite, pure face. No easy solutions for Professor Charles Stone, M.A., D. Phil., D.Litt., F.R.S.L. He was saddled with her for good. Funny that. It should have been a triumph. So why did he feel grey to the very stomach? For good, for good. His parents were gone, Mr Rotherham gone, his childhood bulldozed flat, as if it had never existed. His only link with the world he had lost was this burly stranger, placidly filling his pipe, and more sure of himself than Charles had ever been with a whole army of books at his command. Why had he ever bothered?

'Time I got going,' he said. 'It'll be after the children's bedtime before I get back.'

'I'm glad you came,' said Clegg.

'I'm glad, too. I wanted to thank you properly for what you did that night.'

'Believe me, you don't have to thank me for that. It were a real pleasure.' Clegg grinned. 'Any time.'

'I believe you' said Charles.

Driving out through the suburbs, westwards towards the sun and the sedate university town, they passed under the railway bridge again. A tall, middle-aged man, in shorts and running vest, was jogging absorbedly round the cinder track. Grey haired, on spidery legs, cheeks going in and out, in and out, eyes fixed on nothing. Father, thought Charles, if only you could see your beloved allotment now. It's a new world, though not a better one. Your grandchildren wear blazing clothes imported from France, eat at posh hotels and speak with an accent you would have thought ridiculous, but which they and everyone else think of as no accent at all. Not like your accent, or Arthur Clegg's. Not like mine was once before I got on in the world. If that's what you call getting on. I have got on in the world. I am part of the establishment. *The Times* has my obituary on file, probably a whole column of it.

They were in the country now. He drove slowly to the sound of the car radio, the children already half asleep in the back. The light was deepening and the trees cast long shadows. Tonight he would get drunk, but only in moderation. No more theatricals. He felt as if he had been drowning for years in his own fat, in his own fatty life. That was why he had taken the pills: to thrust himself unforgettably down everyone's throat, like a lump of gristle. It was time to have done with such childishness, time to divest himself of himself. *Let us love one another and work.* And if love were not forthcoming, then simply get on with things. Things, not self. He muttered to himself, under the sound of the radio: 'Now you know, professor. Now you've proved what you knew all along. They're dead and gone. Parents, teachers, even the place. You must stand on your own two feet at last.'

29

The rock dropped sheer away beneath him, biscuit yellow in the afternoon sun. Sam pulled round onto the final wall and paused a moment, hands on comfortable holds, to squint between his straddled legs. Between him and the scree a thousand feet below there was only air, cooler now after the midday blaze. He could see a grey ribbon of unsurfaced road, the hut with its tarred roof, a cluster of cars in front of it and tiny pin men dragging their shadows after them.

He called up, 'Christ, what a position,' and heard Jim's laconic 'Aye.' The rope tightened at his waist. 'Don't stand there all day,' came the voice. He climbed on up the last thirty feet, slowly, making it last, paused at the top to look down again, then pulled over onto the flat summit platform.

'Marvellous,' he said.

Jim sat among the coils of rope, his back against a boulder. 'It makes you realize how much free space there is in the world,' he said.

Sam eased off his rucksack, untied the rope from his waist and sat down. He fumbled in the sack and pulled out a plastic water bottle and a lump of rubbery cheese. They drank deeply and chewed in silence. The mountains stretched out in front of them, yellow into blue, seemingly to the end of everything.

'What a climb,' Sam said at last. 'What a beautiful climb.' He lit a cigarette and handed one to Jim. The smoke rose slowly in the motionless air.

The other man said: 'That's what I call happiness: a V.S. to heaven. Not too hard, not too easy, and on warm rock.'

They sat with their backs to the boulder, shirts off, sunning themselves. They heard a car engine start up below and the sound of a cowbell so close that the animal might have been coming across the rocks towards them.

'Weird what the mountains do to sounds,' said Jim.

A swift hung for a moment level with them, then swooped away, downwards towards the hut, paused in midflight, flicked, swooped up again. Effortless. Free.

'Weird what they do to people, too,' Sam replied. 'I feel like I've just been let out of school.'

'So you have, haven't you?'

'In one way or another.'

Perfectly free. His suitcase deposited at the station, and with it his fancy clothes, his notebooks, Julie. All stacked on a metal shelf until he wanted them again. There was no hurry. He took another long drink from the water bottle. Jim looked at his watch.

'Two and a half hours from bottom to top. That's not bad.'

'I'm fitter than I thought I'd be by now.' Only three days before his fingers were swollen like ripe bananas after two hours' climbing and his wrists were numb. The muscles of his upper arms and legs twitched of their own accord. There were blisters on his heels and a leper's scale inside his mouth. Now he simply felt tired.

'Aye,' said the other man, 'you've even got a little colour in your face.'

'If you can call it colour.'

'If you can call it a face.'

The air was dusted with gold, the shadows were beginning to thicken.

'I suppose we should be getting down,' Jim said reluctantly.

'What's the rush? This is the best part of the climb. Why spoil it? Let's have one more smoke.'

Another swift dipped towards them out of the void, hesitated in mid-swoop, then flicked away. The cracks and chimneys of the peaks nearest them were shadowed with blue now, like the eyes of a mannequin. Beyond them, the blue merged into violet, became hazy. So this it what it is to be happy, thought Sam. It has nothing to do with love. How could I ever have dreamed it had? He tried to remember Julie's pale body and inviolable face, but the picture wouldn't come. Already she was as remote as the horizon. It was less than a week. Gone, gone.

Jim stood up and began to coil one of the ropes. 'Time to go.'
Sam got to his feet slowly and picked up the other rope. As he
looped it steadily into his hands, he began to sing:

O-oh freedom, o-oh freedom, oh freedom, glory be.
  Before I'll be a slave
  I'll be buried in my grave.
Coming home to my Lord to be free.

Gone, gone. Like his broken heart. And so soon.

They collected their gear, shouldered the ropes and sack and
walked slowly in the golden air along the track to the point where
they could begin to rope off the mountain, back to the hut and the
first beer. Gone.

He sang on quietly: *O-oh freedom . . .*

30

The rain had ceased and the clouds had rolled away like a dirty curtain. The whole place was flooded with sunlight. The old people stretched round the sparkling pool gratefully soaking up the heat. Julie lay a little apart from them, peacefully, peacefully. The usual couple swam sedately up and down, so slowly they hardly disturbed the turquoise sheen. Up and down, up and down.

Her body had come to a stop and was gathering in to itself. Nine weeks now. So at least it wasn't Kurt's baby. Charles's? Sam's? Odd that she would never know. Dr Klaus had examined her carefully with square, scrubbed fingers. There would be no problems. The operation would take only a few minutes. In a couple of hours she would be up again. He could foresee no complications. His voice was as neutral as his hands, like a man arranging a loan. He could foresee no complications, excising the past and the future. It would take only a few minutes and in a couple of hours she would be up again. But the core of darkness at her centre would remain, the black jewel for which she had waited so long. All this brightness, the sunlight dazzling off the water and the white walls of the buildings, the emeralds and agates of the brooding forest edging the skyline, all of it was a refraction from the core of blackness in her heart. Wanting nothing more of life than this black peace: no more babies, no more husband, no more lovers. Of course she would go back to Charles. Of course there would be other men. But none of that mattered. She was untouchable now, as shut off as a nun in the austerest convent. There would be no more violations. All the wounds had closed at last into this black knot of certainty.

She stood up. A jet was travelling far overhead, unravelling its white thread behind it. Soon she, too, would be off. She dived into the pool and began to swim lazily. The water was cool after the rain and as clear as the first morning of creation. Lucid. She swam two lengths, then rolled onto her back and floated quietly, her eyes half closed against the brightness, watching the jet trail spread into white fur against the blue. She had forgotten how vivid the world was, how coloured, restored after the rain, after the long years in pallid England. Pallid and chill, like the people, who eat you alive and then spit out the pieces disdainfully. Never again.

When she saw the white-coated attendant out of the corner of her eye she swam obediently to the ladder and climbed out. Cool and fresh like the first morning.

'The doctor is ready for you, Frau Stone.'

She towelled herself vigorously. She felt restored, alert. Once upon a time the doctor's colleagues had murdered her father. But that was all past, long past. Now the doctor himself was going to free her from the past. Once and for all. A simple operation. By tomorrow she would have forgotten all about it. She tied the belt of her white towelling coat – the clinic's name in white, white on white, over her left breast where her heart beat pleasurably – threw her damp towel over her shoulder and followed the attendant through the plate-glass door. She was surprised not to be afraid.

The doctor was right, after all. She felt nothing, neither under the blinding lights, hearing the clink of instruments, nor later lying eliminated between white sheets: white face, pale hair, her eyes a sliver of blue. There were fresh roses in the vase by the window, thick red, as though weighed down by their own rich colour. Their scent filled the room.

The doctor tapped discreetly on the door. Two nurses followed him into the room. All three wore stiff white coats, so heavily starched that they stuck out a little from their bodies. They looked like angels on a Christmas tree. My ministering angels, she thought.

The nurses pulled back the sheet gently and removed the pads. The doctor bent to examine her. A small, dark man with a ramrod back, bending forwards from the hips. His expression was attentive but neutral.

'So.' He straightened up and stood at attention over her, while a nurse changed the pads. 'It is most satisfactory. There has been only moderate bleeding. Tomorrow you may get up, if you wish.'

'I'm sure I will wish.' She smiled at him. 'And there will be no trouble travelling on Saturday?'

'My dear lady, by Saturday you will have forgotten it ever happened.'

'I believe you, doctor,' she said truthfully.

One of the nurses tucked in the sheets and smoothed the counterpane. They all turned to go.

'Doctor,' said Julie, 'I want to thank you for what you've done. I want to thank you and all your colleagues.' Past and present. Thank them all.

'It was very simple, *gnädige Frau*. There were no problems at all.' He bowed slightly, bringing his heels together with the ghost of a click and smiling his professional smile.

'For you, maybe. Not for me.'

'When you have slept you too will think it simple, I am certain.'

'I'm grateful, anyway.'

He bowed again and went out discreetly.

She lay inhaling the scent of the roses, watching the light fade in the window. The past and its fevers were over, the ghosts departed. There was nothing left to fear. Her father had been laid to rest at last.

The nurse who collected her supper tray brought her a sleeping pill. But she didn't take it immediately. She lay for a while, her head empty, until the corridor outside was silent. Then she got up quietly, took the phial of cocaine from its hiding place in the wardrobe and flushed what was left of the white powder down the lavatory. She filled the handbasin with water and washed the phial carefully, then damped her eyes and forehead. She went back into the bedroom and dropped the little plastic cylinder into the wastepaper basket under the table on which the roses stood indolently. It was time for a new start. Her sleep was dreamless and profound.

She was packing her suitcase when Kurt wandered in. He didn't knock. He simply drifted in as though he belonged and flopped into the chair by the table. The curve of his arm and hand over the arm of the chair, the slight arch of his foot: graceful by instinct. If I were a painter, she thought, I'd be in love with him.

'You've been avoiding me,' he said.

'I've not been well. But I'm better now.' Is that what this indifference is: better? She carried an armload of dresses from the wardrobe to the bed and began to fold them into her suitcase, the bright colours slipping through her fingers like coloured liquids. He wondered why she always wore dull clothes. Maybe she was ashamed of looking so young.

She saw his puzzled expression and laughed: 'Now you know my guilty secret. I buy them, then I never wear them.'

'Why on earth not?'

'They look fine in the shop, but once I get them home they feel too . . . too festive.'

'And home is never festive?'

'What do you think?'

'You neither?'

She shrugged and went on packing, golds and reds and greens and blues slithering into the suitcase.

Without looking at him, she said, 'Is it true about your father?' Her voice was light, faintly teasing.

'What makes you think it isn't?'

'What makes you take drugs?'

'You don't think it's because of my father and his history?'

'That's a bit neat, isn't it? A bit easy? You might have invented it all to give yourself an excuse.'

'Of course I might. But by this time how would I ever know?'

She went back to the wardrobe, passing close to him. When she returned he stretched out his hand and stroked her thigh. She did not pause.

'And what about your father?' he said, 'Is he your excuse?'

'Probably. Anyway, he's dead. I don't know when exactly or where, but that doesn't matter any more. Everybody dies sooner or later, including you and me.'

'But with us it takes longer, no?'

She laughed. 'A little. Do you mind waiting?'

'Sometimes I do, sometimes I don't.'

'Well then . . .' She smiled at him quite fondly. There was no longer any contest. She was on her way.

He helped her fasten her suitcase. They kissed like old friends, without heat.

'I'll miss you,' he said. 'We're two of a kind.'

'I'm too old for you.'

Kurt shrugged. 'What does that matter?'

'Oh, it matters,' she said. 'Believe me.'

She looked quickly round the room to make sure she had forgotten nothing. The sunlight flooded through the window onto the scraps of Kleenex, an empty, unstoppered bottle of cologne, a glass of beaded water on the table. The roses were beginning to wilt. Their heads drooped, the edges of their petals were touched with brown.

Julie looked at her watch. 'The taxi should be here by now.'

'Shall I come into Munich with you to see you off?'

'God forbid.'

'Have you got my address? Just in case.'

'Of course,' she lied. It was crumpled in the wastepaper basket, along with the empty phial and Charles's letters.

Kurt followed her down the passage, lugging her suitcase to the hall where the doctor and a group of nurses waited to say goodbye.

*

As she went through Passport Control, she could see Charles and the children waiting on the other side of the glass wall of the Customs Hall. Nose lifted to the weather as usual, feet planted astride. My husband, she thought. Responsible, domestic, laborious, immovable, flat. He'll do. The customs officer waved her through and she followed the porter towards the screened doors, smiling, waving, surprised by the excited, apprehensive faces of her children.

More about Penguins
and Pelicans

Alison Lurie

Love and Friendship

For her first novel Alison Lurie wrote about the stresses
and strains of a marriage in an American academic
community.

'The unfaltering aptness of the dialogue and the acid
penetration of the commentary provide steady,
uninterrupted delight' – Anthony Quinton in the
Sunday Telegraph

The Nowhere City

Alison Lurie holds up life in Los Angeles for her ruthless
inspection.

'Very rarely does one come across a novel so well
constructed that it surges with life on all levels. It is a
remarkably penetrating story of a city without an
identity' – *Daily Telegraph*

The War Between the Tates

The miseries, the bewilderments, the ironies – and the
pleasures – that can attack a middle-aged marriage.

'Stylish, comic, detached, tender . . . she evinces rare
wisdom, wit and compassion; and she writes like an angel'
– *Sunday Times*

Elaine Feinstein

Children of the Rose

The château of Alex Mendez is in Provence, near Avignon:
a rich man's hideout. But for Alex and his estranged wife
Lalka, there is no retreat from their past. Images of war
and childhood still haunt and deform their lives. Both Alex
and Lalka have to discover their true inheritance.

The Crystal Cave

In a Swiss scientific research institute, Matthew and his
colleagues are on the point of a new discovery. Outside,
they belong to a disparate group of characters, carrying
their love for each other like a burden. But someone
decides to rearrange the pieces of their predicament and,
once broken up, things can never be the same.

The Amberstone Exit

Emily lies in the maternity ward, awaiting the moment of
giving birth. Her waking merges with obsessive dreams,
flickering images spinning through her mind as though
on film.

The Circle

Poet Elaine Feinstein probes the sore spots of a marriage
and finds that a wife must accept her separateness – and
that of her husband.

A novel for all those who know – and want to know –
about the loneliness (and the magic) of being married.

Penelope Mortimer

Long Distance

A nightmare journey through a horrific institution where reality is blurred with fantasy, sanity with madness and age with youth. The author of *The Pumpkin Eater* has surpassed herself in this fine, desperate novel.

'The sexual and spiritual progress of female middle age has rarely received such an excitingly imaginative treatment ... Mrs Mortimer is witty as well as tragic ... Enthralling' – Ronald Blythe in the *Sunday Times*

'The overall combination of clarity and mystery and coherence is very impressive indeed' – A. S. Byatt in *The Times*

'Mrs Mortimer's best novel yet' – Elizabeth Harvey in the *Birmingham Post*

Paul Theroux

The Family Arsenal

A novel of urban terror and violence set in the grimy
decay of South-East London.

'One of the most brilliantly evocative novels of London
that has appeared for years ... very disturbing indeed' –
Michael Ratcliffe in *The Times*

'An uncomplicated pleasure ... with this writer the
thrills are never cheap and obvious' – Robert Nye in the
Guardian

'This is a thriller, tightly plotted, terribly evocative' –
Elizabeth Berridge in the *Daily Telegraph*

The Great Railway Bazaar

Fired by a fascination with trains that stemmed from
childhood, Paul Theroux set out one day with the intention
of boarding every train that chugged into view from
Victoria Station in London to Tokyo Central, and to come
back again via the Trans-Siberian Express.

And so began a strange, unique and hugely entertaining
railway odyssey.